The Eclipsed Heart

Kimberly Thomas

*To Barbara Quinn
Kimberly Thomas*

Comfort PUBLISHING

Copyright ©2011 by Kimberly Thomas
Library of Congress Control Number: 2010926050

The Eclipsed Heart

All rights reserved. The author guarantees all contents are original and do not infringe upon the legal rights of any other person or work. No part of this book may be used or reproduced, stored in a retrieval system or transmitted in any form or by any means without prior written permission of the publisher, except in the case of brief quotations embodied in critical articles and reviews.

For information, address Comfort Publishing, PO Box 6265, Concord, NC 28027. The views expressed in this book are not necessarily those of the publisher.

First printing
Book cover design by Colin Kernes
ISBN: 978-1-935361-27-5

Published by Comfort Publishing, LLC
www.comfortpublishing.com

Printed in the United States of America

This book is dedicated to my sons Daniel, Brendan, and Christopher for being my everything; to Ellyssa (the daughter I will never have) for always inspiring me to keep writing; to my parents, Manuel and Lou, for believing I have talent; to my brother Kendall for being the best big brother ever; to Kevin because, although I ultimately ended it all, I gave you my heart and you took that for granted and in some odd way, I appreciate that you taught me to never believe in love even though I will always love you; to Aiden and Neil because I regret not being able to give you the lives you deserve – just remember to never give up the fight and always strive for more; to Anthony because I should have known the grass wasn't greener on the other side and I regret ever hurting you; to Thomas because you wanted to be listed and I miss my best friend and because even though you try my patience, you still make me laugh; to Lee Harkness for being an awesome photographer; and to all the good and bad people in my life who inspired my madness and made this book come to existence.

Yea, though I walk through the valley of the shadow of death, I will fear no evil: For thou art with me;

Excerpt, Psalm 23, KJV

Angry hearts drifting in the night
Feeding on the misery of others
While the innocents live their life
Without any regard
To the anger, and fear, that exists.

-- Kimberly Thomas

Prologue

"I need more money."

Mike had flipped open his cell phone and read the text message from his son, the blaring white screen casting an unnatural glow in the darkened gentleman's club that he frequented.

"He needs more money?" He said the words to no one in particular as he flipped the phone closed and grunted.

A young girl, possibly eighteen but he suspected younger, clung to his arm and watched the current dance on the stage with feigned interest and desire. With slurred speech affected by too many shots of Jager, something that he had willingly provided to most of the dancers that night, she leaned onto his arm closer with as much seduction as she could muster in her state of drunkenness and moaned, "I need more money, too."

He wanted to slap that insolent bulging face of hers, but instead he just chuckled and patted her softly on her bare knee. In the darkness, she could not see his disgust for her. She was an ugly girl of about five foot tall and probably 180 pounds, much too large to be taking off her clothes to dance in front of men. Her face was riddled with acne and she was missing several teeth from decay, which resulted in a putrid smell wafting from her mouth with every word she spoke. Her appearance was the reason she was here at 4am, because the clientele at 4am didn't care too much about size, or anything for that matter. Most of the men there at that hour were usually the scum of the earth, himself excluded of course, and these men were more than willing to drink so heavily until these women became supermodels or at least "do-able."

Mike, however, did care about the appearance of women. He cared about hair color and eye color and body shape. He wanted the perfect woman, beautiful, pliable, and silent. The women here, at any time of day, did not fit that description. At one point, perhaps years prior, they might have been beautiful but the lives they had lived had made them hardened and repulsive and now they were simply vessels for sexually repressed and deranged men.

Mike had experienced the perfect woman once and the thought of her beauty still excited him. She had been perfect –a classic beauty with a wonderful personality that was accented by her perfect body, lovely face and the darkest, most beautiful hair. She had escaped him so many years ago! That had not stopped him from searching for her, expending a significant amount of hours, energy, and money simply to find her and bring her back to him. He had thus far been unsuccessful.

He was older now and life had interfered with his search so he had tossed the torch to his son, giving strict instructions to find the woman and bring her back at any cost. His son, too, had so far failed.

Mike was too tired to search for her anymore and these young women who worked for dollars threw themselves at middle-aged men with such passion that he rarely spent time alone. They were easier than his perfect woman anyway; they did not care about love or relationships; they wanted nothing more than money and drugs and in return would allow him to use them however he pleased, at least for the right price.

He leaned over to the chunky woman by his side.

"I have to make a phone call."

The woman rolled her eyes and giggled with disinterest as he stood up to exit the room. He paused momentarily near the stage to stare at Peaches, the woman who danced seductively near the pole. He had known her for years – from the time when she had been young and beautiful instead of this plastic elderly version of herself. She responded to his presence, as always, subservient and with a cat-like walk on her hands and knees towards him. Pleased, he threw a dollar down for her. She blew him a kiss as he proceeded out of the room.

The room where girls danced on the elevated stage surrounded by mirrors was dark except for the bluish glow from the black lights. Outside the darkened area, the room was occupied with two pool tables and florescent lighting so bright that dancers sometimes refused to go out in it because their flaws – cellulite and bad faces and bruises and even their true age – would be exposed in its brightness.

Steven, the bouncer tonight, was a 6 foot tall muscular man and was all of nineteen. He stood nonchalantly guarding the entrance, usually taking cover charges and making sure that no fights broke out. At this time of the morning, there was little to worry about other than the few stragglers who would refuse to leave the parking lot, hoping for one last chance to hook up with their favorite dancer.

There were only two bouncers who worked at the strip club – Steven and Brian. Mike liked Brian better because he was more easily influenced. Steven was all business and was more likely to call a cab for him than let him drive home drunk. He didn't like leaving his car at the club – the car was his baby, after all. Mike could toss Brian five dollars and Brian would roll over and play dead like the good puppy dog he was but Steven was not that easily bribed.

Knowing full well that Steven would question Mike's sobriety, Mike flipped open his phone to begin dialing and nodded at Steven as he walked, or more or less stumbled, outside of the club. Steven's voice trailed him outside of the door,

"You better not drive out of here, old man."

Refraining from flipping Steven off, Mike ignored the remark and looked again at his phone. His fingers fumbled over the numbers, intoxication making his vision too blurry to dial with ease.

He finally managed to dial the number and the phone rang once and then twice and then three times and then a voice came on the line – a young woman's voice.

"You've reached the Crabtree residence; leave a message at the tone."

He flipped the phone shut and then after a few mumbled curses, flipped it open again and dialed a second number.

The phone rang again, once, twice, and then after the third time the voice of his son answered.

"I'm busy. Leave a message."

Mike sighed, and said to no one in particular, "Voice mail."

The voice mail system beeped and Mike spoke in a slurred voice,

"Who do you think I am? Your bank?"

Without another word, he slammed the phone shut and sat on the curb, his head spinning from the alcohol. The phone vibrated in his hand.

Opening the phone up and clicking the little button on the side of the phone to use the speaker phone, he garbled,

"Hello?"

"Dad?"

"Whatdya want?"

"I need more money."

"You're a big boy, get your own."

There was a pause and then his son spoke again, "Do you want me to find her or not?"

"I don't think you're even looking."

"I'm close, dad, I really am. I just need some more money or otherwise I'm not going to be able to focus as much time on searching for her."

Mike sighed and set the phone down on the curb next to him. The night sky was dotted with sporadic stars and the thump from the music in the club still exuded outside the thin walls. Mike's head hurt and thinking made it reel in agony.

"Dad?"

Mike growled at the phone that still set on the pavement next to him.

"Hold on, I'm thinking."

Mike did not want to tell his eldest son that he had spent most of the money he had acquired, because saying that would be admitting that he had lied about how he made his wealth. His sons believed he made all his money as a construction worker; Junior knew part of the story but he would never know the whole truth. His two boys were ignorant forever, believing that a construction worker could acquire the kind of wealth he had, but then he hadn't intended on raising rocket scientists. He liked stupid people – stupid people didn't ask questions.

Even though the money was running out, he did not want his son to stop looking for his perfect woman, Lisa , because he needed her. Even after all these years, he needed her. Of course, he'd still have the women at the strip club on the side, but with Lisa on his arm he'd be like royalty – better than everyone else or, at least, everyone would be in awe of him.

He sighed, struggled to stand up and grabbed the phone as he did. He slipped and almost fell and then walked slowly and carefully to his car.

He sighed and then spoke softly, "I'll get you some money."

Before his son could reply, Mike hung up the phone.

Mike struggled to get his keys out of his pocket and, in the process, set off the alarm on his Corvette. He silenced it and got into the car. The roar of its engine excited him and he slammed the car into reverse, backed up and then sped away, sending a shower of stones behind him. Steven was nowhere to be seen, oblivious that he had once again let a drunken man leave the place behind the wheel of a car.

He headed towards Vertueux his home and his destination tonight. The gentlemen's club he frequented was not near the town – there were no gentlemen's clubs near Vertueux, something that the townspeople had always managed to maintain -- that sense of virtuosity even in this less than virtuous world.

His destination was Jeremiah Odium's house. He had warned his own children to avoid the old home. After all rumors had it that the house was haunted but Mike knew the house was not haunted. In fact, he had actually started the rumors to keep people away from the house. He was a pure genius, he thought.

Jeremiah had been ridiculously wealthy – so wealthy that most of his belongings were worth thousands, maybe millions, of dollars. Amazingly, his sons had never suspected that he had stolen from the Odium house and even more amazing was that no one in the town had ever gone to pillage the house – that was Mike's own personal looting ground. Perhaps the good people of Vertueux were a little more respectable than him or perhaps he was the only one with the brains to ever take from the rich and give to himself.

"Stupid town," he thought silently.

He had actually only gone to the Odium mansion once but between the hefty life insurance policy payout on his dead wife and what he had stolen, from Jeremiah he had thrived these past eighteen years. He'd invested wisely at first, but lately, the stock market had not done him any favors and his penchant for liquor and women and personal belongings had run him almost dry, that and his needy son who kept asking for more and more money.

The monthly allowance he gave his son, Junior, to scout for his beloved Lisa, was proving to break him, but he was surely not going to give up looking for Lisa. His only option was to go back to the house and steal again for surely there were more jewels or gold or *something* for him to steal.

He paused when he reached the dirt road that led to the Odium place. The mailbox still stood next to it as if time had not erased the memory of that man – that wretched man who had stolen his woman. He turned his car quickly onto the dirt road and drove fast along the bumpy road towards his destination. In the breaking dawn, he saw the house before him. The redness of the sun inundated the house and made it look as if the house was either on fire – or covered in blood. To him, though, the house simply looked ripe for the picking; a fruit that looked bland on the outside but inside held sweetness beyond compare.

He smiled stupidly and turned onto the gravel driveway that led to the massive expanse of the house. Parking his car in front of the substantial steps, he jumped out and staggered up the steps. When he reached the big doors to the house, he knocked. There was no answer.

Of course there was no answer; the man had been dead for years and the house left to rot and decay like his corpse now lying in the ground.

Laughing at himself, he reached for the door knob and turned it.

The door, with a tiny push from Mike, opened up wide upon itself as if the hinges had been recently oiled. The house was dark and dusky and he tried his best to see in the darkness, a feat that would have been difficult sober but was near impossible while intoxicated. He walked forward further into the house, and it slammed behind him, kicking up dust in its wake. Not shaken by the sudden gust that had closed the door, for he would be the first to say that he feared nothing - he coughed and then, eyes somewhat adjusted to the darkness, proceeded forward towards the staircase.

He knew where he had to go.

The stairs creaked with every step, and he walked carefully in case the wood, worn from years of stagnation, were to crumble under his weight. When he reached the upstairs floor, he turned right – towards the master bedroom where eighteen years prior he had first acquired wealth.

The hallway was bare as it had always been – no pictures that adorned the walls and only a handful of closed doors. The once dark burgundy carpet that ran the hallway was now dull and dingy, grey with dust. He walked quickly towards the last door at the end of the hallway and stood before the brown door, hand outstretched towards the knob, but not quite touching it.

The last time he had been at this door, he had been reborn into a new man – a man unafraid to take action. He shuddered, a coldness overwhelming him, but he smiled remembering that fateful day when Jeremiah Odium had died. He grasped the door knob and immediately removed it – the fixture was unnaturally cold and just his hand touching it had burned as if he was standing in Antarctica exposed and naked to the sub-freezing weather.

He grasped his hand in pain. Then he felt it, a soft rumbling below his feet as if an earthquake shook the house, but they were not in an area that experienced earthquakes, there were no fault lines for miles. He stood in front of the door grasping his hand, petrified, for once in his life,

Something unusual was happening. He knew it.

The door to the bedroom flew open in a single gust and he saw Jeremiah Odium lying on the bed, head lulling grotesquely to the side, a gaping gash within his neck spewing blood. The bed was soaked red as the blood spewed forth from him and then, as if sensing Mike's presence, the blood came towards him in torrents like a river overflowing its banks – more blood than was humanly possible. He backed up slowly away from the door, his eyes fixated on the scene before him.

He watched in horror as Jeremiah Odium stood up awkwardly and in his grotesque state walk towards him, his head bouncing uselessly up and down with every step.

Mike turned and ran, stumbling periodically on the staircase as he continuously glanced backwards. Jeremiah Odium followed him slowly, the shuffling of his dead feet across the old carpet a constant reminder that the man – no, the ghost – still followed him. The ghost he had brought into existence.

He reached the door to the house, slammed it open and ran to his parked car – fear making his gait light and fast. Turning the engine on and without thinking he drove away from the house, his eyes focused behind him in case the macabre scene followed him.

There had been no scene of ghoulish morbidity that had followed him. Mike was sure that the ghost – the ghost he had said existed but never believed – was tied to the house and incapable of leaving the realm of its walls. That was how it happened in movies at least. He was satisfied with that explanation and was about to focus his attention in front of him, certain that he had escaped the chilling and macabre scene, when Jeremiah

Odium appeared standing behind him, materializing out of thin air.

There was nothing gruesome about him now, just Jeremiah Odium well-dressed and handsome as he had once been in life. With a hand raised up and a polite and business-like smile, Jeremiah Odium waved as if the two had been life-long buddies parting ways after a pleasant visit.

Mike dared not look backward any longer and turned his head around, pushing the pedal down to the floor. In his frightened and still drunken stupor he had not realized he had driven further into the Odium property instead of away from it or that he had headed towards the chasm that marked the end of the Odium property until he heard the sound of crunching metal and breaking glass as he crashed through the dead end blockade.

By then it was too late.

One

She sat doodling mindlessly on the edge of the notebook paper instead of taking notes. Her doodles were atypical of that of a normal ordinary seventeen year old girl. While other girls were writing notes to their boyfriends or drawing hearts and flowers, she drew pictures of death – tombstones highlighted by morose clouds, hills landscaped with death, and even Death himself, the Grim Reaper.

It wasn't that she drew such morose figures on a daily basis – sometimes she did not draw at all and other times, she drew horses, dogs, faces, or houses, but never things that represented love.

Rachel existed in a constant state of apathy, unsympathetic and callous after years of living in her own tainted world. She, of all people, was aware of her own antipathy and enmity – it was those around her who failed to comprehend that she had converted her own self-loathing into a detestation of all things insufferable.

"Miss Odium. Would you care to answer the question?" The teacher's quavering voice interrupted the rambling thoughts that occupied her mind.

Rachel would have liked to have said,

"No, I would not care to answer the question."

Yes, that is what she would have done and said *if* she was

as audacious as she tried desperately to portray herself, but– instead she simply said, politely,

"Could you please repeat the question?"

She longed to be the epitome of malevolence; the progeny of Satan himself instead of this piteous and extraneous trademark of virtuosity and morality. Guys avoided her because she was unsullied and girls avoided her because she made them look debauched – but their parents loved her for she was the last remnant of eras long passed. But, of course, she knew that was not the real reason the other teenagers didn't like her, it was solely because she was a freak.

Mrs. Crabgrass, as Rachel lovingly called her, for her presence in a room was so overbearing that she wanted to pluck her out like crabgrass out of a yard, waited patiently for Rachel to answer the question. She knew the answer; she always knew the answer, but she liked to wait, eager to not look like the over-zealot geek.

She sighed and rolled her eyes, "1616 – April."

"Very good, Rachel, if only there were more students like you in here", the teacher quavered as she glanced around the room at the students who doodled in their notebooks or hid phones under their desks to text their friends, oblivious to the slander.

"Now who can tell me what relevance Shakespeare had to the literary community?"

She droned on and Rachel stopped paying attention.

Mrs. Crabtree was a reasonably young woman teaching a high school English class. She was in her mid-20s, with flowing sandy blonde hair that fell over her slender shoulders. Without her voice, and that face, she would almost be considered stunning for she had a body that most women would die to have, but her face missed the mark of physical beauty, for her nose was too wide and, her eyes were not a stunning color, but simply a dull light brown; her eyebrows, a darker brown than her hair, were full, unplucked and seemed to almost join together in a giant one.

Yet men seemed to love her, teenage boys clamored on the first day of class to see what Mrs. Crabtree was wearing this year, all the while trying desperately to catch a glimpse of her bulging breasts as she bent over their desks.

Rachel was entirely aware that she was jealous of the attention Mrs. Crabtree's average face and nice body received; the boys never took a second glance at her figure which was hidden behind oversized t-shirts and sweat pants as if she was a cover girl for Goodwill, and they never glanced at the face that was framed discreetly by her coal black hair.

She was, undeniably, a freak.

The bell rang, not only advertising the end of the class, but the end of the school day. Rachel gathered her books quickly, tucked them into her backpack and started heading towards the door.

She was walking up to the classroom door when the sound of that voice, like fingernails on a chalkboard, split through the uproar of her fellow classmates voices. "Rachel."

She was tempted to just keep going, feigning ignorance of her call, but sighed and turned around, ever the compliant student, and pushed through the unyielding crowd of teenagers that rushed towards the open classroom door to their homes and to freedom from the doldrums of this mediocre existence.

"Yes, Mrs. Crabtree?" Rachel exhaled noisily, displeased of this disruption in her efforts to leave.

"I'm sorry… I'm sorry." Her face was contorted in agony – not physical pain but as if something else bothered her, something more frightening.

"Sit, please… I won't keep you long."

Turning the chair next to her desk to face her instead of the classroom, Rachel sat down and patiently waited for her to speak. Mrs. Crabtree did not speak, intently watching as the remnants of the remaining students slowly dawdled around the room.

Something was different about Mrs. Crabtree today – more morbid. Perhaps the abnormal lack of color in her outfit – a grey turtleneck, an odd choice for a warm day in May, matched up with black slacks – brought out the morbidity in her persona. She was one to always wear bright colors, no matter what time of year it was, saying, in her own defense, that the most renowned writers were those who did not fit the social stereotypes. She was not, nor would she ever be, renowned.

The last remaining student slowly shuffled out of the classroom without a word. Mrs. Crabtree turned towards Rachel unhurriedly, with a melancholic despondency that made the girl's heart beat faster for fear of what provoked this after class meeting.

"How is your mother?" she said with a weak smile as she glanced once again at the closed door to her classroom.

Rachel smiled and chuckled lightly. "She's good – well as good as you can expect for someone who only has a few months to live." Her mother had only a few months to live for the past three years.

"My father-in-law passed away last week." She said sullenly, making the statement as if she had not heard Rachel's reply to her question or perhaps had not truly expected a reply.

A substitute had been provided last week due to a 'death in Mrs. Crabtree's family' – the class had not known who it was that had died.

"I'm sorry." Rachel said it almost questionably because a father-in-law did not sound like something she should be overly saddened by – not saddened to the point of her current dour state.

Mrs. Crabtree smiled softly.

"Oh, no, no, it's fine. The man was a self-righteous bast…" She stopped herself. "I'm sorry. I kept you here because of what I found in his belongings -- something I think you might find interesting." She reached in her desk drawer and pulled out a manila envelope out of the desk. Speaking softly, she continued, "I had to make copies of these few because when my husband found out that I was reading them he…well he wasn't too happy." She rubbed her neck softly. "Whatever you do Rachel…" she whispered, "…don't tell anyone you have these. They are only for you and maybe, maybe, your mother, but no one else." She glanced around the room as if someone had magically appeared through the closed door, and then mysteriously added, "I just thought you should know."

Rachel had never been one to interrupt Mrs. Crabtree – because Mrs. Crabtree obviously did enjoy the sound of her own voice – so trying to avoid another diatribe, Rachel, without a word, reached for the envelope and tucked it into her backpack.

"Promise me." She continued. "Promise me you won't tell anyone."

"I promise." Rachel smiled softly. Mrs. Crabtree was beginning to freak her out with her unusual behavior. In a rush to get away from her, she added, "I have to go now. My mom is expecting me."

"I understand. Tell her I said 'hello'. Have a great weekend, Rachel."

She smiled softly, wincing as she moved her arm to pat Rachel gently on the shoulder.

"You, too, Mrs. Crabtree; see you Monday."

Rachel scuttled for the door as quick as possible, curious as to what the contents of the envelope contained but also anxious to get home before her mother returned from her "doctor's appointment."

Rachel walked through the empty school quickly and proceeded briskly along the two blocks to her dilapidated apartment building.

The apartments had been built in the 1970s. Intended to be a government-subsidized apartment community, a management change in the mid-1980s allowed a less socially-acceptable crowd to start renting at the apartments. The neighbors Rachel saw now were mostly drug dealers or drug users or prostitutes and then there were the few like her mother and her who were just "down on their luck". For the past five years, the city had been trying to tear the building down and make way for some high-rise buildings – for this was prime real estate, the only remaining reminder of the poverty in this portion of the city, the eye sore in this well-to-do neighborhood. Luckily, the owners had not caved in yet, but it was inevitable that once the price-tag was high enough, greed would set in and Rachel and her mother would be out of a home.

She opened the door and slipped inside the cool, dank darkness of the apartment. A smell she could only associate with death, for it lingered long after scrubbing and cleaning and air fresheners, greeted her at the doorway entrance an unwelcome reminder always that they were, and seemingly would forever be, poor. She flipped the light switch, and the one and only light in the room flipped dimly on – leaving a foreboding shadow on the few pieces of furniture that they actually owned.

The couch had been donated from someone at the doctors' office after hearing that her mother slept in the only available twin bed in the one-bedroom apartment and that Rachel slept on a ratty old blanket on the devastatingly putrid and soiled carpet. Rachel had grown accustomed to the floor, as it had been her bed from birth to the age of fourteen.

The old couch had been dropped off several years ago now, and using clothes that she had outgrown, she managed to patch up the holes that constantly seemed to pop up on it The couch now looked like something even a homeless person would not accept as charity, for it was a shambled mess of small portions of t-shirts and sweat pants and panties; for her, however, it was where she slept, where she read, and where she laboriously worked on enhancing her knowledge so that one day she would not be subjugated to this embarrassing lifestyle.

She liked to read; it was something that pre-occupied her time since television was not an option in this dull and gloomy living room. Even if they could afford a television, they would only have local television channels, utilizing whatever signal was available through the air, and from the few times she had seen programs on television, well, she just felt smarter reading a book, even fiction, than watching the mindless dribble that they shown on free TV. Of course, she knew that most people would probably tell her that is what all poor people say and, sadly, she'd laugh and probably agree with that opinion.

The rest of this tiny room was the combined kitchen/dining area. There was a small card table sitting in the dining area next to what was called a kitchen - although that area only had a sink, stove and a refrigerator. When she and her mother ate together, they sat on cold metal chairs and stared blankly at each other, never knowing what to say to each other. Anyway, it was rare that they ate together. Monday to Friday Rachel ate the free meals that the state provided to underprivileged kids at school; she never ate dinner. Saturday and Sunday she usually had no time to eat because she spent 15 to 20 hours a day cooking at the diner down the street. She usually had a few bites of food here and there when there was a mistake in an order, but she rarely ate a full meal. When her mother was 'dying' three years ago, her mother had stopped working altogether, but she had barely worked previous to that time.

Now, with the job at the diner Rachel made just enough to keep up on the rent and keep the electricity on. Welfare paid the rest but she hated, more than anything else in her life, being a welfare recipient.

There were two doors inside the apartment; one went to the shared bathroom and the other to her mother's bedroom. The bedroom was so small that only the twin bed covered in a blanket could fit in the room, and even then there was barely room to move about. Her mother kept a small suitcase under the bed, in which, Rachel assumed that her mother kept her spare clothing but she did not dare investigate it further. The bedroom was her mother's home, for she spent 99% of her time in that bedroom, refusing to come out except for the seemingly less than frequent visits to her doctor.

Her mother was in her early forties; at least that is what Rachel believed. She had seen a picture of her mother in her youth once, only briefly, because when her mother saw her looking at the picture she ripped it from her hands and destroyed it in a ripping frenzy that left the picture in a thousand pieces, too small to piece back together. Her mother had been beautiful – slender, coal black hair and eyes, just like Rachel's, a smile that could dazzle even the grinch himself, and a body that far surpassed even Mrs. Crabtree's voluptuousness. She would be beautiful now too, even in her age, if it wasn't for the look of poverty that made her eyes too sunken and lifeless and her once firm body sagging under the weight of the years. Her mother was also sick or at least that is what she had told Rachel.

Three years ago she had been to the doctor quite frequently and three years ago she told Rachel she only had a few months to live. Three years later, she kept telling Rachel that "any day now, you're going to wake up and I'll be a corpse lying cold and dead in that bed over there." "Don't have faith in the living."

That was her mother's creed.

Rachel loved her mother, no matter their dysfunctional relationship. Rachel had no father, no grandparents, and no extended family, just her mother.

Now, while her mother had never spoken of a father, Rachel, even in her virginal naivety knew that she had to have been fathered for she was *not* the product of divine fertilization. Rachel had always assumed that her mother had been raped or somehow otherwise emotionally scarred by the man who fathered her because she couldn't imagine that her mother had always been in this constant state of depressive catatonia; after all, the photograph she had seen so many years ago indicated that at some point her mother may have been normal.

Rachel knew better, however, than to ever ask of her father's existence – her mother would bar herself from the world if she were to ever question her on her past.

When Rachel was eight years old she had asked her mother for a baby sister or a baby brother, ignorant of the fact that her mother would need a man to create said sibling. In corollary, her mother locked herself in her bedroom for a month without saying a word to Rachel.

Eight years old and Rachel had somehow walked herself to school every day, fed herself, and otherwise led an independent life; no one knew the wiser. She was aware at a young age that the state frowned on such unacceptable behavior by parents and that her mother, by anyone's standards, was unfit. She sometimes wondered if she would have had a better life if she had just informed someone of her plight, but then she would always remember that her mother always needed her more than Rachel needed her mother. It was her duty as a child to suffer this intolerable existence just to protect her mother.

Kimberly Thomas

With her thoughts now back in the present Rachel plopped herself on the sagging couch and opened her backpack. Grabbing the manila envelope in one swoop she leaned closer to the dim light as she ran her finger under the seal to open it.

Her heart skipped a beat as she heard the lock on the apartment click and the door open. She hid the envelope in her lap, even though she knew her mother would not notice or care. Her mother, angelic in the radiant glow of the sun behind her, slipped into the apartment. She did not say a word or glance at Rachel but proceeded silently to her bedroom. Her tattered grey dress, the one piece of clothing Rachel remembered her wearing for the past three years, flowed gracefully around her. She floated with a grace that betrayed her poor surroundings and made her look out of place, like a Ming vase in a dumpster.

"How was your doctor's visit?" Rachel said.

In her shockingly sultry voice for a woman who looked near death, her mother replied without turning around,

"Nothing new. One of these days…"

"Yes Mom, I know…one day I'll find you dead in your bed." Rachel smiled softly although even if her mother's back wasn't turned towards her, she doubted that her mother would have seen it.

"Mom? One more thing…"

Her mother had already reached her door and with an intense portrayal of disgust, she turned around and looked at Rachel.

"What?" Her anger and disgust did not surprise Rachel ;it only saddened her now.

"Graduation is next Friday. Do you think you can come?" Rachel said the words softly, fearing the answer.

"No, no, no." Her mother shook her head violently. "I don't go out in public, you know that. One day," she paused, "one day you're going to have to figure this out."

She opened the door to her bedroom and slammed the door behind her – Rachel doubted that she would see her mother for the next two weeks.

Rachel wasn't surprised with her answer. The only "public" her mother ever exposed herself to was the doctor's office and even then Rachel sometimes didn't believe she ever actually went to a doctor; the last bill or notice of new appointment she had seen was three years ago, just prior to the notification of her mother's impending demise. She imagined a doctor would probably think her mother crazy and institutionalize her, and they probably would be right. Her mother was an odd one all right and every word out of her mouth confounded Rachel to the point that she feared she might one day grow to be as bizarre as her mother, confused to the point of lunacy.

The envelope summoned her, however, so she quickly ignored the internal ramblings on the oddity of her mother to focus her attention on it.

Flipping the seal, she slipped the pages carefully out of the envelope. The pages were copies of handwritten notes, dating 1990 to 1991. Rachel sat in the dimly lit room and flipped through the pages - there were five letters, all written to a Lisa, which was coincidentally her mother's name, and signed by Mike.

The first letter was dated January 2, 1990 and written with beautiful penmanship.

"Oh my dearest,

I saw you at the New Year's party, with your hair beautiful in the night sky, the fireworks glowing on it. I saw you with Jeremiah – of all people, Jeremiah. You smiled at me as you held his arm and I knew that your heart was mine. I hate him, I hate him, I hate him. Come to me, my dear and, leave that callous old man behind. I must know your name and your face and that beautiful body of yours. This, my dear, is what love at first sight is all about – I will have you.

Love forever,

Mike"

It was a sappy love letter and Rachel laughed, having long since given up on the ideologies behind love – and she definitely had no faith in love at first sight.

The second letter, dated March 31, 1990.

"Lisa, Lisa, Lisa,

The two of you walked alone in the park, or so you thought, but I was there behind you all the way. Why are you not true to me, my love? Why do you insist on staying with that man when I, your one true love, wait patiently for you? Is it my wife, my son? I will forsake them all just to have you by my side. I wish Jeremiah were dead so I can take you in my arms and have you love me.

Forever yours,
Mike"

The third letter, December 25, 1990.

"Merry Christmas Darling,
I missed you today of all days and I wanted to wish you a Merry Christmas and tell you that you looked remarkable in that red evening gown that you wore with him a few days ago. I saw a ring on your finger, a big diamond ring, and I heard rumors... terrible rumors...that you were engaged. Are you a whore? Marrying Jeremiah solely for his money? You are a whore because I love you with my heart and you just love him for his money. If I were rich would you love me? Because I would kill and maim and steal just to have your love. What more can I do for you to make you stop being a whore and love me?

I'm sorry, I'm sorry. I love you so much and I can't stand seeing you with him. This I promise to you and this I swear to you, he will soon be gone from our lives forever.

Your heart will be mine,
Mike"

Rachel couldn't help but think that Mike was a strange man who seemed bi-polar to her; definitely unstable.

The fourth letter, dated January 2, 1991.

"Dearest Lisa, the love of my life,
I saw you with him last night, naked in his arms, even though you are not his to have. You are mine. I saw you lying in his bed, doing things only the married should do. But, you are mine. I was outraged by your betrayal and in that brief moment wished you were dead. But I cannot hurt you; I love you too much to hurt you. So I did something – something bad but something that had to be done. Now that he is gone, you will be mine.

Kimberly Thomas

Mike"

The fifth and last letter, dated August 31, 1991.

"Lisa,

You have long since left, the death of your lover having forced you away from me. You know this is a small town and even though you are far away, I heard rumors that you carried his child and that not too long ago you gave birth to his daughter. Rachel, I believe that is her name and she, will be his only heir. I've looked for you but I cannot find you; they say you moved to the city but I looked and I cannot find you. No one knows where you went.

Come back – marry me and we will live off his wealth forever in harmony. My wife, if she is what stopped you from loving me, is dead. Please, I only did what I did for you, my love, because we deserve forever to be happy. Please mail me, call me, anything. I have attached my information in case you lost it.

Love forever,

Mike

P.S. I will forever regret not mailing these letters to you, but your beauty frightens me.

The address of Mike was on the back of the page – some obscure address in some town of which Rachel was unfamiliar.

Rachel had never heard of Vertueux. Was it simply coincidence that the letters were to Lisa – her mother's name – and the rumored daughter was named Rachel – her name? She knew that she would have to ask Mrs. Crabtree on Monday.

She organized the papers and slid them back into the manila envelope. A crunching sound stopped her from continuing so she extracted the papers once again from the manila envelope and dumped the remaining contents of it on the couch next to her and then slid the paper back into the envelope.

A yellow post-it note lay crumbled on the couch. She gathered it cautiously and opened it slowly, half-expecting it to be some new terroristic technology and explode in her hands. In Mrs. Crabtree's familiar handwriting, the note simply read

"It is you."

Two

It had only been a week since his father's death and life at school was more unbearable than ever. Sympathetic teachers let him slide on homework assignments and his friends didn't bother asking him to the pre-graduation parties that were surely going on this weekend for fear that he might not be in a jovial partying mood. It was starting to perturb him that he was being treated as if the world had ended, when, in all reality, he considered this the start of his life – his rebirth.

His father's death was just another day in his already dull existence – it had been inevitable for his father to die so young because his father was, after all, an appalling representative of the human race and even some would have been less kind in their description of his father.

He had sometimes wondered how he had ended up as he had, for he did not look or behave like his father.

Perhaps he looked like his mother, but his father, swearing that the loss of his wife had just been too traumatic, destroyed all pictures of her after her death. He had been told that his mother had had died of complications during childbirth. At least that is what his father told him – and, of course, his father always reminded him that it had always been Tom's fault that his mother had died. Living in a small town of only a few hundred people like Vertueux, the rumors had spread quickly that his mother, who had been labeled a patron saint in the town, had died under suspicious means. No one ever clarified and no charges had ever been brought against anyone on the murder of his mother, and the death certificate specifically stated that she had died of cardiac arrest.

If his mother had indeed been a patron saint, then Tom was more like her than his father. His father, a construction worker – vulgar with a penchant for hard liquor – was an average looking man, big and bulky at around 6 feet tall and 250 pounds, mostly muscle, although in the later years most of that muscle settled around in his mid-section as a beer belly. Tom's father was a womanizer, yelling at Tom to stay in his room while women laughed and cavorted in his father's bedroom. The women didn't stay around long though, because inevitably he'd either tire of them, or the women just gave up putting up with his random anger streaks and his proclivity towards the more unusual sexual behaviors. It had been almost traumatizing and definitely unfortunate for Tom to realize his father's partiality towards the masochistic forms of sex – that was a story in and of itself and Tom really didn't like discussing it.

On the other hand, depraved as his father was, his mother, they said, "was a good Christian woman who saw the good in Michael Crabtree and fell in love with him from the day she met him". Now, if you could believe the townsfolk of Vertueux, his mother had overlooked the fact that, even during marriage, his father had liked the ladies – sometimes not coming home for days. That's *if* you could believe them, but Tom wasn't into believing everything they said – there may have been some truth to their rumors, but those old busybody ladies knew how to spin the truth and it was quite obvious that they never liked Michael Crabtree.

Tom didn't want to think that his father had always been the way he remembered him, for Tom believed that love really could have conquered all and the death of his mother surely would have traumatized his father into living a life filled with beer and women instead of the good clean and socially-acceptable married life he surely must have had with his wife.

In all, however, the townsfolk agreed that Tom was the spitting image of his mother both in looks and behavior and Mike Jr., his older brother who had since moved away, was "going down the same path as his poor unfortunate father, both in looks and aggression".

Tom stopped in the school hallway when he saw Mica leaning seductively against her locker talking to her friends. He only flirterd with the darkest haired women in school; perhaps their dark hair and mysterious eyes intrigued him, or perhaps it was just some long-engrained genetic tendency to fall for the dark haired women, but Mica would probably be the prettiest girl in this school even if she had been blonde. Mica was a junior, still a few months shy of seventeen; she was head of the cheerleading squad, the first junior ever to accomplish that feat at Vertueux High. Slender and athletic, with the unfortunate breasts of a tween, she had, nevertheless, the face of an Italian goddess. Chocolate brown hair and naturally tan skin, she was the girl that everyone in school wanted to date.

And except for the geeks and uglies, Mica had dated them all – except for Tom.

"Hey Mica." He said more loudly than he meant.

She jumped, startled. "Oh. Tom, how are you doing?"

Her voice had a hint of seduction, a siren's voice intent on stealing his soul. She placed her cold, long, dark fingers on his arm. She had the fingers of a pianist but had the talent and brains of someone in a coma – most guys liked that about her.

"I'm good. I'm good." Eager to circumvent the potential conversation of his dead father, he continued, "Where's the party at tonight?"

She smiled and ran her fingers behind his head seductively, pulling his ear towards her full lips and open mouth, and then after a quick flick of his ear lobe with her tongue, whispered, "My place."

He pulled back, amused that she was so assertive and, with as much strength as he could muster reminded himself that she was well used in all senses of the word and that he, albeit a teenage male, was not attracted to the easy ones. It had been difficult this past year turning down Mica but he did enjoy the challenge of the hard-to-get ones and Mica, by no means, was hard-to-get. This mentality of his was probably why he just turned eighteen and still had not been laid – of course this was not something high on his to do list, and as strange as it was, true love was what he sought, not sex. With nothing better to say in retort to Mica's invitation, he just simply replied, "Where else?"

She sighed in disgust, upset that she was turned down again – she, the prom queen of Vertueux High and voted most popular girl in school.

"I don't know, go ask someone else." She tossed her hair over her shoulder and skulked away, friends promptly in tow.

He smiled, delighted that, once again, he offended the almighty Mica, and then proceeded to walk out of the front doors of the school, heading home for the weekend. He climbed into the 1979 Chevy Camaro that his brother had left him after leaving for the big city. Starting the car, enlightened by the roar of the engine, he backed up and headed home.

Home – it was empty now. It had been empty before – bereft of love and emotion – but now it was physically empty. His father, even on his meager salary, had managed to provide them with a house full of the finest things – big screen televisions, all the gaming consoles, plush leather couches, name-brand clothes – but his father could not provide a house full of love.

It was odd, not really sad, that his father was really gone, killed in an automobile accident a week ago. There hadn't been much left to salvage of the mint-condition 1965 Chevrolet Corvette, or of his father for that matter. The police said that he had been drinking and driving, which was nothing unusual, and on that fateful night his car had careened off the cliff near the old Odium place, ending in a fiery pile at the bottom.

No, it wasn't surprising that he had been drinking and driving, or that he was dead. Tom was more surprised that his father had actually been close to the Odium place. His father had placed strict rules on his two sons to never venture near that "ungodly ground" rumored of being haunted by old Jeremiah Odium who still pined for his lost love. Even the mention of Jeremiah Odium would send his father into a rage.

In response to the news of their father's death, his brother and sister-in-law had rushed to the house and had been there since the news. They had come to help out with the funeral arrangements but seemingly more for his brother to pillage through his father's belongings. As much as he and his brother disagreed, it had been a welcome reprieve from the morosely silent house. He wasn't sure he would have been able to handle the funeral and everything else, for that matter, had they not been there.

He liked his sister-in-law, and wondered sometimes why a woman that pretty, even though she was not his type, would stick with a brute like Junior. His father had been a genius naming his first-born after himself, because Mike Jr. was his father re-incarnated. Tina, however, was quiet around Junior, and demure – probably some engrained behavior pattern where Junior preferred her to be seen and not heard.

Without Junior around, however, Tina was a talker – her broken, saddened voice telling stories to Tom about her teaching job and her students and more information than Tom cared to hear about her life. He felt bad for her, and never made her stop even though her voice eventually got on his last nerve. He had spent eleven years with Junior and he could only imagine that her one year with him was enough to make her mad.

The two had been there a week when on Thursday night Tom had come home from work and their bags had been packed, setting in the grand foyer near the front door. Tina was sitting on the couch crying and Junior, his brother, was nowhere to be seen.

Junior had hit her – that was obvious from the red marks on her face and the budding bruises on her neck. Tom had not known what to do – holding her while she cried would have made his brother take his anger out on him. Unsure of what action was best, he simply walked away and went to his room, staying out of their sordid affairs. He was never one to just walk away from an accident, but this one, this problem, was too close to home. He was as scared of his brother's anger as he had been of his own father's temper.

By Friday morning when he awoke, Junior, Tina, and half of his father's personal belongings, including the safe, were gone.

Today, the empty house was a welcome reprieve because he did not care to have another episode of the Crabtree drama unfold before him again. His father was dead but his anger existed through his brother. Tom was thankful he was like his mother more now than ever.

He pushed the button on the garage door opener and once the door slid up, he parked the Camaro in the now bare garage, once occupied by the two cars, now only by one. He was not saddened by that thought as he felt he probably should have been, granted he had lusted after his father's Corvette, but if losing the Corvette meant freedom, then it was a much welcomed loss. He slipped out of the car, and into the house, closing the garage door behind him.

Hungry, he walked to the refrigerator and after opening it, started pulling some lunch meat out, only to drop the food in fear when he heard his father's voice.

"You've reached the Crabtree residence; leave a message at the tone."

He laughed at himself for his ignorance and edginess – he'd have to change that message soon before it freaked him out again.

The answering machine beeped and there was the sound of static – only a loud hissing static that hurt his ears. He rushed towards the answering machine in the living room to stop the noise when he heard a woman's voice, crackled and somewhat familiar say, "Come" and then more static again and then "Now".

The line went dead. He had reached the machine just as the recording ended. He picked up the phone receiver and looked at the caller ID – unknown number.

Kimberly Thomas

Star 69 did not work either.

There were three messages on the answering machine – one of which was the odd one just left. He clicked play.

"Friday. 8 AM. Hey Tom." It was the voice of his best friend Alex. "Was wondering what you're doing tonight. I hear Mica wants to hook up with ya." Alex laughed on the line. "I'm going to the lake if you want to come along. Yeh, yeh, I know I'm supposed to be in school." Alex laughed again and the call ended.

"Friday. 12:30 PM. Tom." It was his sister-in-law, Tina. "I don't know who to turn to; I found some stuff of your dad's, something that…well I can't really say here. I'm scared. If I don't make it, I need you to find a girl named Rachel – she is in my English class. I told you about her, the smart ugly girl… remember? Oh, it doesn't matter, please, there's something weird – something weird going on." The voice on the machine paused and then in a whisper, she continued, "Please help Tom."

"If I don't make it…" What the hell was wrong with her? he thought. He did remember the girl she had told him about. She was always dressed badly, she rarely smiled, she knew all the answers, was a genius at every subject matter, and had no friends. Tina had said she was ugly – but, of course, Tina thought everyone besides herself was ugly. Of course, the girl did sound rather on the ugly side, but that wasn't relevant right now. Why did Tina have to think that he was interested in her problems? Did she not notice him ignoring her just yesterday? He didn't want to get involved in his brother's marriage problems. He sighed and continued to the next message.

"Friday. 3:50 PM." Loud static. "Come." Loud static. "Now."

He picked up the phone and dialed his friend Alex.

Three

Rachel was awake at 4am, out of the door by 4:30am, hair pinned back in a tight pony tail and regulation work-issued slacks and polyester shirt, cleaned, pressed and ready to go. She knocked on the back door of the diner; the doors didn't open to the public till 5:30am.

The diner was retro, reminiscent of those of the 1950s with the outside being a shiny aluminum or metal-like substance accented with bright red and blue awnings and windows, lots of windows, and a curved shape that seemed unnatural for a rectangular building. A big neon sign lit up the top of it reading "Maude's Diner" – the sign was actually turned off right now since the diner wasn't open ,but soon it would proclaim that Maude's Diner was open today for business. The only thing missing from the diner was a parking lot full of classic cars and girls in poodle skirts, although the waitresses were required to wear retro-1950s clothing to keep up with the aura of the times.

It was Maude herself who let Rachel in the back door. Maude, as indicated by her name, was an old woman – she joked and said she was around for the great flood and was best friends with Noah,but Rachel would say she probably was only around 75. Maude and her husband, Dennis, had opened the diner in the mid 1950s and throughout the years they had been an integral part of running the business. Her husband had died about 10 years ago, and to keep from going crazy, she spent every waking hour working in the restaurant. Her frail frame and wrinkled exterior was only a guise for the youthful exuberance that Maude still portrayed. Rachel knew that if she had a grandmother, she wished only for her to be Maude.

"So Friday, eh?" She said as Rachel slid through the back door.

Rachel smiled a huge smile. "Yup, this coming Friday."

Maude was referring to graduation - she said she'd never let Rachel work during the week because of school but she paid Rachel more than other people to work extra hours on the weekend because she knew she needed the money.

"I have something for you." She grabbed Rachel's wrist in her hand and pulled her towards the office door.

"No, no, no." Rachel said as Maude ushered her in the office, a big smile on Rachel's face betraying her reluctance.

"For graduation – my gift to you - you can't refuse a graduation gift – it's against the rules of social etiquette." The wrinkles in her face deepened as she gave off a smile that beamed from ear to ear.

Inside the office was a box, not wrapped, sitting on the office chair. Rachel looked at her quizzically as if she were too dense to realize the box was hers.

"Open it." Maude said softly.

Rachel pulled the box off the chair and laid it on the desk, opening it gingerly. Inside was a black dress. A mix of cotton and rayon, the dress was strapless with a slim waistline that was accented with a corset that tied up into a bow and then flowed downwards. It was a beautiful dress that would seemingly be fit for a movie star, not the self-proclaimed Goodwill cover girl. Rachel held the dress to her chest.

"Do you like?" Maude said softly as she reached up and pulled another box off of the filing cabinet. "Shoes to match." She shoved the box in Rachel's hands. "I expect to see you wearing this on graduation day."

She smiled sweetly. Rachel put the shoes and dress down and leaned over and hugged Maude tightly. She didn't hug her for the shoes and the dress but for the fact that Maude wanted to celebrate her graduation when her own mother did not care.

"I love it, Maude. What would I ever do without you?"

Had Maude really known that Rachel had worried about how she needed a dress to wear for graduation – something that was sadly mandatory at her school – or was this just Maude's usual generosity working at the most opportune time? Rachel was baffled and amazed at Maude.

"Time for work," Maude said, never the dawdler. "You can leave your stuff here and pick it up when you are ready to leave."

Rachel kissed her lightly on her wrinkled old cheek, "Thank you."

They went to work, flipping pancakes, scrambling eggs, cooking bacon and making toast. The rush on Saturday usually started around 7am and ended around 10:30am when the diner switched to the lunch menu. Maude usually let Rachel take a break around 10:30am. The rush helped the time fly by so hot and tired, it was 10:30 before she knew it.

"You're looking way to skinny, my girl." Maude said as Rachel took off her cook apron for break and hung it on the wall. Maude handed Rachel a plate of bacon and eggs. "Eat."

Rachel smiled at her and graciously took the food. She was starving, and admittedly looking "way to skinny".

Sitting in the silence and darkness of the back stock room, Rachel ate, thinking of the dress and the shoes and graduation and the letters from Mike to Lisa.

Maude walked back into the stock room, interrupting her thoughts, and said ,

"Break's over Rach, we need you to help out with the tables."

Time had flown by too quickly. "One of the waitresses didn't show up today. I wouldn't ask you but you know Butch and Nick can't do it and I'm just way too old to be waiting tables. It's your time to shine, my little star."

She smiled softly, her grey curls lit up in the glow of the fluorescent lighting. Maude knew Rachel hated dealing with people and Rachel had been adamant from day one that she did not want to wait tables even if the money could potentially be better than what she was currently making as a cook.

Butch and Nick were the afternoon cooks – fully capable of working the kitchen without Rachel but not capable of ever dealing with the public. They both looked as if they were on work release programs – tattooed from neck to wrist and thick as a sumo-wrestler on steroids, they would only frighten away most of the clientele who frequented Maude's diner.

"OK." Rachel consented with a sigh, afraid, albeit illogically, that if she did not agree Maude would take away her job. "Just this once, though, ok?"

Maude didn't answer and simply handed Rachel a waitress apron, a different shirt and a poodle skirt and then quickly told her to change and then,

"Get out there and help."

Rachel wasn't sure how Maude knew what size she was or how she happened to have spare uniforms just for her when new waitresses had to wait a few days, but Maude was a miracle worker who could pull coins out of thin air if asked and Rachel would even venture that she could probably turn water into wine.

Rachel went to the bathroom, closed and locked the door behind her and then looked at herself in the mirror – she never saw much in the mirror that was worth a continual gaze so she proceeded to change. She slipped off the polyester cook shirt and hideous cook pants and slipped on the t-shirt that the waitresses wore and the poodle skirt. Rachel tied the apron around her waist, gathered up her cooking clothes, and walked out of the bathroom. The shirt was too small, and, having been cursed with a small waist line and oversized breasts – something that she had always hid in the hand-me-down clothes she wore day to day, her breasts pushed on the front of the shirt as if trying to escape.

Butch, waiting patiently in the hall for the bathroom, looked Rachel up and down and then whistled. She blushed and scurried off to the dining room without a word.

Rachel went into the dining area for the first time as a

waitress. Maude was standing at the front desk taking money from customers and Rachel slipped up behind her and whispered "What tables do I have?"

Rachel knew enough about waitressing to know the basics of the job – on the job training by osmosis. Maude turned around and looked at Rachel and with one glance up and down said, "Dang girl."

Rachel blushed again.

"Take 14, 15, and 16. Fourteen just got there, so haul your cute little butt over there before they walk out on us." She smiled at Rachel as if Rachel was her progeny and she was proud of her; Rachel liked how that made her feel.

The feeling of euphoria soon escaped Rachel when she walked over to table fourteen. She sighed when she saw the table; Tony, Randy, Dana, and Danny were sitting there chatting mindlessly as they periodically glanced at their menus.

Tony was an eighteen year old high school dropout who seemed to still hang out with all of his old friends as though he was still a part of the high school crowd. He was average looking, 5'8" around 150 pounds with dirty blonde hair that hung loosely over his face and dull blue eyes. Most girls found him to be attractive mainly because he played the 'bad boy' persona up as if he invented the role. Rachel thought he was callous and rude and downright insincere; he used his girlfriends like he'd use deodorant – they kept the smell of nastiness off of him but once he was done with what he needed from them, he tossed them away.

Randy was the class clown, although he was rather on the large side for the cool kids, being all of 250 pounds at 5'7", he was so funny that even in Rachel's truly apathetic states she'd inwardly laugh at his jokes. She'd only laugh at his jokes that weren't at the expense of others, however, and, sadly, most of his jokes were making fun of other people. He was a red-haired, freckled boy of eighteen whose parents were so rich that every year since sixteen he had a brand new Audi to drive, so with that trait alone, he was never in short supply of friends. Rachel always thought she would have liked him if it weren't for his arrogance and his inability to just be nice.

Dana and Danny were twins. They were so similar in appearance that only their gender told the two apart. They were both freakishly skinny with light brown hair and freckles and the most beautiful blue eyes that Rachel would imagine could make the Caribbean jealous. Dana and Rachel had been best friends in first grade until Dana had found out that Rachel was poor; after school one day mid-year in first grade, Dana had decided to come to Rachel's house and play, only to leave in disgust when she saw the state of Rachel's apartment – at seven, she had no bed to sleep in and no one to clean the house but herself. And, besides, she really didn't have anything that Dana could have played with – toys were a commodity they couldn't afford. Dana, having been born into affluence with a father who was a plastic surgeon and a mother who was as plastic as a Barbie, was "traumatized" by the dereliction of her best friend's living conditions and to this day, told every one of how Rachel wasn't just poor but "oh my god, like so nasty poor that I'm surprised she doesn't live on the street."

Dana was cruel and vindictive while Danny on the other hand was sweet and caring and was so oppressed by his sister's cruelty that he was forced to live the lie of the smug teenager. At least that is what Rachel had hoped because he had never said a cruel word to her and, in sixth grade when Rachel had asked him to go with her to the middle school dance, he had said 'yes' but then later said his sister told him he couldn't go – not with Rachel, at least. So Rachel had gone home and cried and then told herself that love was a lie .

To this day, she still believed it.

Rachel stared at the table when she walked up, fearing eye contact.

"Can I take your order?"

She said the words so meekly and softly she was surprised they had heard her.

Dana spoke up first. "Aren't you Wretched Rachel?" She

didn't wait for an answer, but continued. "Shouldn't you be out collecting welfare?" She snickered, and Rachel looked up just in time to see Tony and Randy snickering with her.

Rachel had not heard that nickname in a long time and it didn't hurt her feelings anymore.

"Can I take your order?" She ignored Dana's rhetorical questions.

Tony spoke next, "No freakin' way is that Wretched Rachel." He looked directly at Rachel's chest when saying, "You are too freakin' hot."

"Can I take your order or do you need a minute?" She said it rather gruffly, partly because Maude was just about to seat another table in her section and partly because she was in no mood to deal with these goons.

They rattled off their order, both drinks and food, and Rachel scurried off to the kitchen to drop off the ticket, but she wasn't quite far enough away when she heard Tony say,

"When the hell did she get hot? I'd sooo tap that. Mmmm. Mmmm. You guys need to tell me these things."

In some odd way, as disgusting as Tony was, she thought it felt good being 'eye candy' instead of ignored as always.

Table 16 had been sat, then 15 and then 14 left, finally, and then re-sat. Hours later, her feet hurt and she was tired of being devastatingly friendly and social and she was sure as hell tired of guys staring at her chest – age didn't seem to matter, from 15 to 80 they never made eye contact with her.

Maude patted her on the back softly. "One more table and then you're done, sweetie. You've done well; I think I may keep you out here more often." Maude winked and then smiled softly and Rachel hoped-no, prayed- that she was just joking.

Rachel walked up to table 15, just recently sat. Mrs. Crabtree and a man that Rachel did not recognize sat silently staring at the menus.

"Mrs. Crabtree. How are you doing today?"

Mrs. Crabtree looked up at her, shock and then panic crossed her face. She glanced over at what Rachel assumed was her husband and then back at Rachel.

"Good, good. We're good." Her voice was shakier than usual.

The man with her glanced up at Rachel. He was much more handsome than Rachel imagined. He was a big man, muscular, with sandy brown hair and a strong jaw line. He stared at Rachel, intently, not at her breasts as all the others had done that day but at her eyes. He finally broke his gaze and looked at his wife,

"Well, are you going to introduce me?"

"This is one of my students." She said softly. She was acting very strange.

He held his hand out towards Rachel. "I'm her husband. The name's Junior."

Rachel smiled softly, and started, "I'm---"

Mrs. Crabtree jumped in, "Her name is Raquel, and she's one of my best students."

Rachel looked at Mrs. Crabtree strangely as she had never mispronounced her name before; in fact, Rachel couldn't imagine that anyone in the history of time had ever confused Rachel and Raquel.

"We'll have two Cokes." Mrs. Crabtree quickly stated before anyone else had time to speak.

Rachel nodded and then walked away with a quick statement that she'd be right back only to overhear Junior tell his wife,

"She's quite the looker - looks really familiar."

Rachel poured ice and then Coke into the two glasses and stared at Mr. and Mrs. Crabtree from the beverage station. As a teacher, Mrs. Crabtree seemed to be loving and doting; she never seemed flustered or frightened; she was always carefree. With Mr. Crabtree, she seemed to be on edge, always looking left and right, never right into his eyes. Rachel didn't know anything about love, but she could only imagine that they should be holding hands and staring into each other's eyes and whispering sweet things that no one else should hear.

Their drinks delivered, Rachel asked the Crabtree's for their order; Mr. Crabtree stared at Rachel's face.

"Do I know you? You look so damn familiar." He said gruffly, his voice not as grating as Mrs. Crabtree, but nonetheless had an otherworldly tone to it – masculine, and frightening.

"Nope. I don't think so." Rachel said softly and confidently, because, in truth, she had never met the man. Something about him alarmed her though – perhaps Mrs. Crabtree's behavior around him or just some natural aura that exuded from him.

"Rachel!" Maude called in a sing-song voice from across the virtually empty diner.

Rachel looked over at Maude, apologized and told the Crabtree's she would place their order and have it right out, and then walked away.

Maude handed the telephone to Rachel when she reached her, "You got a call."

Rachel looked at her like she had lost her mind because no one ever called her, but she took the phone anyway.

"Hello?"

No answer.

"Hello?"

Still no answer. She couldn't help but feel as if the line wasn't completely dead though because an icy chill passed over her spine as if Death himself had called. She did not say hello again. Placing the phone again on the receiver, she looked at Maude and shrugged her shoulders.

"It was some kid, probably chickened out when you answered. Think it might have been one of those kids that you waited on earlier today, one of them kept asking about you." Maude winked at her. "The 1950s look good on you, girl."

She chuckled and walked off.

The food was up shortly for the Crabtrees since they were the only customers in the entire diner – after all, it was now 9:30 at night. Grabbing the food out of the service window, Rachel dropped it off at their table. Mrs. Crabtree would not make eye contact with her – she almost looked like she was crying, and her hands tapped nervously on the table as her back shook slightly like her breathing was ragged and torn by tears.

Mr. Crabtree broke the awkward silence.

Kimberly Thomas

"So, Rachel, how is school?"

Rachel did not miss the fact that he called her by her correct name or that he gave a cutting glance to his wife who did not look up from her food. He took his fork and mixed the gravy into his mashed potatoes, not glancing up at Rachel.

"Good." Rachel said softly.

"How's your mother?"

"Good." She said, her heart beating louder now.

"And your father?"

Rachel paused -- upset that he would ask such a question but also vaguely aware that he may not know her situation.

"I wouldn't know."

She said it harshly, uncaring as to how he reacted. She looked at him with a look of anger but he still sat destroying his mashed potatoes with his fork, unaware of her reaction. She knew there was no way he knew her situation but not wanting to clarify or continue the conversation, she quickly added, "I have to go back to work now." He laughed, a vicious, heartless laugh, callous and intimidating, that warned her he might know more about her than just the unfortunate story of her mother and her lack of a father.

She was also vaguely aware that she was tired and perhaps just a little bit paranoid.

Rachel quickly glanced back at the table as she was walking away and stated, "See you Monday, Mrs. Crabtree."

Mrs. Crabtree did not reply, staring indifferently at the food on her plate.

Rachel would ask Maude to finish the shift; after all it was so late now. She was determined to not subjugate herself to the troubling events that seemed to be happening at the Crabtree table and she knew that Maude, her ever-doting wannabe grandmother, would understand.

Four

Tom and Alex had been friends as long as he could remember, and having got the call the night before to hang out at the lake, he had jumped at the idea. Unlike the other teenagers of the small town, Tom and Alex were the good kids, never drinking or doing drugs. It's not that they stopped the other kids from doing it, they just never joined in.

The two of them had spent the night staring at the stars, fishing poles propped up, and talked – well, that was until Alex's girlfriend Andrea showed up. Andrea was the only African-American girl to attend Vertueux High and sometimes Tom thought that Alex only dated her because she was "taboo". Having come from a long line of Irish-Americans who could trace their history back to royal ancestors in Europe, his parents had become flustered and threatened to throw Alex out if he didn't dump the girl immediately, afraid that their good name would be marred if anyone in the town found out that their son was dating a black person – of course that's not the word they used but the word they used was so antiquated and vulgar that Tom would never repeat it, even for dramatic effect.

Alex had not dumped Andrea, in fact, happy that he could cause such distress to his parents, he increased his devotion to Andrea, and six months later, Alex and Andrea were still going strong.

Tom didn't really have anything against Andrea; she was a nice girl and in her own way was beautiful, but she was loud and obnoxious and always spoke her mind. Tom, was a poet at heart, a hopeless romantic and Andrea was lackadaisical about true love

When Andrea showed up, he knew that Alex would end up elsewhere, either steaming up the windows of Alex's car or moaning too close nearby and disturbing the peace and tranquility of the lake. Sometimes he hated Andrea for taking away his best friend, but Tom also knew that when he finally found someone that he'd leave Alex hanging alone too. It was sad, growing up, all those years of building close-knit friendships, only to betray them for sex.

Inevitably, Alex and Andrea had gone to Alex's car – personally Tom would have preferred the ground, making love under the starlit sky, holding his lover in his arms afterwards and just wishing on every star that the moment would last. But, Alex was not Tom and Andrea was not a romantic. And, in all reality, he was glad they chose the car for the sounds of lovemaking would have made him wish all the more that he wasn't alone.

He laughed at himself for thinking such things and, embarrassingly getting worked up over the idea of romance – it was not sex he desired, for he wanted romance interlaced with lovemaking – nothing animalistic about it; he wanted perfection.

The silence was broken by the rhythmic squeaking of the car under Alex and Andrea's movements and Tom thanked God that he did not hear more than just that.

He smiled, closed his eyes, and drifted into sleep.

He saw her face – pale, thin, covered half in coal black hair, one dark eye peaking from the side uncovered by her hair. She sat in darkness, only her face irradiated by some unnatural glow. She smiled a dazzling smile that set his heart ablaze, and tucking her hair behind her tiny ears, he saw that she was indeed the most beautiful woman he had ever seen. She reached out with her long fingers and caressed his face – it was warm and he wanted to hold her but he couldn't reach her. She opened her mouth to say something and he heard "Dude" in a voice not that of a woman but of his friend Alex.

He opened his eyes. The sun had come up and he blinked to regain bearings. Andrea sat next to him and tapped his thigh.

"Good dream?" She smiled scandalously as she glanced at the bulge in his pants.

"I have to pee." He said it harshly, looked at her in disgust, pulled himself off the ground, and shuffled off to urinate in the bushes a little way off.

It was not Andrea's place to judge, he thought. He had not seen that woman in his dream as sexual, simply beautiful and perhaps the one who held the missing piece to his heart. He felt warm inside because he had a feeling that the woman he saw was real, not just some dream, and that somewhere out there she was waiting for him to save her from whatever kept her in darkness, whatever was keeping her from him. He longed desperately to go to sleep again just to see that face one more time, to be close to her.

He walked back to Alex and Andrea, who were kissing on the blanket where he had just awakened, and he said, "So, what now?"

It was Saturday morning, and he did not desire to go home.

"Want to go to my house and play the PS3?" Andrea said, quickly.

Alex still wasn't allowed to bring Andrea to his house and although he loved upsetting his parents, he loved the roof they put over his head better. Even though Tom had all the cool stuff at his house, they all knew instinctively that the less time Tom spent in his house, the better. So, they agreed and drove to Andrea's house on the far side of town.

They parked in front of her house and went inside. The boys sat down on the couch in front of the 27" television and waited for Andrea to grab sodas for them.

Andrea lived in a little house with her mother and three brothers. The house wasn't run-down, just an older house that had long since seen its prime. The yard was filled with crabgrass and dandelions and the outside of the house was peeling paint. Andrea's mother, having been left for some "cheap ass ho" by her "deadbeat" husband, did everything she could to keep the family fed, and, working 60 plus hours a week, she was rarely home. Compared to the house that Tom lived in, Andrea's house was a shack; compared to Alex's house, it was simply a starter home. But this house had something that Alex and Tom's houses lacked…love, and whether or not Andrea's mother was home was irrelevant because this house exuded the love that the siblings had for each other and that the mother had for her children. Tom envied Andrea because he knew that all the belongings in the world could never be better than what they had here.

The PS3, subjugated to analog display through the old 27" television – a crime in and of itself - was a purchase that Andrea had made with her very first paycheck. A gift, not only to herself, but for her three little brothers who she inevitably had spent most of her life raising and whom she loved more dearly than life itself. That was the one thing Tom did love about Andrea – her dedication to family.

The three of them took turns playing some racing game that he failed to catch the name of, mainly because it was irrelevant since he inexorably sucked at racing games. He had no clue why he could handle his Camaro at any speed on a real road but in video games he always managed to drift into walls and run smack into the back end of other cars. They usually had a good laugh at how bad he sucked.

Tom's cell phone rang right in the middle of a race. He ignored it, hoping desperately to beat Andrea to the finish line. He did not beat her, which was not too terribly surprising.

"I was distracted," he said jokingly. "Damn cell phone."

Andrea punched him lightly on the shoulder, "So what about all the other times, huh?"

He smiled and grabbed the cell phone out of his pocket, checked the time, and then looked to see who called.

"Work." He sighed.

Always on Saturday they called him, someone inevitably

called in sick and he was their most reliable backup. Without even checking the message he called the number and ascertained that he was, indeed, requested to work. He finished the call with,

"I'll be in as soon as I can."

Andrea immediately prompted, "You need to learn to say 'no'."

Tom smiled, knowing full well that he should learn the meaning of that word, but it had never been in his vocabulary – always the compliant employee, student, and friend.

"Well, it's been fun but I guess I have to get out of here. See you two lovebirds later. Don't have too much fun without me!" He winked at the two of them.

Andrea and Alex had already proceeded to start another race. He walked out of the house without a word knowing that as soon as he reached the car, those two would be racing for her bedroom instead of the video game finish line.

He drove home with the radio blaring loudly to drown out his own thoughts, the rhythmic thumping of the bass over the reverberation of the car engine lulling his thoughts into oblivion.

His house was deathly silent and abnormally cold when he arrived in through the garage door. He rushed to the thermostat and turned it down, waiting for the sound of the air conditioning compressor to shut off before walking away. The thermostat was set at 75° which was warm enough that the house should never get cold, not unearthly cold as what he felt right now.

Tom walked to his bedroom, grabbed a change of clothes, and headed towards the shower. His father's room had been at the end of the hall, opposite of the bathroom and halfway across the house from his own bedroom. When he walked towards the bathroom, he noticed that his father's room was open, door ajar at least six inches. Tom thought to himself that Junior must have left the door open but he didn't recall seeing the door open on Friday .Of course, Tom was thinking, he was prone to miss things like opened or closed doors. Walking towards the door slowly, cautiously, he began to feel that it was colder here, as if the icy hands of death had settled on the former bedroom of the now deceased.

Kimberly Thomas

He chuckled at his own insecurity and superstitions – something that he wasn't used to feeling. Closer and closer he moved towards the door, the cold was nearing painful levels, until finally he reached the door and in one burst of adrenaline he pushed the door completely open. In an instant, he saw a glimmer of something – a shape, something unnatural, something hideous and demonic; he saw something fall to the ground; and then the room was warm again.

Now, one would think that having seen something that was as disturbing as the glimmer of a shape in a room of a deceased man, one would run away, but Tom was not one for superstitions and what he saw was no doubt just a cloud that blocked the sun and caused a shadow and some abnormal coldness in the house and a draft, a draft that knocked something to the floor, that had to be all it was, that is what he told himself. Without fear, Tom walked forward to where the shadow had been and where he had seen something fall. On the ground before him was a photograph, and he picked it up and glanced at it.

He gasped and as his heart beat loudly in his chest, he stared at the photograph for on it was the woman he had seen in his dream.

Five

Rachel sat on the couch in disbelief.

Two hundred dollars.

Two hundred dollars for only a few hours – well more like eight - of work, and that didn't even include the paycheck she'd get on Friday. No wonder people preferred waitressing to cooking. Now, granted she had seen most of the people she waited on before, and most of them knew she was poor, so she probably got some pity tips but still, TWO HUNDRED DOLLARS!! Maude had told her that Tony had left her $20, which was surprising since the waitresses at the diner always complained at how the teenagers always left bad tips.

But, what could she say; she was 'tappable' now. She laughed; one outfit and she already had a different opinion of herself other than that of the Goodwill cover girl. She had been transformed into something, maybe not beautiful, but at least 'tappable' – that was a definite improvement.

She never had enough money to start a bank account so any spare cash she had was stored in a frozen pea box inside of the freezer. At first glance, no one would know it wasn't frozen peas, but tucked inside was around a $100 and now as she tucked the money safely in the box, Three hundred dollars.

She went back to the couch and grabbed the box with the dress that Maude had given her. She was drooling over it and desperate to try it on. She slid into the bathroom, slipped on the dress, and to the best of her ability, looked at herself in the tiny vanity mirror – the only mirror in the house. From what she could tell through the old glazed mirror was that she looked amazing. A perfect mix of cotton and rayon, the dress did its best to make her look out of place in this humblest of homes.

Among her many talents, Maude apparently was a fashion genius.

Rachel took the dress off, put back on her baggy t-shirt that she slept in, folded the dress back up and slid it and the shoes next to the couch, and laid down to sleep – 4:30 a.m. would come early when it was already close to midnight. Her dreams, typically devoid of action, were wrought with Junior chasing her, Mrs. Crabtree in tears and pain, and a figurative knight in shining armor, who, face disguised from her in her dreams, rescued her from this tormented hell in his white sports car.

The alarm on her watch destroyed the silent sanctity of the night and reminded her that morning always came too soon. She reluctantly arose from the couch, showered and then slipped out of the house decked in cook attire – another day, another couple of dollars.

She would like to say she was always anxious to go to work and that she loved her job, but there were times, especially days like today when four hours of restless sleep did not help, that she wished she were like the other kids in school; some parents were so wealthy that the kids only worked for spending money, not because they had to pay the bills.

Rachel smiled tiredly at Maude as she walked in through the back door of the quiet diner, yawning; she asked what Maude needed her to start on for her morning work. She listed out the things and then added, "Next week, I want you to start waitressing."

Rachel smiled listlessly, and without a word, went on to do her daily opening duties. The day dragged on for what seemed like forever. She was only supposed to work till around 6 p.m. when her replacement would come in and take over. Maude came in around 5:45 – Rachel feared that she was going to tell her to stay late.

"You must have made some friends yesterday; I've had several people call and ask when you were working again." Maude kept talking..

"Of course, you are working today I told them, but only as a cook. Next weekend, you'll be transformed again into my little 1950s waitress." Maude's smile beamed across her face.

Rachel wasn't sure how to respond. She liked the money; there was no way she could say she didn't, but she wasn't really sure that she wanted to wait tables again and be subjected to the scrutinizing eyes of the diner patrons.

"Oh, something else, something came for you." She smiled mischievously, a look Rachel had always loved on her – a look that brought out her youthful glow.

"Come now, the boys can handle the orders. You're done for the day."

Maude took Rachel to her office and opened the door, pointing gracefully at a bouquet of red roses that set the dark office aglow.

"Those are for you."

Rachel looked at her befuddled and then reached for the card that stood like a blank spot on a bloody canvas. Opening the envelope, Rachel read the card aloud:

"From a secret admirer, MJ"

Maude laughed. Her laugh was the sound of angels, soft and rhythmic. "One day as a waitress and you're already acquiring a fan base. Now go home and take those allergy-inducing flowers home with you." She smiled and tapped Rachel lovingly on the butt, pushing her towards the back door. "Come on now, get out." She laughed softly.

Rachel laughed in response, "Yes, mother."

Rachel slipped out of the back door of the restaurant, flowers in hand, albeit awkwardly and headed towards her apartment. The sound of cars and traffic – being much too close to the highway – was a welcome sound from the hustle and bustle of dishes rattling and orders being called out and profanities being ejected when things didn't go just right. Rachel did love working with Maude and the pay was good, but sometimes fresh air, as much fresh air as could be expected in a big city like this, was welcomed.

A horn honked behind her, scaring her. Rachel scooted further into the sidewalk closer to the wall, immediately assuming that the driver thought she might be too close to the road - drivers were so rude sometimes. The horn honked again and she looked towards the sound of the horn, half-tempted to throw up her middle finger at the rude driver, something that she rarely ever did and only reserved for the most callous of offenses.

She was shocked, surprised, and somewhat alarmed when she saw Mr. Crabtree hanging halfway out of his silver Mercedes sedan window, driving with his head out of the window, slowly edging forward with every one of her steps.

"Mr. Crabtree?" She asked, incredulously.

"Junior." He said in his gruff voice, the voice she was sure most women found stimulating. "Call me Junior. You need a lift?"

All the talks in school about taking rides from strangers slipped through her head like hurried nightmares, almost eighteen she was still able to be overcome by someone of his stature. She said softly,

"No, no, I'm fine. I'm just going around the corner."

Which was the truth, but she was almost equally scared to accidentally lead him to her apartment, at which she'd even be more susceptible to whatever harm he had in store. God knew her neighbors would be of no use, so subjected to such intense violence that they just ignored the cries of others, now.

"Tina told me all about you." He paused; the puzzled look on Rachel's face must have told him what she was thinking. "My wife, you know, Mrs. Crabtree. Anyway, you know it's the last week of school, Tina said you always look like a poor kid and I wanted to take you shopping, get some new clothes for your last week. Make you look pretty."

Rachel swore he said "Make you look pretty for me", but she had to have been mistaken. Rachel's head filled with angry thoughts. Mrs. Crabtree would surely never tell people that she looked poor. Mrs. Crabtree was annoying, yes, but never had she just been downright rude.

Without a word, Rachel stared blankly at him, her mind elsewhere, and he continued, "I promise it'll be okay."

Rachel shook her head in protest. "I don't think that's a good idea. Maybe if Mrs. Crabtree came, but I don't know." She shook her head fiercely, as if the shaking alone would deter Junior from whatever his intentions were, "Besides, I don't like charity."

He looked saddened.

"Well Tina was going to come," he said softly, "but she's not feeling well. She came down, with something." He smiled impishly, a smile that sent chills down her spine, and then continued, "She'd be disappointed if you didn't come." The smile on his face looked more devious than friendly. "And don't consider it charity, consider it an investment in our future."

"Our future?"

"No, no, that's not what I said, I said your future." He smiled and again, chills went down her spine.

A little unnerved, she politely replied, "I'm sorry, Mr.... Junior. I can't." She turned her head back towards the diner and then towards her apartment building – both in running distances.

He took the hint.

"Well, if I can't drive you to the mall or something, then at least take this." He held his hand out, rolled up money lay in his palm.

Rachel walked towards the car slowly, not knowing if she should take the charity or run away, and, in the back of her mind, thinking that she wanted to avoid the appearance of looking like a prostitute picking up a John. When she was close enough to the window, he grabbed her hand firmly and placed the money in her palm. Holding her hand almost to the point of pain, he said ever-so-softly and somewhat seductively, "Come closer."

Rachel balked, trying to pull her hand out of his, but he held tighter and she was forced to move closer to him. With his other hand, he grabbed the back of her head and pulled her face into his car and them firmly kissed her – nothing vulgar just a simple kiss on the lips but still she felt her stomach clench as if she would spew the food in her stomach, and then as quick as it had started, he let her hand and her head go.

She stumbled backwards, money still cupped in one hand, roses held in the other, and he said "See you around", winked, and then drove off at breakneck speed.

He had left five one hundred dollar bills in her palm but the disgust she felt was not erased by the money she held.

She had been used.

Common sense would have said to not use the money, to give it to Mrs. Crabtree on Monday and tell her what happened. Human nature told her to use the money and do just what Mr. Crabtree had said, make herself beautiful for the last week of school. Human nature won.

The mall was not in walking distance from her apartment, and even though she had obtained her driver's license through the driver's education at school, she was not fortunate enough to own a car and public transportation would have been an unnecessary expense. There was, however a free standing department store nearby though, which sold everything from bedding to clothing. After dropping off the flowers in the kitchen of her apartment and changing into a pair of sweatpants and a baggy shirt, she walked to the department store.

An hour later, she was two hundred and fifty dollars poorer but five dresses and one pair of shoes richer. She chose the dresses because they were one piece and would end up costing her less to purchase than if she had to coordinate outfits. Frugality always led to simplicity.

Skipping all the way home, she slipped into her apartment and lay on her couch, staring at the ceiling and wishing, for once, for school to start.

In her exuberance, she had failed to notice the roses scattered on the kitchen floor.

Six

*H*e wouldn't have called his job work because he always had fun doing it. The little pizzeria was one of the few remaining non-chain pizza places in the small little town. The owners, an older man and his wife, entrusted him with more responsibility than they did their own son. Tom was the delivery driver, the cook, the host, the server – whatever they needed -he never said 'no'.

Anthony, the owner, would tell Tom, "Sometimes, I wonder if I shouldn't just will this place over to you when I die, 'cause sure as hell Mikey over there ain't gonna do anything with it."

Anthony's heavy New York accent gave away his origination and the pizza tasted like a little bit of heaven; he couldn't imagine pizza tasting any better even in New York itself.

Nancy, Anthony's wife, doted on Tom like she was his mother, always making sure he was eating enough and not "doing the drugs."

Too many years of eating Anthony's pizza had turned Nancy into a heavy-set woman. Anthony and Nancy together were a formidable force, both weighing over 250 pounds each but as jovial as they were round. Mikey, on the other hand ,was short, skinny, and between Nancy's Scandinavian heritage and Anthony's Italian blood line, Mikey had ended up with fiery red hair and freckles.

Mikey was the reason Tom ended up at the pizzeria every weekend – he spent too many late nights drinking. They couldn't fire Mikey because he was their son, so they always called good ol' reliable Tom to pick up the slack. Sometimes Tom wished they would just fire Mikey because he really hated being called in at the last minute.

Tom walked into the pizzeria and was bombarded with pizzas for delivery. Nancy was flustered, shouting out addresses and handing out pizzas.

"I got it. I got it." He said reassuringly.

Nancy smiled, her chubby cheeks hiding the edges of her mouth. She knew she could always rely on Tom.

The night passed quickly, and before he knew it 11pm was fast approaching and it would be time to go home. He never did feel ready to go home – even before the house was empty – but now he was hesitant, almost afraid.

"Thanks for coming in, Tom." Anthony said as he started locking the front doors. "You're always a lifesaver."

Tom, knowing it was out-of-context, asked "Anthony, how long have you been in Vertueux?"

"Hmmm…about fifteen years now, I guess. Nancy's been here forever though…born and raised." Anthony looked back to where his wife stood cleaning the counters and smiled lovingly at her.

Tom pulled the picture out of his pocket that he had found in his father's room. "Do you know this woman?" He showed the picture to Anthony.

He whistled. "Nope, but sure would like to." He winked at Tom, and then winced when Nancy walked up behind him and whacked him on the head.

Tom chuckled. Nancy grabbed the picture out of Anthony's hands.

"Yeh, yeh, I knew her – a long time ago, probably before you were born. Name was…" she paused, "…something with an L… Lana, Laura, Lisa…Lisa that was it. Married that Odium guy and a day later when he showed up dead, she just up and vanished."

Anthony was humming background music as if the story Nancy was telling was frightening. Nancy chuckled and handed the picture back to Tom. "Where did you dig up that old picture?" She said inquisitively.

"I found it." He paused. "Do you know where she," he pointed towards the picture, "disappeared ?"

"Nah. Some people say she killed old Jeremiah and then ran off to hide; others say she was pregnant at the time and went off to have his child in the city. But, you know how the people around here like to talk. There is no telling where she went off to – a woman that beautiful though, she probably went somewhere better than this small ass town. Probably found her another rich husband to kill…" She chuckled. "…ooh I'm starting to sound like the other old women in town." She laughed heartily and her enormous chest heaved up and down with her laugh. "Thing is, if she really did kill Jeremiah for his money, she never came and got it because," she whispered even though the restaurant was empty except for the three of them, "from what I hear, the money is sitting in an account accruing interest until she returns."

"Or his heir." Anthony said, as if he knew the story.

"It's probably billions by now." She whispered.

Anthony rolled his eyes and walked back into the kitchen to start cleaning up, yelling behind him, "Get out of here Tom or she'll keep you here all night spreading rumors."

Tom chuckled and tucked the picture back in his pocket, said good night, and headed home.

The house was abnormally warm now, because Tom had forgotten to turn the air conditioning back to its normal setting. He fixed the setting and then went to go check the phone messages – perhaps Alex would like to hang out again. God knows, he didn't want to hang out in this house alone tonight.

There were eleven messages on the phone.

"Saturday. 10:25 PM." Static, static, and more static, followed by a blood curdling scream. Message ended.

"Saturday. 10:27 PM." Message ended.

Kimberly Thomas

"Saturday. 10:28 PM." Message ended.
"Saturday. 10:29 PM. HELP." Message ended.
"Saturday. 10:30 PM. ME." Message ended.
"Saturday. 10:40 PM. HELP." Message ended
"Saturday. 10:41 PM. ME." Message ended.
"Saturday. 10:59 PM. RACHEL." Message ended.
"Saturday. 11:02 PM. PLEASE GOD." Message ended.
"Saturday. 11:05 PM. RUN. SAVE. RACHEL." Message ended.

His heart raced fast in his chest, beating so loudly it seemed to reverberate against the walls in the house. What the hell was going on?

"Saturday. 11:10 PM." A whispered, somewhat scratchy but familiar voice – unlike the voices in the other messages which had seemed almost mechanical – said,

"It's too late for me now. Save her."

The phone rang, he jumped backwards startled, heart racing wildly in his chest. Grabbing the phone, he yelled,

"Who the hell is it?"

The other side of the line was silent and then a broken voice but clearly the voice of his brother said,

"Tina's dead."

It was almost midnight and he was tired and this news, given only moments after he had listened to the odd and unusual messages on the answering machine, shocked him.

He sank against the wall; the questions rolling through his mind were not coming out through his mouth. His brother kept speaking relieving him of the need to speak,

"I went out." He spoke softly, his voice seeming to crack under the strain, "She jumped. She jumped, right out of the apartment window."

"When?" It was all Tom could muster in response.

"I don't know. Today sometime. The cops, they were all up here tearing through stuff, I don't remember when they said she jumped, something like 10:25 to 10:30 when it was reported. It doesn't matter, she's dead." He paused. "Fourteen floors and then splat right on the pavement."

Tom sympathetically spoke.

"I'm going to drive up tonight, okay?"

Tom swore he heard in the most demonic of voices, "No, no, no, she's all mine, all mine." But when asking "What?" his brother simply and coolly replied, "You don't have to, I'll be okay."

Tom feared that his brother might be taking this all too well, and replied matter-of-factly, "No, I will be there. You shouldn't be alone." He hung up before his brother could reply.

The matter was settled, and Tom, gathering up a bag of clothing, headed towards his brother's apartment in the city. Two deaths in two weeks, and voice mails that were beyond strange – one of which he swore was made by his sister-in-law after her supposed death.

Kimberly Thomas

Seven

*R*achel had noticed the roses on the floor the morning after as she prepared a bowl of Fruity-Os – the cost effective version of the name brand cereal for breakfast. Her mother would not speak to her until after graduation – that she was sure of – but this inexplicable display of irrational behavior was absurd even for her. She felt like intruding on her mother's privacy and objecting to her display, but she chose against it for it would only take her mother longer to come out of her shell.

After all it was the first day of school where she would not be dressed in hand-me-downs, first day not dressed as the Goodwill cover girl. She picked a light floral dress that tied just below her chest and not only provided a quite stunning view of her cleavage but also made her look like she had the perfect hourglass figure – something that wasn't too difficult to achieve when she was dressed in clothes that fit her. She pulled her hair back into a ponytail and slipped on her new sandals, looked approvingly at herself in the tiny bathroom mirror, and proceeded to walk to school.

She had a different bounce in her step today, head held high instead of turned towards the ground, back straight, and a big smile as a rolled down car window let a cat call escape from the occupants. Had she seen the silver Mercedes parked on the side of the road, she might have been frightened, but she was oblivious to everything but the happy little song that played in her head.

She felt it as soon as she entered the doors to the school, an air of despondency and grief in the hallways – something quite alarming for the last week of school. It was a solemn atmosphere that left a dark foreboding cloud on the school.

She saw Danny in the hallway, for once, separated from the twin that shared his face. He smiled at her politely and she touched his arm as he passed,

"What happened?" she said softly, hoping that she was not the only one that felt this upsetting ambiance.

He looked sad and then staring at his feet, muttered,

"A teacher died, they aren't saying much." Then pulling away from her walked on to his classroom.

If this had been a cartoon, her jaw would have dropped to the floor, instead awe-struck and in shock, she intuitively and mindlessly walked to her first class – the happy song that once portrayed her mood now replaced by something more vile and dismal, a song of death.

Each class that day explained that Mrs. Crabtree had died; no one said how, no one said when, just that she had passed away. Lunch was quiet with subdued rumoring of the murder, no the suicide, no the accidental death of Mrs. Crabtree. Rachel dreaded the last day of the class when they had to face the substitute who would replace their Mrs. Crabtree for the remaining week of class.

When it did arrive, they all walked in sadly and sat quietly at their desks waiting for the substitute, Mr. Timothy, to begin. Mr. Timothy, who refused to let the students call him by his last name, simply because it had very few vowels and was long enough to confuse even himself in pronunciation, was an older gentleman of around 65 who, having retired from the business world, wanted to give something back to the "younger generation".

Mr. Timothy began today's class with a somber reminder in

his cultured voice that "we must cherish those while they live and cherish their memories when they are gone." With that said, he proceeded on with the lesson. She was sure that the entire class was thankful for that quick and to-the-point discussion on the death of Mrs. Crabtree, for her death, as tragic as it was, was not what they were here to discuss, and class-after-class, Rachel and her fellow students had to suffer through moments of silence and discussions about her death all day.

The day was nearing an end and the students, casually glancing at the clock on the wall, kept hoping for that bell to ring to indicate the end of the school day and a release from this prison of remorse and sadness that they had been subjected to this entire day of school. Instead of the bell, however, the class was interrupted by a commotion outside the room.

A woman's voice,

"You cannot go in there right now. Not until after class." The voice sounded vaguely as that of the school secretary.

A male's voice, gruff and appallingly familiar as that of Mr. Crabtree, said,

"I can do whatever I want, she was my wife."

Another voice, sounding out of breath, said, "Just wait Junior, wait a few minutes."

"Get the hell out of here, Tom, I told you not to fuc---"

The bell rang and the voices were blocked out. No one jumped up to leave as usual, but the entire class casually and slowly put their books in their bags. The three figures from outside opened the door and walked in.

Ms. Palaid, the school secretary, was a large old woman who, never married, had made the school her replacement husband, apologized to Mr. Timothy for the intrusion and introduced Mr. Crabtree.

"Tom, was it?"

Junior glanced around the classroom; Rachel ducked behind the tall boy who sat in front of her so he couldn't see her.

Mr. Timothy, annoyed that the student's were sitting around

even after the bell, said "Come on now, all of you, go home." Pausing, he added, "Rachel." He glanced over the class. "Uh. Rachel Odium?"

It had always amazed Rachel that even though Mr. Timothy had taught the class on numerous occasions during Mrs. Crabtree's frequent absences, he still had failed to associate names with faces.

The tall boy in front of Rachel stood up and pointed at her, snickering as he pointed, apparently still seeing Rachel as the geeky Wretched Rachel, not the butterfly who emerged from her cocoon – Rachel couldn't say she wasn't disappointed. Junior and the young man who they had called Tom both turned to look at her. Rachel, refusing to make eye contact, stared straight at Mr. Timothy.

"Yes?"

"I have something for you. Mrs. Cra---." He glanced at Junior and then continued, "---well, there was some stuff left in the desk for you. Old papers or something. Come get them please."

Rachel stood up and nervously walked towards the front of the class and grabbed the envelope out of Mr. Timothy's hands – another manila envelope, sealed. She glanced at Junior who licked his lips seductively – or at least that is what she saw, but the other two men did not seem to notice the vulgar display. Quickly averting her eyes, from Junior's gaze, she glanced at the one they called Tom. Tom was breathtakingly beautiful with green eyes flecked with gold and a face that was so cherubic that she would bet under his shirt he hid a pair of wings. He was shorter than his brother and not as muscular but was so stunning that he could easily be confused as a model or movie star; he looked nothing like the raw, rugged handsomeness of his brother.

Even in this most somber of days, Rachel felt her heart beat faster just looking into his eyes and the smile he gave left her knees weak and she thought to herself, re-designed her entire purpose for living. He outstretched his hand,

"I'm Tom, Mr. Crabtree's brother."

Rachel placed her hand out to reach his and grabbing it felt a shock of energy pass through her. She felt as if she were going to pass out and she had no energy to even tell him her name – but she was also aware that he already knew her name.

Out of the corner of her eye, she saw the look that shot from Junior's eyes, and letting go of Tom's hand quickly, she clutched the envelope to her chest, and promptly said good-bye.

Clutching the envelope for dear life, she rushed from the classroom and ran all the way home, looking back periodically to make sure that Junior did not follow.

Eight
🦋 🦋 🦋

The drive to his brother's apartment was only about six hours but after getting a late start on the trip, by the time he reached the city, it was early Monday morning and his brother was not at the apartment. He had not expected that his brother would have stayed in the apartment for the night because the reminder of his wife and the aura of death would have been bitterly strong. Had he and his father been close, Tom felt that he probably would have never been able to return home with the constant reminder of the person he had lost but Tom was a sentimental and emotional person. Junior would no doubt be in grief over the sudden loss of his wife.

Tom had spent the morning driving around, constantly calling his brother's cell phone and trying desperately to find the silver Mercedes that his brother drove – afraid that if he did not locate his brother that his brother might be in danger. He had no luck.

After hours of fruitless searching, late in the afternoon, on a hunch he had decided to check the school where Tina had worked. Something inherent and primal had led him to the doors of the high school and fortunately, Tina, always sharing too much information, had shared with him all about her time at the high school – name and all.

Arriving at the school, he had immediately gone to the front office where he found out, as women scattered around like hens looking for feed, that sure enough Junior had arrived at the school before him.

One of the flustered women in the office spoke up in a squeaky voice that sounded like it came directly from the PA system, "Mr. Crabtree, uh, your brother, he just came in here and demanded that he be taken to his wife's classroom - said he wanted her stuff. Ms. Palaid, our secretary, she's down there now trying to stop him from going in."

Another woman piped in. "Class ends in about three minutes. But your brother shouldn't bother the students, they've had a tough time with her death…everyone, everyone loved her." She glanced towards the ground solemnly.

He had only arrived a few minutes shy of his brother, which the women found to be quite fortunate on their behalf since they had no way of stopping the hulking and unwieldy body of his brother on a mission. Tom asked politely for the location of the classroom and ran, ran as if the school was on fire, to the door of the classroom.

As he approached the classroom, he saw a large woman, most likely the secretary the hens had mentioned, and his brother arguing in the hallway. In a vain attempt to keep his brother from going in a few minutes before the bell, Tom said,

"Just wait Junior, wait a few minutes."

But after his brother started to yell at him about coming there in the first place with a few choice profane words the bell rang and the secretary slipped them into the class as if no altercation had occurred in the halls.

He was embarrassed, not only because the class was still sitting down but because they had obviously interrupted the learning environment and it was obvious by the look on the instructor's face that the class had heard the argument outside their door.

Amazingly, unlike at his school, the students still sat there, putting their books up in the backpacks slowly and robotically. He did not stare at their faces, simply glanced over the room and proceeded to follow his brother – determined to not have his brother make a fool of himself, which would be a feat in and of itself.

The secretary made the introductions to the instructor as Tom stood staring at the chalkboard – not reading it, but simply staring at it blankly. His attention was drawn away from the white lines on the black background when the teacher interrupted by calling the name "Rachel." That oh so familiar name. And then, "Rachel Odium." Rachel, the ugly girl who was Tina's prized student and the girl Tina, in her odd voice mail, said he had to protect. She had never said that Rachel's last name was Odium – it was probably coincidence. It was not likely that she was related to the long-since deceased Jeremiah.

He turned, half-expecting a morphed version of the Hunchback and a witch, but was stunned as the picture of angelic beauty, bathed in the glow of the fluorescent lighting of the school, stood and walked towards him. Her hair was long and black, her eyes the color of coal shone like diamonds in the rough, her body was perfect, curved in every way that every man would want and that every lust could ever desire.

She was the girl in his dream, not the one in the picture.

He stared at her, longing for her to turn to him and talk, or perhaps just to grace him with a smile.

She turned to them and he outstretched his hand in introduction. He was aware that his brother's breathing had changed but he did not look away from that face – This was the woman with whom he wished to spend the rest of his life.

She placed her hand in his and he felt as if he was going to fall to the ground for she was magnetic and she energized him in ways that only his wildest dreams could have imagined.

Her hand fell from his and as quickly as she had arrived in his life, she was saying good-bye as she walked away, school secretary waddling behind her. He was too stunned to stop her.

When the door closed behind her, the teacher whispered to Junior, "Smart and beautiful, they don't make them like that anymore. If I were thirty or forty years younger…"

The teacher chuckled softly but was immediately silenced as he noticed the expression on Junior's face - a fierce look that even Tom had not seen from either Junior or his father before; Tom, disinterested, turned to watch the door.

The door had closed behind her and her very scent, and the sensation of her presence, departed with her. He longed to see her again; he had to see her again. His life would be forever complete with her by his side. He sighed softly.

His yearning was interrupted by Junior – big and burly – leaning over the teacher threateningly as he asked in a gruff, low murmur, "What did you give her?"

The teacher stammered and moved backwards against the wall, "Just an envelope - something Mrs. Crabtree – uh, your wife – had left for her. Papers, I guess."

Tom had to step in to keep his brother from towering over and possibly destroying the now shuddering teacher. There was a look of pure, unadulterated evil in Junior's eyes, something that he had not seen before – something uncharacteristic even for his easily-angered family.

Junior backed away but as soon as Tom let go of his arm, he rushed towards the teacher who cowered against the wall, and whispered something into the teacher's ear.

"Out, get out now." The teacher in a voice trembling and frightened screamed at Junior.

Tom pushed his brother gently out of the classroom, telling his brother they could come back later for Tina's belongings. They exited the classroom, and to Tom's dismay, there was no sign of his angelic Rachel in the hall.

Nine
❦ ❦ ❦

*R*achel sat panting and out of breath on her couch, still clutching the envelope to her chest. In the rush to exit the building, she had left her backpack sitting under her chair. She was not inclined to return for the bag today; it would and could wait until tomorrow.

After her heart stopped racing like a greyhound chasing the rabbit at the races, she sat under the dim glow of the light and, again, sat anxiously as she opened another manila envelope from Mrs. Crabtree. If Mrs. Crabtree had this envelope on Friday she would have given it to her, because Mrs. Crabtree was well-known by the students for her inability to hide good or bad news. At some point this weekend, in some futile attempt to hide information from her husband, she had gone to school and left the paperwork in her desk to be given to Rachel on Monday.

Her husband, whom in only a few brief encounters she had concluded was a psychopath, because of the events in the classroom earlier today, now knew that his wife had provided information to Rachel – something that Mrs. Crabtree had been adamant about keeping secret.

The link between the pages Mrs. Crabtree had provided her before and Junior's sudden interest in her life still escaped her – although the obvious connection to Mrs. Crabtree's father-in-law was quite obvious. Rachel slipped open the seal on the envelope and again extracted the pages from this package, something that eerily felt like a call from the grave.

Expecting another post-it note, she turned the envelope upside down – there was nothing.

The first set of papers in the package was an old term paper Rachel had written called "A Modern Day Approach to The Scarlet Letter". It had been one of Rachel's best papers she had written during her junior year - an expose on the current applications of discrimination against women who are labeled adulterers. She sat the paper aside, disappointed.

After shuffling through the pages of her former term paper, she found, in Mrs. Crabtree's handwriting, a note written to Rachel dated May 10, this past Saturday – the day Rachel saw her at the diner.

"*Rachel,*

I write to you in great urgency for I fear my life is in danger. My husband has always been a violent man but he changed even more when his father died and I fear that my husband, possessed by the same psychosis as his father, will rid himself of me just to get closer to you and your mother.

I pray that you do not take these matters lightly and that you and your mother will run and hide for these obsessions will kill us all.

Tina"

Rachel wasn't sure how to take that letter; on one hand it seemed as though Mrs. Crabtree had predicted her own death but on the other hand, the letter seemed a little on the paranoid side and perhaps the paranoia had taken the best of her. After all, suicide was something that Rachel had always considered an option for the weak – those who could not learn to cope with their fears and insecurities.

A knock on the door interrupted Rachel's musings and her readings. Heart being loudly in her chest, and feeling as if Death himself stood at her door, she slipped the pages from the envelope underneath the couch, afraid that Junior had somehow found her. She peaked through the peep hole in the door and saw Maude.

She unlocked the door and let her in.

Maude had never visited her apartment before; she only had the address because it was required by law for tax purposes. Rachel was embarrassed of her living conditions and ducked her head in shame. Maude said nothing as she came in; she simply wrapped her arms and hugged Rachel.

Rachel let her hug her as long as she desired.

Maude finally spoke, "You look beautiful today, dear."

Rachel smiled, but did not speak.

"I heard about your teacher – that Mrs. Crabtree – what a shame, what a shame." She shook her head in disbelief.

"Suicide - and she had so much going for her."

There was a brief moment when Rachel thought better of her next steps, but she had to share this burden of information with someone, and who better than her quasi-grandmother, Maude?

"I have something." Rachel said softly, almost inaudibly. "I want you to read this, tell me what you think."

She extracted the first envelope that Mrs. Crabtree had given her from behind the back cushion of the couch and handed it to Maude as she sat on the far end of the couch, closest to the light.

"Read these first."

Rachel pulled the second envelope and the contents from underneath the couch and held those until Maude was done.

"Interesting." Maude said, confused. "Who gave these to you? And are these about you and your mother?" She glanced at the closed bedroom door of the apartment.

Rachel nodded. "Mrs. Crabtree said it was, but I don't know. I've never even heard of that town and it could be all coincidental – the names and all."

Rachel handed her the note from Mrs. Crabtree, Maude read it quickly and then responded,

"You need to give this letter to the police, dear. If she thought she was in danger, then they may want to investigate her suicide a little further."

"I haven't had a chance to read the next couple of things in this package. There isn't much," Rachel flipped through the pages, "just this one letter it looks like and some badly copied pictures."

"Well, read the letter out loud then." Maude said, never one to duplicate efforts when it wasn't necessary.

"It is dated May 10, 2008. It's from Mike." Rachel read the date incredulously because the last letter she had seen from Mike was dated in 1991. Excluding the fact that the handwriting was different than those letters from the early 90s which could have been logically attributed to age, according to Mrs. Crabtree, her father-in-law who Rachel had assumed was Mike had died a week prior to the date that this letter was written. She continued reading, despite it being chronologically unsound.

"Lisa,

I have found you, alive and well in the city, along with a daughter who has grown to be as beautiful as you were, perhaps even more beautiful. You have changed, however, into an old shell of a woman who, perhaps affected by the death of Jeremiah, has become such a useless person that even I would not want you.

If you have truly lost all hope in living because of the death of your beloved, then know that he pines for you in his house, stewing with an anger that cut me down and started me anew. Your precious Jeremiah should be accredited for me finding you and his child.

Go to him because I have found my new love in your daughter. Good-bye forever.

Mike"

Rachel's hands were shaking as she dropped the letter next to her and grabbed the pages of copied photos that Mrs. Crabtree had sent along, eager to deviate herself from the letter which moved Mike's psychotic obsession from mother to daughter.

The first was a dark photo of a house, more like a mansion reminiscent of old movies like Gone with the Wind, pillars tall and wide accentuated the massiveness of the home. The home looked overgrown with weeds but the majesty of the home still shone through even the dilapidation. Windows dark and shadowed covered the mass expanse of the two floors, placed several feet apart and wide as they were long – as if the house, in days of old, would have been lit only by the light of the morning sun than by the electricity of the modern world.

The photo had no relevance, however, and Rachel placed the photo down and grabbed the next page. This photo was a close-up of one of the windows. She was casually glancing at it, and then glanced at Maude who was looking at the photo of the house.

She held the photo up to the light and then pointed at something, "Do you see this?" Her finger shook slightly as she pointed towards a window on the second floor.

"Probably dirt." Rachel said, for the smudge in the window looked like nothing more than a flaw in the photography or the photocopy – the photo had been taken from such a great distance that it could have easily been anything.

Maude reached over and grabbed the paper Rachel was holding – the photo with just the window. "There, see it's there too." She pointed at a similar smudge on the photo of just the window.

Sure enough, there was something on the photo in exactly the same spot as the window in the larger shot. Maude grabbed the next and last photo out of the pile of papers and held it up to the light. Gasping, she dropped the photo to the floor.

"What, what is it?" Rachel said quickly.

Maude's face had turned to a paleness that made her look her age – old and fragile.

Rachel grabbed the paper off the floor, and holding it up to the light, she gasped as she saw an ethereal and unearthly, but strangely familiar, face staring back at her out of the window. She too dropped the paper to the floor and muttered, almost incoherently to Maude,

"I need air."

Maude nodded and they walked out of the apartment, heading nowhere in particular, and not speaking a word.

Ten

*N*ineteen eighty nine.

She remembered it all too well; a year when Driving Miss Daisy won over the world and students demonstrated in Tiananmen Square and the world gasped when the Exxon Valdez destroyed the sanctity of our precious oceans and spawned a new era of activists. Of course, that is just what happened in the world around her, the most important part of 1989 was meeting Jeremiah.

She had been twenty-one years old, working at a locally-owned department store in Vertueux, when Jeremiah Odium, wealthy heir and current owner of the department store had walked in and bought a tie. She had thought it odd, in her naiveté that he would purchase a tie from his own store, when he knew full well that they sold nothing that was anywhere near his standards in taste, but she had assisted him diligently, albeit shyly, in picking a tie that best accentuated his deep green eyes.

She had thought about him for days after that chance November meeting for he was everything that she had ever dreamed of in a man, even though he was ten years her senior. It wasn't his wealth that attracted her but the power that exuded from him, the way he carried himself, and the face that was soft but rugged and reminded her of an old western where Jeremiah Odium would be the one who would be called to rescue the damsel in distress.

She had loved him from the moment she had seen him.

It was nearing Christmas time when she had been called into the manager's office and told that she was out of a job, fired, even though she had always been an exemplary employee. Her manager, Mr. Smith, was a cold callous old man who smelled vaguely of onions and wore old polyester suits that should have been tossed in the trash simply to spare the rest of the world from having to see them. Without so much as an explanation, he handed her an envelope with "Lisa Sanchez" written in a script too fine to be his and then told her gruffly to get her belongings and get out.

She was near tears but held them back. Of all the times to lose a job, Christmas was not one of them. For all intents and purposes, she had no Christmas plans. Her mother and father had decided to spend a good chunk of their retirement years touring Europe and had called recently to say, "We're sorry dear, but we won't be making it home in time for Christmas."

Her father had tried his best to use a fake Irish accent, as at the time of the call he was downing a pint of Guinness while mother cavorted with the locals in the background. She had not expected them to return in time anyway.

With feelings hurt but feigning strength, she grabbed the envelope, went back to her station, grabbed her purse and exited the building. She walked home, which was her usual routine because she enjoyed the coolness of the November air and she loved the time to think. She slipped open the envelope and read the letter enclosed.

"*Miss Sanchez,*

I do apologize for firing you on such short notice and at such an inopportune time but I cannot get you out of my mind. I have spent a month thinking and thinking about you and decided that I cannot ethically ask you out if you were an employee of mine. Please accompany me for dinner tonight and if things do not work out between us as I hope they do then you may have your job back tomorrow. I will pick you up at 8 p.m.

Forever yours,
Jeremiah Odium"

She had laughed warmly and was immediately excited about

the upcoming date, no longer upset of her loss. She tucked the letter back in the intent on keeping that letter forever for it warmed her heart every time she read it.

The date had gone miraculously well, so well that throughout the rest of the year and the year after and the beginning of the next year, they spent every waking moment of their lives together.

It had never been sexual. They had enjoyed each other's company so much that they had opted to refrain from anything more physical until the day they married, which they both knew from the beginning was inevitable, for their souls were destined to be together forever.

A few days before Christmas in 1990, walking in the park hand-in-hand, he had gone on one knee, and with eyes glued to hers, he had asked her to marry him.

It had been a big scandal that he had dated and then proposed to a woman who once worked for him; of course she had been labeled a carpet bagger and by some, worse than that, for they saw her as wanting simply to marry him for his money. That had not been true; she had loved him and she had married him secretly on December 26, 1990, and unbeknownst to either of them at the time, had conceived his child on the same day they had consummated their marriage.

She did not dare remember the days following December 26th, for they were too painful to remember. She did not dare despair over the reasons why Jeremiah chose to leave her or why he had chosen to not take her with him. But these eighteen long years, these desperate and dangerous years, she had been forced to live – if what she did was called living - without him and she was forced to see him in the face of his daughter.

She had wanted to die but feared suicide would take her to hell while Jeremiah was no doubt up in heaven looking down on her. She even had tried to convince herself she was going to die, but day after day she suffered through this meaningless existence staring at the bland and shabby ceiling above her with nothing but hopelessness to endure.

Kimberly Thomas

On this day in May, a few days after her daughter had asked for her presence at graduation, she had heard someone come in the apartment, which was unusual because neither she nor Rachel had friends, and, being honest to herself, no family. She sometimes regretted never being a mother to her daughter but she couldn't stand looking into the face that reminded her so much of her precious Jeremiah. She sometimes regretted just not having her parents' raise the child but she had spoken to them only once after she left that dreadful town and they did not know they had a grandchild. She didn't even know if her parents were still alive.

The voices of both her daughter and the unknown visitor in the room were muffled. Afraid that whomever had sent flowers to her daughter had encroached themselves upon her house, Lisa walked slowly towards her door and opened it quietly and cautiously. As little maternal instinct as Lisa had towards her daughter, she was also very aware that Rachel had no right finding love for love was something that was destructive as and would leave death, destruction and mayhem in its path, as much as a Category 5 hurricane.

It was not a man who had visited, as Lisa had suspected, but an old woman, small and demure, who sat on the couch near the light while Rachel sat clouded in the darkness. They were reading something or looking at papers, she couldn't really tell. The old woman looked flustered, frightened, and in disgust she threw a paper down on the floor. She saw Rachel's frightened face as she reached to the floor and picked up the paper that the woman had thrown down and then watched as both promptly fled the apartment.

Curiosity killed the cat – and today Lisa was the cat. She slunk out of the room as if she was walking through a mine field and grabbed the tossed aside paper. She moved towards the light, eyes not accustomed to the dimly lit room, and gasped. That face – that shadowed face -- she grasped the paper like a school-girl with a photo of her crush and plopped herself on her daughter's couch. "My Jeremiah." She muttered the statement softly over and over again.

She smiled a smile reminiscent of days long passed.

Eleven

*T*om had silently followed his brother all the way to Junior's car, padding behind him like an obedient puppy. Junior muttered incoherently, fists flailing periodically like a mad man; he seemingly was oblivious to Tom's presence. They reached the Mercedes and Junior - as if somehow just made aware of Tom's presence - turned around and, grabbing Tom by the neck, threw him against the driver's side of the Mercedes, door handle pushing painfully into Tom's body.

"Stay away from her. You understand me?" He spit saliva as he sputtered the words in Tom's face.

"Who? Who do I need to stay away from? Tina's dead, bro." Tom was confused as to his brother's reference.

There was a darkness in Junior's eyes that Tom had never seen before, as though something possessed him, as though he was crazed. It was a darkness that one would surely find in serial killers and lunatics, a demented madness that Tom knew would not end well. Tom shuddered for he feared his brother was capable of just about anything, more now than ever, and at this moment, he feared that his brother was capable of killing – of killing him, his own flesh and blood – simply for whatever insanity possessed him.

Hand still firmly on his neck, Junior spat, "You know who. I saw the way you and that despicable old teacher looked at her."

His brother's hand tightened around his neck and pain shot through him. In an effort to please his brother, he said weakly, "OK, OK, I'll stay away. Sheesh, just let me go. Are you trying to kill me?"

His brother let his hand slide.

"Sorry, sorry."

He muttered as he pushed the button on his keychain to unlock his car.

Tom moved out of the way so the bulky body of his brother could slide into the car. Without a word, Junior slipped into the car and started it. Tom quickly rushed towards his vehicle before his brother could back out.

It had come to him quite remarkably that he should probably follow his brother – for his brother lacked the wherewithal to control his anger – as witnessed by this recent outburst. Tom slipped into his car, and aware that his car, with its beefy engine, was loud and obvious, drove several cars lengths back from his brother's vehicle and tried desperately to keep vehicles in between them for fear that his brother might see him in the rear view mirror.

His brother had not driven far, maybe four blocks. He pulled up to a diner, silver and lined with red and blue, the evening sun glimmered in radiant colors off of the windows and Tom, glancing at the building that was dedicated to a former time, had a sudden desire to see cars from the 1950s and girls in poodle skirts and to listen to some Roy Orbison tunes. He had always longed to have lived in more innocent times. He laughed at himself, and then watched his brother, who, having parked the car, was now walking into the diner.

Stomach grumbling, Tom reluctantly passed the diner, made a u-turn and parked on the opposite side of the street to face the diner so he could wait for his brother's next move.

Tom watched as the analog hands on his watch slowly clicked minute-by-minute until it seemed as though his brother had been sucked into a black hole and that he would never return. An hour had passed and he had not left the diner.

His mind focused on tracking his brother, he was suddenly distracted by movement on the right side of his vehicle. Perhaps it was the jittery state he was in, tailing his overly aggressive brother or perhaps it was something else, but his head turned just in time to see his angelic beauty, Rachel, walking slowly with an older woman who clutched her hand tightly.

He reached over to the passenger side door and rolled the window down – cursing the window for not being automatic and being so difficult to open.

Yelling, because they had now passed his car by at least a few car lengths, he called "RACHEL!"

She turned, eyes wide in terror, and then letting go of the old woman's hand, she bolted, running as if Satan himself was nipping at her heels, her dress fluttering around her bare legs. He wanted to follow after her, to find her and tell her that everything was going to be all right but at the same instance, he saw his brother leaving the diner. His heart wanted to go after Rachel, but he knew also that he must keep an eye on his brother.

The old woman had kept walking, only glancing back once at the young woman, he assumed her granddaughter, that ran away in fright. She had not seemed too confused or concerned about the display and maintained a sense of calm that even Tom could not have even mustered in a time like this.

The woman reached the parking lot of the diner and Junior approached her, arms flailing in emotion, as he spoke – or better yet – screamed at the old woman, for Tom could hear a semblance of the conversation even at the distance he was away from the two.

The dusky sky left a shadow on the parking lot and masked the two individuals who stood in it. The parking lot to the diner was empty and the road Tom had parked on had been virtually empty except for a periodic passing car. It was now reasonably late on a Monday night and most people were home with their families – except for Tom, Junior, the old woman, and his beloved Rachel.

Had the streets been packed and the diner been busy, he would have doubted that Junior would have taken the action he did with the old woman. Flailing arms in a conversation that was obviously one-sided, Junior cemented his opinion with an open-handed slap to the old woman's face. Their father had failed to teach them that women should never be hit – in fact, he had preached the opposite, but both Junior and he knew that it wasn't right. Tom shuddered in his car and grabbed the door handle as a thought briefly crossed his mind to go help.

The old woman bravely stood there and took the hit, which, knowing Junior, only infuriated him more. As Tom expected, Junior continued with a flailing of fists that knocked the old woman to the ground.

Tom, hand posed on the door handle to open it, hesitated, again afraid of what would happen to him if his brother knew he had been following him. He was so mortified and terrified of his brother's anger that he did nothing, instead he simply sat in the comfort of his car and watched in utmost horror of the scene that unfolded before him. The old woman's frail arms that were shielding her face were no match for Junior's muscular punches.

Mercy finally showed up when a car turning onto the street, its headlights briefly lighting the darkened parking lot, pushed Junior into a quick retreat, and racing towards his car, he backed up the Mercedes and drove off.

Tom had not seen Junior run over the old woman, for if he had, he would have been more prepared for the scene when he had arrived at it. As soon as his brother's Mercedes was nowhere to be seen, and forgetting his mission to protect his brother from violent outbursts, knowing that he had failed to protect the old woman, Tom ran towards the old woman, cell phone in hand, already dialing 911.

He had expected to arrive at the woman's side only to see budding bruises on her face and maybe some broken facial bones but nothing more. Instead, running, trying his best to tell the location of the diner to the 911 agent, he stopped suddenly, his stomach churning, when he saw her broken and twisted body on the parking lot.

One leg, bent backwards now, had a bone protruding from

the skin; the other leg was underneath the broken one with probably additional damage. He didn't dare move her or look more intently for he was determined to maintain his cool and to not heave the non-existent food out of his stomach. He went to her side, and stared at her face.

Her breathing was ragged but her eyes were open, clear, and full of pain but she was alive. She muttered something, ever so lightly.

Tom replied, "I'm sorry, what?" He moved his ear closer to her face.

"You..." she paused, breathing ragged. "...You must save her."

He thought to himself, "Not this again."

The sounds of sirens grew closer.

She continued, "Protect her from your..." She gasped for air, holding by a string onto consciousness. "Protect her from your father."

The ambulances arrived and Tom had no further opportunity to talk to the old woman as they carted her off and took her to a hospital.

He wanted to call out to her, "But, my father's dead." But, besides the fact that such a statement would have seemed ultimately callous at such a time, it would have gone unheard for she had since slipped into unconsciousness.

He thought to himself, "How can I protect Rachel, when I couldn't protect you?" Feeling useless, he moved away from the bloodied scene and sat on a curb in the parking lot and placed his head in his hands.

He knew the rest of his night would be spent explaining to police officers how he didn't see who did it or what kind of car it had been and how he had just happened to be driving along when he saw the old woman laying in the parking lot.

He hated lying, but Junior was his brother after all.

Twelve

*O*ut of breath, Rachel had arrived home, and locking the door behind her, she leaned against it and stood gasping for air. Twice this happened – twice in one day. She was never one to run from confrontation but there was something dark and foreboding at work here – something for which she did not want to sit idly and wait for.

    She had simply reacted when she had heard her named called as she walked with Maude back to her diner – something deep inside of her told her to run for only a day before, Junior had followed her from the diner and she knew there was something that she needed to fear from that man.

    While running away like a frightened cat, she had glanced back only to notice that the only vehicle in the street was a white Camaro, not a silver Mercedes, but she had no clue what fleet of vehicles were at the command of Junior and his psychotic dementia.

    She walked, having calmed herself somewhat, to the couch, and gathering up the papers that Mrs. Crabtree had given her and that Maude and she had strewn across the couch and she haphazardly threw them back in the envelope, trying desperately not to glance at the words or pictures. She vaguely remembered at least one of the papers being on the floor, there were none on the floor now – simply on the couch – but in the rush to get fresh air it was surely possible that they had left the paper on the couch instead. She was not too terribly concerned about it, and having placed all the papers back into the envelope, she tossed the envelope behind the couch. This would not be one she would re-open and re-read; the idea of burning both envelopes had seriously crossed her mind.

The sound of sirens in the distance – a very common sound in this neighborhood – lulled her to sleep.

She saw Tom's angelic, white, pure face – the brother of Satan himself. She focused on Junior then – not by choice, but because she could not dictate her dream world into conducting itself according to her will. Junior's evil laugh echoed through her mind and he seemed to exude flames and intense heat as horns sprouted from his head and his eyes turned blood red.

Now she saw herself, lying exposed and naked on a concrete block similar to those used in ancient cultures for the sacrificial slaughter to the gods. Junior, knife held high above her, moaned seductively as his grotesque and demonic face stared at her with nothing but lust. He stood poised and ready to plunge his knife inside of her.

Tom, angelic as he was, stood there silently staring, not at her or his brother, but at the floor below him. She screamed for him to help her, to protect her from this deviant that was ready to take everything from her. Tom finally looked up at her and his eyes were red with fury as he pushed his brother away, the knife falling with a clang to the floor below. Tom reached down and grabbed the knife and she saw it glistening again above her, this time, perhaps to cut her bonds. He smiled at her softly and before she could see what happened next, the dream turned itself into something else.

She now stood in a marbled entrance way, glorious in its richness. Dressed in her black graduation dress, beautiful and remarkably changed from the poor girl of a week ago, she stood looking at her reflection in a mirror that was as tall as her and as wide as she was tall. In the mirror she could see a doorway that led to a dining hall that had a table that could probably hold a hundred people. Music played in the background, a classical piece from Mozart or Beethoven or Bach – something familiar but something that she couldn't quite place. A man and woman danced gracefully around the table. In the reflection she could see that the woman was beautiful - her red dress flowing around her legs, her black hair, long and beautiful, flowed around their arms.

She could not see their faces for they hung in darkness, his face clouded, her face clouded – simply a red dress and the hint of a tuxedo, white shirt seeming to glow against the black background.

She walked closer, wanting to see them – intrigued by their elegance and refinement. As she came closer, the woman turned and, with a smile, she said in a voice so sultry and remarkable,

"Come, child, I have someone I'd like you to meet."

She stared at her in awe, for it was no doubt her mother – her mother reborn into the woman she had seen so many years ago in the picture, beautiful and stunning. The man she danced with walked towards her in darkness and as he outstretched his hand towards her, she grabbed it. With her hand in his firm cold grasp, his face suddenly became clear as if her eyes had somehow become adjusted to the darkness, and letting go of his hand suddenly she backed away for the face she saw now was the same as the ethereal face she had seen in the photograph.

She woke cold and sweating, with a fear that things were only going to get stranger, for she had felt that dreams, even though they rarely came true, were warnings of things to come. She did not know who the man in the picture was or why Mrs. Crabtree felt it was important for her to have those pictures, but she knew beyond a shadow of a doubt that she would gladly turn back time just to be her old self rather than living in this mystery she now seemed to be subjected to.

She did not sleep the rest of the night; she lay on the couch simply staring at the ceilings with a forlorn hope that tomorrow would not be as strange as today.

Kimberly Thomas

Morning came slowly and the sound of sirens and horns reminded her that her life had not truly changed with her conversion.

She thought of simply going back to school as the cover girl for Goodwill since the attractive version of herself seemed to call for trouble – things had simply become strange since she became this new person. But, she did not always want to be seen as the poor girl and opted to wear another new dress, after all, she had wasted a significant amount of money on clothing when she knew better. She picked a blue dress with floral patterns that hung just to her knees and covered enough to not be too seductive but still showed off her curves. She threw the dress on, combed her hair, and threw her sandals on and rushed off to school – intent on getting there early so she could pick up her backpack.

The lights were on in Mrs. Crabtree's – well the former Mrs. Crabtree's classroom – so she glanced through the window to see who was in there. A large, round woman sat in the teacher's chair. She had been a substitute once before when Mr. Timothy had not been available. She was in her late 20s with around five children and everyone hated her as a substitute – not because she was overly mean or harsh but that she had a foul odor that made you gag when she passed by you – as if she never washed any part of her body.

Rachel took a deep breath, knowing that the room would smell of her, and walked in. Smiling as she opened the door, Rachel glanced at the teacher and said "I left my backpack in here yesterday."

The substitute nodded, and then looked back down at the newspaper where she sat avidly reading the comics. Rachel also did not like her because she was not a very smart substitute – her idea of literature was simply the comics – which Rachel found to be rather amusing as she was substituting for the advanced English course.

Rachel grabbed her backpack, which still sat leaning against her desk, and proceeded to her first class, pushing through the bustling crowd of students who stood in groups talking in the hall.

The day today was not as full of sadness as it had been

before – students were excited about graduating in a few days and other students were just glad the summer break was coming up. Rachel was just glad that today seemed less foreboding and full of doom as yesterday had felt.

There wasn't much to do or learn in any of the classes, for, in all reality, everyone was done with classes on Thursday and finals had been completed the week prior. This was a "goof-off" week where everyone had time to sign yearbooks and take pictures and get addresses and phone numbers of the friends they wanted to keep in touch with during the summer and, for that matter, for the rest of their lives.

Rachel did not have any friends and, for the most part, sat in classes and just read books she had borrowed from the library – eternally the nerd.

Rachel's next to last class of the day was calculus. Danny, the twin who was not only the nice one but the smart one, sat next to her as he had all year. Rachel smiled at him softly when he sat down, and then proceeded to continue with the novel she had been reading all day.

He whispered, "So, did ya hear that we can take tomorrow off to go the Mrs. Crabtree's funeral?"

Rachel looked up at him, confused not only that he was talking to her without being prompted to do so, but that she had not heard the news.

"I hadn't heard that."

She said it simply.

"Well, yeh, that's what they said in her class when I was there earlier. Ms. Smelly is subbing today. I guess Mr. Timothy was sick or something."

Her name wasn't really Ms. Smelly but no one could remember her real name once the new title had been dubbed to her.

Rachel smiled, "Yeh- I was in there earlier today to pick up my backpack and noticed she was there. It already smelled in there this morning, I can't wait to go next period." She laughed softly, hoping that she didn't look like she was flirting – she had never flirted before and had no desire now to flirt with Danny.

Kimberly Thomas

He laughed, and his voice was soothing and calming, unlike the sound of his sister's hideous cackle that sounded too remarkably like a witch.

"Can I ask you something?" He paused, glanced around the room and without waiting for a reply, continued, "You think you might want to get something to eat after school today?"

"With you?" Rachel said, puzzled.

He laughed softly, "No, with the Pope." He smiled, and continued, "Of course with me."

"What about your sister?"

"What about her? She won't be there, if that's what you want to know. We're graduating in a few days and I think it's time that I actually do what I want to do and not what my sister thinks is 'socially acceptable'." He rolled his eyes, and then continued, "I still regret to this day that I didn't get to take you to the dance in 6th grade."

Rachel laughed, "You know until you mentioned it just then I had totally forgotten about that dance." She lied because in all reality that moment in time had been the turning point that caused her to be disgusted both with love and with social interaction.

The teacher interrupted them, apparently still intent on being one of the few teachers to actually still teach up until the end of school. She smiled at Danny softly, whispered "Okay" in response to his original request and then watched as the teacher insipidly discussed Calculus.

The bell rang and they slipped out of class and on to the next one; Danny whispered softly in her ear as they pushed their way out of the class that he would meet her outside of Mrs. Crabtree's class after school. Mrs. Crabtree's class was a madhouse. After her announcement that they were permitted to attend the funeral tomorrow, Ms. Smelly shuffled back to the chair and groaned as she plopped her large body into the tiny little chair. Rachel sat and read while the rest of the class chatted and talked on their phones and shot spit wads at each other and overall, acted like they were still in kindergarten.

Rachel was neither excited nor scared about the upcoming

"date" with Danny – confused, yes, but nothing more. She had always considered Danny the sweeter of the two twins, and even though he was attractive he was by no means drop-dead gorgeous, except for those sapphire eyes that shone so brightly. He was nonetheless popular and would surely be committing social suicide by even talking to her. Even in her current state of "tappable", she was still "Wretched Rachel" and tappable or not, it was still unthinkable to consider being friends with such a loser.

The bell rang and Rachel slowly gathered up her belongings and threw them back into her backpack. She ambled towards the door with a foreboding intensity that she couldn't explain and tried her best to stay out of the crowd of bustling teenagers heading towards to the open door of Mrs. Crabtree's classroom and out to the hallway and freedom.

When she reached the door, she saw Danny standing next to it, grinning softly. He grabbed her hand gently and pulled her along without a word. Rachel did not dare look at the faces of people as she passed them in the hallway for fear that they would glower at her and throw accusations with their eyes as if she were Hester Prynne and she wore the scarlet letter upon her chest; she simply stared at the ground, allowing Danny to guide her out of the school.

Upon reaching the open air outside, she sighed in relief and finally looked up. Teens engaged in conversation stood in groups here and there and a few still scuttled off to their cars – none paid any attention to the two who stood hand-in-hand at the front entrance way – one rich kid, one poor one.

Danny led Rachel to his car, a black Honda Accord – one of two of which had been purchased, one for him and one for his sister, on their mutual 16th birthday. The twins usually rode together to school to conserve gas in these days when gas prices sky-rocketed to abnormal heights. Today, they had apparently taken both cars.

As chivalrously as possible, Danny unlocked and opened the passenger door, waited patiently as she slid into the car, and then proceeded to his door to climb in and start the car.

Kimberly Thomas

They were soon heading out of the parking lot, and Rachel smiled softly at him – not sure if he was doing this solely to forget about the 6th grade dance drama, or as charity towards the poor girl, or just because he truly liked her. Either way, it was a welcomed change and she appreciated the normalcy of all of this.

He had not asked where she would like to eat – probably aware that she did not know what restaurants were around besides the diner where she worked. He pulled into the parking lot of a restaurant and by the name was identified as Italian – Carmelo's Italian Ristorante. Parking the car, he rushed to her door before she could open it and assisted her out of the car.

He was overwhelmingly chivalrous and held her hand as they walked inside the restaurant, head held high as if he held the hand of the princess of some foreign kingdom. A young man, clad in white dress shirt and black pants, asked for the number in the party, and then led them to the table.

The young man smiled at Rachel softly.

As they followed the host to their table, Danny put his arm around her waist and pulling her close he whispered, "You look beautiful today." He kissed her softly on the cheek just before she slipped into her side of the booth and he walked to the other side. She was taken aback by his forwardness, but blushed and smiled innocently at him.

The dinner, lit by a single candle in the center of the table, was both romantic and confusing. He held her hand as if they had been dating since that fateful night in 6th grade where he had destroyed her hopes in love. He whispered softly of her beauty and how he believed he'd always wanted to be with her. Rachel smiled and said not a word.

Uncomfortable, not by his bizarre display of affection but by something else, something in the air, she constantly looked around the restaurant, positive that someone was watching them. Her paranoia was at a heightened state because no matter how many times she looked, there was no one there – no one but the two high school students sitting alone eating an early dinner. Her wariness was growing; she hoped her paranoia would not end as fatefully as Mrs. Crabtree.

When dinner was finished and he had paid the check, he helped her out of the booth and as she accidentally bumped into him as she was standing up, their faces so close together you wouldn't be able to fit a piece of paper between them, he kissed her, ever so gently, on the lips.

Flushed, heart-racing, she backed up and fell back into the bench seat of the booth. She laughed and then he laughed and grabbing her hand, he helped her out of the booth. Rachel couldn't help but feel that the kiss had not felt "right" – at least not the way she had always imagined that it would feel.

She kissed him softly on the cheek, "Let's go before we make a scene."

They left the restaurant hand-in-hand. His face was aglow, proud and magnificent, with Rachel on his arm and she felt as if she had somehow been reborn as if she had undergone extensive plastic surgery and had become someone completely different.

And she was undeniably confused because someone like Danny, high in the social ranks of the teenage hierarchy, should never be proud to be seen with Wretched Rachel. Perhaps she had been right about him all along – perhaps he really was the nice twin and had just been repressed by his sister for all these years.

She smiled at him softly, and gripped his hand firmly; all thoughts of the Crabtrees – both Junior and his cherubic brother Tom – escaped her mind in that single moment. Danny opened the door again for her and she slipped inside and he, again, going to the drivers' side, started the car, and backed out.

Danny drove away from the restaurant and asked if she wanted to go somewhere else – the movies, the mall, the park – anywhere as long as she "could make him happy just a little longer."

It was sadly romantic and she, the harbinger of hatred and bitterness when it came to love, was moved by his display of emotion. It was not something she had expected, this feeling of unencumbered relief that she might be normal for once in her life.

"A park would be fine." Rachel said softly, thinking that the day was cooler than usual and it would be nice just sitting in a park and talking rather than partaking of the noise of the mall or the mindlessness of the movies.

He drove on with a nod and came upon this park labeled simply, "City Park." In the middle of the park was a huge fountain that gushed water ten to twelve feet in arcs of beautiful showers that shone with spectrums of color in the sun that was quickly moving towards the skyline, readying itself for its movement to the other half of the world.

To the right of the fountain was a small park filled with swings and a play set and a slide. A few children around eight or nine years old laughed and giggled as they chased each other around the equipment, their mothers' sitting on a park bench nearby talking and not paying attention to the kids. Danny and Rachel walked around the concrete pathway past the kids playing in the playground to the back side of the fountain.

"We won't get sprayed on this side," he said. She looked at him confused, so he continued, "The wind is blowing the other direction."

He smiled softly and grabbed her hand in his.

"Ah." She said softly and looked back towards the water that tried desperately to reach the heavens but inevitably fell back down into the pool below – doomed to repeat itself forever.

Reaching over he kissed her softly on the lips and she found herself kissing him, her hand placed gently around his neck as his found the small of her back. They would talk and then kiss and then talk some more and she was not sure exactly how long they had been there when they ran away from the fountain quickly, laughing, as the wind turned and drenched them in the cold water that spewed from it.

They laughed and, both noticing that the sun was fading into oranges and purples and beautiful magnificence, he pushed her hair out of her face, and said softly, "We should probably go."

She nodded and they went back to his car. He had wanted to take her home but she told him that he shouldn't, that he should just take her back to school and she would walk home, but he refused – adamantly refused, insisting that "it was too late for a beautiful girl like you to be out walking around at night."

She laughed, and finding his comment almost too paternal, she complied with his request and let him take her to the outskirts of her apartment complex – insisting that she could survive the walk to her apartment door. He had known she was poor from those fateful days long ago when his sister had told everyone of her living arrangements, but she was still embarrassed.

When they arrived at the outskirts of the apartment complex, which in the dimly lit sky looked more like the devastating scene of a bombing than actual homes, he did not appear to care that she lived in such humble means; he simply grabbed her face softly and pulling her towards him, kissed her softly, and grabbing her hand and placing it on his crotch, he whispered "until next time."

She had felt something there; perhaps he had something large stored in his pants. She had gone through the mandatory sexual education classes but she really didn't know the first thing about what guys had between their legs – it surely must have been a phone or something because there was no way he would have been so vulgar after such a sweet date – not Danny, maybe Dana but never Danny.

She smiled at him softly, and, for once, he let her get herself out of the car. She started walking towards the apartment when he rolled his window down and called out, "Are you going to the funeral tomorrow?"

She shrugged. She wanted to go but was positive that Mr. Crabtree would be there – after all, it was his wife who had died.

"Are you?"

"Yeh, probably. If I don't, I have to go to school." He laughed.

She smiled, "Well if I go, then I'll see you there, otherwise I'll see you Wednesday." She blew him a kiss and he pretended to catch it. She laughed, and then turning around walked to her apartment, giddy and excited that for one day her life had seemed normal.

Kimberly Thomas

Thirteen
❦ ❦ ❦

*J*unior, Junior, Junior. He had been sick of that name since second grade when he realized that everyone had hated his father. Now that his father was dead, he was determined to be called Mike now, even though he kept forgetting and still introduced himself as Junior – there had been too many years with that title to change overnight.

Like that stunning waitress at the diner, he'd said he was Junior but he should have told her he was Mike. He had not wanted to be Junior with her, because Junior was a silly puny name, while the name Mike would show her how strong he was and how masculine he was.

It was funny because he had recognized the girl; something deep inside of him knew he had seen her before. It hadn't been until later that night that he realized that Rachel – who his stupid wife had introduced as Raquel – was the daughter of old Jeremiah Odium, the richest man in Vertueux – well, perhaps, he used to be the richest man but he had been dead for almost eighteen years and he guessed that dead men weren't really rich.

His father, right after high school, had provided his son with a substantial amount of money and had told him to go to the city just to find Rachel's mother and that he was, at any means necessary, to bring Lisa back to Vertueux. He had known his father had been obsessed with the woman at a very young age when he had seen his father staring at an old photograph and writing tearfully a letter.

His father, always favoring Junior over Tom, had let Junior in on his little secret, but Junior had always thought of his father as weak for ever letting himself become obsessed with a woman, after all, it was his father who had taught Junior how to make women do what he wanted. His father's obsession had not been clear to Junior until he had seen the radiant beauty of Lisa's daughter Rachel.

His pursuit of Lisa, which had been more of a guise to keep his father's money coming, had come to a complete halt when he had met and married Tina. Not because of her, per se, but Tina had pretty much taught him that women were not worth chasing.

He had only known Tina for a few weeks before he married her, having met her at a bar. She had been there with a group of teachers – mostly elderly or obese women – and her curvy body and sexy smile had intrigued him. After all, she was the only attractive one in the entire bar that night. After a few drinks and some rather promiscuous dancing on the dance floor, they had ended up at his place. Of course, he was well known for always taking the hottest woman in the bar home – he never was without someone in his bed, and the shorter the stay, the better.

The next morning, naked and hung-over, he had regretted the move for this girl's tremulous voice sent shards of pain through his head. He had reluctantly given her his number and she had given him hers, but for weeks neither one had called the other. He had no desire to call her for she was nothing like the woman he wanted in his life – he wasn't sure what he wanted, but she, the insistent talker with a voice that sounded like the squeaker from a dog toy, was not it.

Three weeks later he came home to a voice mail that said "we need to talk" – the voice of the dreaded one-night stand. Had she not told him her name on the voice mail he probably would not have remembered because he usually had four or five one-night stands per week; he probably would not have remembered her at all if it were not for that voice.

He did not call her back.

A day later she called again, this time he answered. He knew if he had looked at caller ID or perhaps if he had just moved or changed or his number or so many other different options, he would not have been in the state he was in right now, but he had answered and it was too late to do anything about it.

"Junior?" She said in a wobbly voice that made him want to punch her.

"Yes." He answered gruffly for he wanted to provide her with no guise as to his disgust for her.

"This is Tina. We... ...we slept together a few weeks ago."

He laughed. "So that's what you call it?"

She chuckled meekly.

"Um...well...yeh...anyway, I'm going to just come to the point, okay? Um...I'm pregnant."

"And?" He knew what she meant, but he'd been suckered into the whole pregnant thing before. Girls saw his rippled, muscular body, his large manhood and his big-screen TV and his Mercedes and thought that he was the guy they'd sucker into marriage. He wasn't stupid.

"Well...it's yours."

"How so?"

"You're the only one I've slept with, silly."

She said it softly and giggled as if the idea of her sleeping with anyone else was ludicrous.

"Like hell."

"I'm serious. You're the only one I've been with and I'm willing to do a paternity test to prove it."

"So you plan on keeping the little bastard, then?"

"Well I don't believe in abortion, so yeh, I do, and he or she is not a 'little bastard'. So you have a couple of choices."

Her voice was more stern and serious as if she just realized that Junior had no intention of taking this matter seriously.

"Go on."

"Well first one is I'll hire an attorney and we'll set up a child support agreement so you can help in the care and welfare of our child."

He sighed and thought "typical woman," and then said, "What's the other option?"

"You marry me now and we raise this child together."

The conversation went on and without raising voices at each other, which Junior had even found surprising, they had agreed, via the phone, that they would marry only after she provided proof that she was indeed pregnant. After all, marriage was the easier and less financially straining of the options she had provided.

For Junior, it had been convenient when three months later and Tina had just begun to show signs of pregnancy that she had miscarried. Now some people, had they known about the fight between Junior and Tina, would have said that the repeated blows he had given Tina to the stomach might have caused the miscarriage, but he wouldn't admit it. That child was weak – a strong child would have survived it; that child did not deserve to live.

He and Tina had fought more often than they had liked each other. Sex was rare between the two and when it was it was brutal and violent for he insisted that she loved the rough stuff. One time he had caught her crying after a night of passionate lovemaking, and since she was pregnant and moody she had been on his last nerves. That was when he beat her so bad she had lost the baby. He had no tolerance for weakness.

They never slept together after that – she slept on the couch and he slept in his king sized bed alone. He was never without sex though for he had a slough of women throughout the city who would throw themselves at his mercy.

The last straw with Tina was her betrayal of his father's belongings. He had seen her going through his father's safe when they were in Vertueux for his father's funeral. He had inadvertently left it open and after going to hang out with some of his old friends, he had come home to find her reading letters from his father to Lisa – the woman he had been told to find.

He was not sure why it mattered that Tina was looking at the letters or why it bothered him that she was looking through his dead father's things but he was tired of her always being around, tired of her in his business, and just downright tired of her.

He had beaten her – albeit not as bad as other times – and then, after telling her to pack their things, he had left to drive around his small hometown.

He wasn't sure what had caused him to drive out to the Odium place, perhaps curiosity or perhaps knowing that his father – now deceased – had forbid it. Yet, here he was sitting in front of it. It was amazingly in decent shape for having been left unkempt for over eighteen years now. The grass and weeds were high in areas but even in the dark of night, it still did not look haunted as he had been told.

He recalled leaving his camera in the back of the car and reached behind and grabbed it. One day, if he found Lisa, this house could be his. He chuckled softly and focused his camera on the front of the house.

Not willing to drive his Mercedes any closer to the house than the front gate, he got out of his car and took a few pictures of the front of the house. Architecturally, it was a beautiful house, stone pillars that reached towards the sky, and windows upon windows that he was sure made the house bright and beautiful on sunny summer days.

In his head he was still thinking of Lisa, the woman his father had been obsessed about – if he could find her, convince her through his own means – which meant violence, of course – this could all be his, this mansion, the millions or billions of dollars that sat accruing interest somewhere. He took a few more pictures and then out of the corner of his eye he noticed movement in one of the windows. He swung his camera up towards it, and zooming in took a few pictures. In the darkness of the night and the lens of the camera he saw nothing but black.

It had been eerie at the Odium place but not as eerie as when his world collided with Rachel Odium – beautiful, young, with a body of a porn star and the face of an angel, and unbeknownst to her, a millionaire – maybe even a billionaire.

Kimberly Thomas

At the diner he had simply known her as Rachel and when he finally realized that Rachel was indeed the offspring of Lisa and Jeremiah – both in looks and name – he had decided that he would have her at any cost. Starting with writing a letter to Lisa, he had expressed his interest and then he decided to politely interrogate his wife on how much she knew about his future wife, Rachel Odium.

It had been Saturday evening when he had gone out, and Saturday night when he returned and Tina was gone from the house. He had not questioned her yet and was angered that she was not around for him to interrogate. He went to find his letter to Lisa so he could put it in an envelope and discovered that it was missing along with several other items, including his camera. Muttering curses, he paced the floor fervently.

When he heard the locks click on the door to their fourteenth floor apartment, it had occurred to him what really needed to be done. He raced to the back patio and opened the sliding doors and then he hid.

She had looked around nervously throughout the apartment and then after calling his name with no reply, walked around the apartment and returned his stolen goods back to their rightful places.

With as much stealth as a cheetah on the prowl, he grunted, "You bitch," and with ease, pushed Tina towards the opened door at the back of the apartment and threw her over the railing before she even had time to scream.

She had plenty of time to scream on her way down and he raced out of the apartment, and although he desired to go see the grizzly remains of his dead wife, he had headed towards Maude's Diner to find his future wife, heiress to the Odium estate and the girl who would make both his financial and sexual dreams come true.

He had called the diner several times that Sunday, always asking if Rachel was working and always told the same thing, "she's on the line cooking, she can't come to the phone right now."

Earlier that day he had ordered flowers to be sent there. He had paid cash and sent them as "From a secret admirer." He knew she would love them although the roses paled in comparison to her intense beauty.

He had sat intently waiting until the time she got off work. It was nearing 6:00 when he finally saw Rachel leave the restaurant.

Even in baggy pants and a dirty shirt, hair disheveled from cooking, she was stunning. He pulled up beside her and honked.

She waved at him and flirted with him and he offered her money for clothes, knowing that women who took money from men would eventually have sex with them and he wanted nothing more than to ravage her right then and there. She had thanked him with a kiss, chaste and pure and he knew that this naive girl would learn much from him – they would be so happy together. He did not remember exactly what he had said or what she had said just that he had been in awe and aroused in her presence.

That had been a temporary fix for him, and stimulated more than he had ever been by any woman, he had contacted one of his many female friends – a brunette, not even remotely as stunning as Rachel, and made her pretend she was Rachel so he could practice for later.

He had gone back to his apartment, dealt with the police and their questioning about the death of his wife and then after calling his brother to keep up with the guise of his remorse, he slept like a baby.

In the morning he went to the high school and waited.

He saw his precious Rachel walk to school, beautiful and stunning in the morning sunshine. Then he waited, waited until the time when he knew she had class in his dead wife's classroom. Under the guise of picking up his wife's belongings, he had gone to the school office. He had not cared about Tina's belongings – he just wanted to see Rachel again.

When he entered the class with the fat secretary and his obnoxious brother, he had looked for her. When the teacher called her, he looked at her in awe. She had been stunning in a little sundress, bought no doubt with his money. He knew that she had worn it just for him. He licked his lips as he watched her walking up towards him and he imagined that dress balled up on his floor; imagined her body on his; imagined her writhing in pleasure as she paid him back for his generosity. He'd have to get his friend a similar dress, he thought, at least until he could have her.

He was quickly distracted from the erotica however when his brother, Tom, gawked longingly at his woman and had held her hand, and then the teacher – old man that he was – made a comment about HIS woman after she had left the room.

Anger coursed through his veins and he knew he must take her now for there were others that would want her and she must know him first in order to be his forever. He must find her.

Upon leaving the classroom, they had discovered she had disappeared, and with a threat to his brother to leave her alone, he left that damned school in search of his love, the beautiful Rachel.

He went to Maude's diner, assuming that he could coerce the owner or manager into telling him Rachel's address, either by financial or violent means – he hoped for a violent ending for violence, especially murder, made him feel alive and he longed to kill again.

Maude, who he had found out was the owner and manager, had not been there when he arrived at the diner and he waited for her for at least an hour before walking to his car. Luck was on his side, for the old woman was walking towards the restaurant as he walked to his car.

He approached her and calmly said, "Hello Maude. I'm curious; do you happen to know where Rachel Odium lives? I have some very important papers I need to give her from my wife." He feigned sadness.

Maude was stubborn and with brevity stated, "I can't give that information out."

She had tried to walk away and he had tried to rationalize with her but she was adamant about not sharing the information. In anger, and hoping to spark some cooperation from the old woman, he slapped her once and then twice and then, when she wouldn't divulge the information, he just gave into the anger that welled up inside of him, and punched her until she fell. He laughed psychotically for it was fun seeing the old woman trying to fight back and protect herself; the thin, weak woman who was no match for him.

When he had heard a car, he ran to his and quickly climbed into it and drove off, ignoring the speed bump that he passed over way too quickly.

"I'm not sure where you are my little angel, but I will find you. For now," he thought to himself, "I need to find that damned teacher."

Kimberly Thomas

Fourteen

*T*om had spent most of the night at the police station giving his statement. They had cleared him, when after scrutiny, stating that his car did not show signs of running someone over and that his fists were clear of any signs of fighting. He was, however, asked to remain local for a few days in case they needed identification of suspects.

He wanted to tell them that his brother was a raving lunatic but the tie of genetics between himself and his brother caused him to protect him. Accessory to the crime, or not, he was not willing to give the cops his brother.

The old woman had been right; he needed to find Rachel, not to protect her so much but solely because he had not been able to get her face out of his mind from the moment he had dreamt of her.

He had rented a hotel room, afraid to spend the night in his brother's apartment. After washing and changing clothes in the morning, Tom had gone to the school and sat in his parked car the entire day. It was after school was out and the parade of students rushing towards the car died down, that he saw her. Dressed in a blue dress, long black hair flowing behind her, she clung to the hand of a skinny little guy. They drove off together, and although saddened that she had apparently been dating someone, he knew that she'd be safe as long as she was with someone. It was not his place to spy.

He walked into the school and went to the main office. The ladies all bustling around squawking rumors and stories looked up when he walked in.

"Hey there. I was here yesterday with my brother."

They consecutively rolled their eyes. The large secretary that had fought with her brother stated,

"He's not here with you, is he?"

He laughed, "Nope, just me today. I wanted to apologize to that teacher yesterday, my brother was…well, he was a little rude."

The large secretary, muttered, "A little?" Then, with a scoff, continued, "He didn't show up today, never called in. Sorry."

"No problem. I was just passing by, thought I'd try." He smiled.

The large secretary smiled and her chubby cheeks hid the majority of her mouth.

"We'll let him know when we see him, okay? See you tomorrow at the funeral."

He had almost forgotten about the funeral; he would have to find his brother just to find that information so he could attend.

Leaving the school, he headed towards his brother's apartment.

He parked in the underground parking of the building and took the elevator to the fourteenth floor. The door to his brother's apartment was ajar and he heard the sound of a vacuum cleaner running inside. He knocked but no one answered, so he pushed the door open gently.

A tall blonde woman was vacuuming the floors. His father had always used a maid service to clean their house so it was not unexpected to see a woman vacuuming his brother's apartment. What was unusual was this woman – tall, blonde, and reasonably attractive - was dressed simply in an apron that barely covered her private areas and left her backside exposed.

Apparently, she had incorrectly assumed that Tom was Junior and had conveniently bent over towards the open door to pick up an invisible object, exposing her womanhood to Tom.

Tom blushed and then turning around, for he did not desire to look upon her nakedness, asked, "Is my brother here?"

"Oh- I thought you were Junior." She had a soft voice and a strong southern accent that gave away the fact that she was a transplant from somewhere else.

She walked around him rubbing her fingertips on his shoulders, and then exposing her backside to him she reached for the front door and closed it.

"So brother, huh? I didn't know he had a brother." She kept talking as if she had not asked a question. "You're cute, though."

Tom stood there as she ran her finger tips across his chest. He never answered her, never responded to her; he just stood there as if he was made of stone.

She continued, "Junior hasn't been around all day. I come…" She chuckled softly as if that was some kind of joke. "…I come here every Tuesday, to clean." She winked at Tom as if he should know why she really came there, although her lack of clothing pretty much told him why she came there. "He better show up soon 'cause his bitch of a wife is going to show up here and then all hell will break loose."

"His wife's dead." Tom said it matter-of-factly and almost felt remorse for saying it so coldly.

She smiled, but in a saddened voice said, "Oh, I'm sorry to hear that."

Tom doubted she was actually sad; in fact, he figured that in that pretty little head of hers she was already calculating a plan to get Junior to let her move in and maybe even marry her.

The lock clicked on the door and the door opened. The girl stood up and ran towards the door and as Junior walked in, jumped on him and planted a kiss on his lips. He had not noticed until the immature display by the girl that she looked all of about sixteen, maybe seventeen; his brother had just recently turned twenty-six.

Junior pushed her off of him and looked straight at his brother. She spoke seductively directing her statement at Junior,

"Your brother is here."

"I can see that."

"He told me about your wife." She smiled smugly.

"Oh?" Junior looked at Tom without the look of anger that

had been there before – without guilt as should have been there for the crimes he had just committed the night before. Junior looked sadly at ease.

The girl continued, "You wanna…" and then she glanced at Tom and then whispered something incoherent in Junior's ears.

He smiled softly at the girl, and then slapping her bottom softly, he glanced at his brother. "What about my bro?"

She stuck her hand down Junior's pants and Tom looked away in disgust. The girl said much too loudly for Tom's liking for it seemed to resound throughout the city, "I can do him too."

She had smiled and winked at Tom, but Tom quickly retorted, "No, no thanks."

"You're loss." She said smugly as she and Junior walked towards the bedroom.

The sounds that came out of the bedroom were much too reminiscent of his father and made him long to just hear the squeaky car with Alex and Andrea – for lovemaking was not the sounds that protruded from the closed door of Junior's bedroom; it sounded more like torture.

Tom pulled his iPod from his pants pocket, and inserting the headphones, turned the volume as loud as it would go.

Fifteen

She awoke in a pleasant mood, enlightened to be alive. It was Wednesday and there were only two more days until her life would change with graduation.

Granted today was not a day that she should wake in a pleasant mood, for today was the day that Mrs. Crabtree would be buried. She had opted to not go to the funeral for fear that Junior would approach her, and she would be more than happy to never see that man again in her life.

She chose a little black and white polka-dot dress and with an upbeat step, walked happily to school. She had known Danny was not going to be at school today but it wasn't for him that she was happy, it was that she had somehow let go of the baggage of her old life of insecurity and hatred.

She sat through each one of her classes with only a handful of students because most had opted for the day off from school, spending a few hours at a funeral rather than spending the full day at school. The last class of the day, being Mrs. Crabtree's class, was empty except for herself and the large smelly substitute.

Although Mr. Timothy had always been the first choice for substitutes and was as reliable as the sun rising, she had not thought to ask about Mr. Timothy' for substitutes were there one day and gone the next and asking the new substitute about the old substitute was just asking for a hard time.

When school had ended, she had almost expected for Danny to have been waiting for her outside of the classroom, his blue eyes aglow with pride when he saw how beautiful she looked in her little polka-dot dress, but he had not, and disappointed, she had slowly walked away from the school – not quite in the happy mood that she had been when she had gone to school – but not really despondent, more as though she was just disappointed that today seemed almost categorically ordinary as part of her old life as the Goodwill cover girl.

As she walked through the parking lot, scanning it just in case Danny's car was in the parking lot, she noticed Butch leaning up against his old Chevy pickup truck. Rusted and peeling paint, he'd curse at it and kick it but when asked why he didn't get rid of it, he'd softly tell everyone that the car was his baby and that he'd never part with her.

She looked at Butch oddly and then walked over to him.

"Hey Butch. What's up? Trying to pick up a young girlfriend who might be attracted to that old truck of yours?"

He chuckled softly but he wasn't his usual self. As big and mean as he looked, Butch was a big teddy bear and Rachel swore on numerous occasions she had seen him cry, although he swore it was just the onions. She never believed that story.

"Something happened." He said softly. Butch was around a foot taller than Rachel at 6'4" and his big bulky body and tattoos scared most people, but when he was sad as he was now, he looked as frail as a baby.

"What? What happened?" His sincere sadness frightened her.

"Maude." He said it as if she should know what happened.

"What happened?" She repeated the question as if he hadn't heard her.

"Someone beat her up, and then ran her over. She's not dead, but she's badly hurt. We've been trying to catch you but you're hard to find."

He looked at the ground and shuffled his feat.

"Where is she?"

"St. Mary's Hospital. I can take you if you'd like."

Rachel agreed to take the ride with him. She climbed awkwardly into the old truck and he sped off towards the hospital with the urgency of an ambulance carrying a dying patient. She had to grasp the door handle for dear life for fear that any turn would send the dilapidated truck into shambles. Her heart raced in her chest and she dared not speak for fear that the questions that were running through her mind would reveal answers that would send her into tears. She was too strong to show fear – to show emotion.

Butch parked the truck in the visitor parking and they walked side-by-side into the hospital. The hospital was cool and the smell of cleanliness masked the smell of sickness that would be expected in such a place. The hospital doors opened into a foyer that was so unlike a hospital that she almost had to glance and see if they had indeed gone to a hospital and not a mall or a five-star hotel. The nurses and doctors in their scrubs were the only tell-tale sign that they had indeed gone to a hospital.

Butch led her to the elevators where they proceeded to the fourth floor. She watched the numbers change on the digital read-out for each floor they passed, until it settled on the number four. The doors opened and a nurse walked past silently, her purse on her shoulder, obviously going home or going on break. Her name tag read "Lauren" and she smiled softly at Butch and them Rachel.

Butch put his hand inside the elevator door to keep it open. "How's she doing?" He said it softly, the voice so uncharacteristic for a man of his stature.

Lauren replied, softly, "She's doing as well as can be expected." She glanced at Rachel softly and smiled.

Butch thanked her and then removed his hand from the door. Lauren reached over and pressed the button for the floor where she was heading and the door closed behind Butch and Rachel.

Maude was in room 410. They stood in front of the door for a moment and Rachel stopped Butch from opening the door.

Whispering, she said softly, "Before I go in there..." She

paused, desperate to maintain a composure of maturity. She sighed, "…Before I go in there, what is wrong with her? What is wrong with her exactly?"

Butch whispered, "The doctor's aren't real sure." Butch reached over and moved a piece of hair out of Rachel's face in an act that was much too paternal for him. "She got beat up real bad, lots of broken bones and stuff, and she had some internal bleeding." He paused, and wiped a tear from his eye – Rachel did not know how he'd blame that tear on onions. "From what I understand – and you know I don't understand that medical lingo too well – but what I gather is that it's possible for her to survive but she just doesn't have the will to do so."

"So, she's dying?"

"No, she's not. But the doctors say she's determined that she is. I don't know much more than that kiddo."

In a sign that he was done with the conversation, Butch opened the door for Rachel and then stood inside the door, waiting.

The room held two beds – one of which was unoccupied. There was a small television hung on the wall that was turned off and a lot of medical equipment that beeped and gave off an eerie glow to the room.

Maude, all broken, lay in the occupied bed. Her face was a blanket of bruises, her legs both in casts were propped up by pulleys. She lay asleep and if it were not for the rhythmic beeping of the heart monitors and the gentle movement of her chest, Rachel would have feared she was dead for she looked too peaceful.

Rachel sat in the chair next to the bed and watched her while Butch stood near the door, silent, his head tilted to the ground as if he was paying his respects for the dead.

Maude's eyes fluttered and then opened and in a voice so weak and dry she said, "Rachel, my dear, you came. I have been waiting just for you."

Rachel placed her hand on Maude's cold wrinkled hand and took it gently.

Maude continued talking in a weak voice, "He wants you, and he tried to get to you through me." She smiled and winced in pain when she did so. Several of her teeth were now missing. "He wants you bad but that other boy, that other boy will protect you. I saw it; I saw it all as if I had been there. He may have to die to protect you, but he will protect you."

She paused, gathering up more strength. Rachel did not say a word – she knew who she was talking about for she had the same dream where the angelic brother of the devil himself had appeared to save her. And, if she spoke, she knew that she would cry, for the pain and suffering that she heard in Maude's voice far outweighed the bruises and the bandages that were on the outside; there was more wrong with her than just that.

"I'm sorry I won't be there for your graduation, dear, but know that I will be there in spirit. Don't worry your pretty head about me, okay."

She paused and gasped for air.

She looked to the other side of the bed and stared lovingly at the open area next to her and then continued speaking, "Dennis will take care of me from here on just like that boy will take care of you." Her voice crackled softly and she turned to look again at Rachel. "I love you my little Rachel."

A tear fell from her eye and Rachel knew that Maude was saying good-bye. Rachel laid her head on Maude's chest, and tears falling, muttered, "I love you too."

She lay there for a while, comfortable in her warm and loving embrace and then Butch interrupted softly with, "Visiting hours are almost up Rach."

Maude whispered, "Thank you for bringing her, Butch."

He smiled softly and nodded a good-bye. At the door, Rachel blew her a kiss and with tears in her eyes, whispered, "Good bye." She knew that would be the last time she saw Maude.

Sixteen

Dressed in black, he and his brother had left together for the funeral. Tom was confused as to his brother's behavior – not only the extreme violence but the narcissistic behavior that would allow him to take another woman to his bed only days after his wife's suicide. Perhaps his brother was more indifferent than he thought. It was still beyond his grasp of understanding how two people could marry each other and not be constantly ecstatic for the opportunity to please the other. Yet, he had always known that he and his brothers were as alike as ice and fire.

They drove to the chapel at the funeral home in silence. His brother was dressed in a white dress shirt and tie with a pair of black slacks, while Tom had chose a black sports jacket and black slacks, white dress shirt and no tie. He had perused himself that morning in the full length mirror and had thought that he had looked good – good enough that perhaps Rachel, who would surely be there, would notice him and come say 'hello'.

He was disappointed when he had not seen her.

The chapel was a quaint little place with stained glass windows depicting scenes from the birth of Christ to the death of Christ. The pews, covered in red velvet, were packed with teenagers and adults – so full that people were forced to stand.

Tom thought to himself that Tina should be proud that her life was so remarkable that so many would show up to mourn her loss. His father's funeral had only garnered a handful of people – mostly family who were required to show.

When the crowd settled and the ceremony started, the pastor came up and spoke some kind and remorseful words about the loss of such a young woman; a few students came up and spoke about their experiences with Mrs. Crabtree; Junior did not speak. He simply sat on the front pew next to Tom looking around in boredom. Tom even thought he had seen his brother doze off once during the sermon.

Tom had to admit the ceremony was quite dull and his mind had drifted several times. He had felt bad, however, for it was the responsibility of all attendees to be thinking of the deceased and to be saying their prayers for her soul. Yet, his mind drifted to the face of beautiful Rachel – her soft skin, her radiant body, the eyes so dark and mysterious that he only imagined that behind them lay the spirit of a wild mustang waiting to be freed.

Awakened, he was happy to see that the final speaker had sat down and that the urn, as there was nothing salvageable of the body to merit a casket, was brought to Junior, who stood and wiping the non-existent tear from his eye, sadly grabbed the urn from the preacher's hands.

Junior and Tom, the only family to attend the funeral, were subjected to stand in front of the chapel and soulfully accept the condolences of the attendees for their loss. He had wished that it was in him to look more melancholy, but with each passing face he searched for his beloved Rachel – but to no avail. His only sadness was not for the loss of Tina but for the unfortunate realization that Rachel had not attended and that he risked never seeing the woman of his dreams again. Tina would have probably been upset that she had not attended – and had she been alive, he would have been subjected to an hour long discussion of why Rachel is "just another teenager who has no respect for anyone or anything".

There had been a mixture of students and adults. He had recognized the large secretary who had fought with his brother, and a few others from the office. As person after person passed with their condolences, the faces became irrelevant and the end of the line was all he sought. As the last of the mourners grew nearer to them, Tom sighed in relief. Twins stood at the end – skinny with light brown hair and had it not been for their gender Tom doubted anyone would have been able to tell them apart. The girl shook Junior's hand and then moved to Tom, whom she chose to hug. The twin brother, who now closer looked familiar, shook Junior's hand and then as he was on his way to Tom tripped and fell to the ground.

The twin looked at Junior in disgust and Junior just shrugged. Instead of shaking Tom's hand, the twin stood up with his sister's help and then stomped out of the chapel, upset.

The chapel was empty except for a few people who were quickly cleaning up, most likely preparing for the next funeral.

"Let's get out of here." Junior said quickly and then proceeded out the front door without a word. He did not realize he had left the urn sitting on the table behind him and Tom, wishing not to be left behind, did not bother to pick it up.

Tom was quickly in tow, knowing that if he didn't follow Junior that Junior would surely leave without him, as he had been known to do when Tom was too young to drive.

Tom noticed the twins getting in a black Honda and then realized that this was the same boy he had seen Rachel with only the day before – that had been her boyfriend. He found it odd that Rachel would not have attended the funeral with her boyfriend but hoped that perhaps they had broken up and that is why she had not come. He smiled to himself.

Junior had quickly shuffled into the Mercedes and Tom, noticing that his brother had started the car already, had to race to the passenger side, open the door and slide into the car, all while it was already backing up.

"Why the rush, bro?" Tom laughed.

His brother did not look at him or answer, instead, with eyes gazing on the road with ferocious intensity; his answer to his question was met with speed as the Mercedes slid up behind the black Honda. The occupants inside seemed oblivious to his presence.

The Honda had gone onto the highway and Tom grabbed the

door handle as Junior, slipping in through tightly packed cars, kept at a ruler's distance from the back bumper of the Honda Accord. There was no doubt in Tom's mind that the twins now knew that the Mercedes was following them – the girl who sat in the passenger side kept looking back and the boy who was driving was making equally dangerous merges through traffic at speeds that were best left for the raceway.

Flashing through his mind were the words his brother had spoken to him only a few days ago, "Stay away from her." It had not been his dead wife he had been referring to; it had been Rachel. It all fit now, the dead wife, the warning to his own brother, the attack on Rachel's grandmother, and now this, the flagrant harassment of Rachel's boyfriend.

"What the hell are you doing?" Tom asked loudly.

Junior did not respond.

"Stop or someone is going to get killed."

Junior still did not respond but the smile that crossed his face was answer enough, that death was what he sought.

They had been on the highway for fifteen minutes and Junior had not backed off the bumper of the Accord. In one swift movement, the driver shot up a middle finger and the Accord slipped onto an off-ramp across two lanes of traffic, trying to ditch the Mercedes that hung onto it like a leech. It did not work. Junior was on the off-ramp in time to see the Accord attempt to cross the intersection of the service and main road.

Junior slammed on his brakes and pulled off to the emergency shoulder as he proclaimed they "might as well watch the show".

The light ahead at the intersection was yellow when the Accord had exited the highway and had for a few seconds been red when the car had crossed into it. It had happened so fast that he doubted any of the parties could have stopped anything. The driver of the moving truck going north on the road slammed on his brakes unsuccessfully and the cars going south tried desperately to avoid the Accord, but none were successful. Like an accordion, the Accord crunched on all sides in a painful wailing that would forever haunt him. The car screamed as metal crunched against metal. Tom imagined that the occupants of the Accord were screaming too, for there was no way in that brief instance that they could have survived – only by some divine miracle would they have escaped death.

"Well, guess we're not going that way." Junior laughed and then putting the car back into drive, pulled back into the traffic on the highway.

Tom's heart was pounding in his chest as if the entire percussion section of the symphony resided where his heart should be. He had no words to say to his brother – no words to say at all.

Both silent, Junior continued driving away from the city. There was little that Tom could do but sit in silence and wait for his brother to stop – he was a prisoner in his brother's car. Afraid to confront his brother or to say anything at all, he sat staring blankly out the window with a thousand thoughts running through his mind – how had it come to this? This insanity that overwhelmed his brother for a girl – she was beautiful, yes, but worth killing for?

As an hour had passed, neither had spoke, Tom never looking at his brother. Junior drove until they reached a lake – albeit this was not the lake where boats and swimmers and families would come for picnics. This lake was filled with trees that stood naked and bare within it giving it an oppressive look as if the water had overtaken a forest and drowned out the life within it. The road was empty, the lake even emptier, and a feeling of desolation and loneliness exuded from this place. Normal lakes had houses that skirted up against it with docks that housed big yachts; this lake had none of that – there was not a house or car or even sign of wildlife in this forbidden place.

Junior parked the car on the bridge and then looking around, commanded firmly, "Get out."

Tom sat there, frightened.

"Now!" Junior demanded. Tom was afraid – afraid that his brother would kill him and dump him in this vile lake where his body would show up months later as decayed and putrid as its surroundings. But he was compliant and did as told.

Junior was at the trunk when Tom finally made it out of

the car. He popped the trunk with his car remote and the smell that exuded from the trunk was as abominable as this lake. Holding his breath, Tom glanced inside the trunk. Wobbling and nauseated, Tom stared at the dead body of the substitute – the one whom Junior had threatened.

"Grab his hands." Junior said the statement as if Tom should not be concerned that a dead body was in his trunk, that this should be all commonplace – but of course it wasn't normal at all.

Tom hesitated and backed up.

"Grab his hands, you little pussy, or I'll throw you in the lake with him."

Tom grabbed the hands which were cold and clammy and lifeless and fought to keep from puking. As they pulled the body out of the trunk, the head fell listlessly towards the ground and Tom turned and puked as he saw the empty eye sockets and the ripped open neck that exposed the spinal cord below. He did not, however, let go of the hands, ignoring the drips of vomit that still clung to his mouth. He believed his brother meant the threat and he did not dare risk it.

Junior muttered obscenities as he pulled the body and Tom with it towards the edge of the bridge.

He lifted the legs of the body -- the legs which were tied to a cinderblock -- above the edge of the bridge and Tom did the same with the arms. In one swift movement, the body was over the side of the bridge and then dropped to the putrid water below. In one splash, the body floated and then sunk into the ghastly depths – disappearing into the darkness as easily as his brother had sunk into insanity.

Tom puked again over the side.

Patting Tom on the back, he stated matter-of-factly, "Grow some balls, dude. Now let's go and you better not puke in my car." He laughed as he got in the car, and Tom, obediently and silently, got in the car with him, his face ashen and disturbed.

They again did not speak the entire ride but Tom thought about nothing other than how to protect Rachel from this mad man – his brother – who had been unleashed upon her.

Seventeen

*M*aude was not only the woman she had been spent the last couple of years working for, but more importantly the woman who she believed to be her confidante and the woman she would have gladly called grandmother had genetics been on her side. Maude was alone now, except for her beloved Dennis who watched over her from heaven, or from whatever place that the formerly deceased went – she had no children, and no grandchildren - only the restaurant.

Rachel had cried herself to sleep that night when Butch had dropped her home, wishing for once that she had a mother who she could just talk to or who would at least hold her while she cried – but she, like Maude, was truly alone. Her reason for existence on this futile planet was illogical; she surely should have never been born.

There was an evil voice inside her head that told her that everything was somehow her fault – the state of her miserable mother, the death of Mrs. Crabtree, the impending death of Maude – somehow had she never been born these things would have never happened. In her dreams, Death had spoke to her, his silver scythe hanging menacingly over her head, and he had told her in a whispered voice that she was better off dead, and when she awoke in the morning, she felt as if he was right. Her existence surely was the instigator for all things destructive.

She dressed in the morning in yet another new dress – red and flowing, the dress represented to her the blood that should be flowing from her veins, a reminder that she did not deserve to live. Perhaps she looked stunning in the dress but she did not feel stunning – simply disturbed and repulsive. She walked sullenly to school, head hung low as in past years when she was her former self and not this newly reborn version of herself that seemed to bring about great harm. Her thoughts elsewhere and the sounds of cars and people were not heard.

The school was reminiscent of Monday – and three days later, the feeling of sadness that overwhelmed the school was even stronger than that of Monday, stronger than the loss of a favored teacher. It was the first period class when she had found out the twins had been killed in a grisly car accident. The school officials said very little about the deaths except that graduation would continue, as planned, the next day. It would not be postponed for a simple tragedy – life would and must continue on.

And, yet another death clouded her ominous existence, as if everyone she touched, everyone she cared about, would die. She was apprehensive now, afraid to talk or look at anyone, for fear they might self-combust into a ball of flames and die right before her very eyes. She longed to be the Goodwill cover girl again for it seemed as if this morphed butterfly that she had become was venomous, deadly and destructive.

She had sat in each class silent, holding back the tears. Only two days ago she had held Danny's hand, kissed his lips, said she would see him again – and now, the only way she would see him would be in a casket, his young, frail body now lifeless and useless – all his hopes and dreams trashed in a moment. The more she thought of him and Maude and Mrs. Crabtree, the more she wanted to cry, and the more she held it back. She had not loved Danny in a sense that she thought they would spend eternity together, but she had loved him as a friend – perhaps her only friend.

Each class came and each class passed until finally the bell rang and Ms. Smelly told them to go home and be back for graduation practice the following day.

School was over on the most somber of occasions and tomorrow's graduation ceremony seemed like it would be more fitting as a death march.

She had opted to not return home after school but to walk the thirty blocks from school to the hospital where Maude lay broken and beaten. She could not bear the thought of not seeing her again, not when everyone around her was dying. She needed her Maude – she needed her more now than ever.

The air was warm and humid and her dress clung to her uncomfortably. Her sandals flipped softly thump-thump, thump-thump, with every step. The sound of the city drowned out her thoughts and she walked vacantly to the beat of its music, each honk a crashing cymbal, each siren a crescendo – its symphony beautiful and catastrophic.

She slipped through crowds of people clamoring in the city streets unnoticed, her head down towards the ground, her eyes glued to the ground below her for she did not dare gaze upon those around her for fear that she would look up into the empty eyes of Death. For even though it was seemingly fit that she should be erased from this existence, some semblance of fear still held her glued to this miserable world – this world that was taking away everything from her.

She was tired and sweaty by the time she reached the hospital, entering through the wide automatic doors that kept the coolness of the air conditioning and the smell of sickness inside. The hospital doors were a gaping mouth that swallowed the occupants whole, subjecting them to the cold, cold dissolution that this building was meant to heal, when, she knew that this was where you went to die. "Don't have faith in the living." Her mother had been right all along.

Rachel was surprised by her own morbidity for even she, having lived a life destitute and impoverished, had been always optimistic. But today, having lost too much already, she was in no mood for optimism.

Kimberly Thomas

She walked the well lit hallways on the cold tile floors and up the elevator to the fourth floor, to the room that held her friend – the woman who should have been her grandmother. She stood on the outside of the closed door and stared at it. Staring at the patterns in the wood and the large cold handle, she stood afraid – no, aware somehow – that the room was empty.

A small blonde woman walked towards her donned in blue scrubs and a nametag reading "Lauren." Rachel remembered her as the nurse they had seen the night before when she had visited Maude.

The young woman put her hand softly on Rachel's shoulder, and in a voice that obviously had given the news too many times in her career, said softly

"She's gone."

Rachel had known she'd be gone – she just had hoped it would not be so. She needed her more now than she had ever needed anyone in her life – her Maude.

She did not cry; she could not cry – not now. Nodding her head towards the young woman, she simply walked away.

"Don't have faith in the living." That was her mother's creed and perhaps a foreboding warning of these days – these days in this terrible existence where she would lose everyone and everything.

The thirty two blocks back to her apartment were made in the same manner as when she had gone to the hospital – silent, staring at the ground, refusing to think, she let the sound of the city orchestrate itself around her. It was not the beauty of the city she heard, but the death – crunching metal as bumpers met, violent curses spouted in anger, gunshots, and screams, and the derelict voices of the homeless whose lives were somehow more fruitful than hers.

It was not until she reached the comfortable familiarity of her home – imbibed in the smell of destitution – that she allowed herself to cry – for Maude, for Danny, for Mrs. Crabtree.

Eighteen

He was shaken to the point that he could not eat or drink or sleep. He could not bear to look at his brother, the only living remnant of his family. His brother was not like his father after all, but worse – his brother was Satan himself, born solely to reap havoc on this world. As much as Tom had despised his father, he knew his father would have never been able to commit murder but Junior – Junior was a vicious lion preying upon helpless victims just to get what he wanted.

They had known all along – Tina and Rachel's grandmother – telling him that he must protect her at all costs - but, at what price? Tom was enamored by the girl - that was sure - but no matter what magnetism drew him to her; even if she was his soul mate, would death be too great a price to pay for love? He feared it would be and Tom did not believe that he could protect anyone from the brute force of his brother.

That night he half-slept, half-stared at the ceiling blankly, thinking seriously of just leaving and going back to Vertueux where he could be rid of this violent drama that unfolded before him. Yet her face haunted him, innocent and pure, she called to him – she had called to him before he had even met her and he knew he had to protect her.

A knock on the door Thursday morning had woken both Tom and his brother. The blonde "maid", dressed in a pair of shorts and tank top – neither of which left much to the imagination, but of course Tom had seen more than he had cared to see the other day – stood at the door.

When Tom had opened the door she said in disgust in her thick southern drawl,

"You still here?" and then with a brush of her fingers on Tom's bare chest, added, "Change your mind yet?"

As her fingers drifted further south, Tom backed away from her in answer and walked to the couch where he grabbed a t-shirt and put it on.

Junior, completely naked, stood in the doorway of his bedroom holding a beer in his hand. Tom looked away and the girl went running. The door closed and squeals immediately were coming from the bedroom; Tom gathered his keys and wallet and walked out.

Tom wanted to find the old woman, Rachel's grandmother, but he knew nothing about her except for the location where she had been taken – courtesy of the local newspaper. Without a name, however, he could be there for years searching for her. With nothing more than Rachel's last name – which could very well not be hers – he went to the location of the diner.

The diner was beautiful in the morning sun; it irradiated a glow that looked like it could warm the heart of even his cold-hearted brother. He knew that was impossible, however. He parked his Camaro in the parking lot and walked towards the door. A big burly man, with tattoos down both arms and a shaved head, stood at the entrance way holding in his fingers a cigarette that funneled little curls of smoke in the air.

Tom said "hello" as a general courtesy and reached for the door handle.

A voice too soft for that of a man so tall and wide said,

"I think I might be waiting for you."

Tom, not sure he heard correctly, said, "Excuse me?"

"I think I might be waiting for you." The voice was louder

this time, but still unnatural for the size of the man.

Tom turned around

"I don't think so. I think you have the wrong person."

"No, no, I think you're him."

As the man moved closer, Tom grasped the door handle and opened the door, saying in a single breath, "I don't think so."

"You're the one; you're the one who is to protect our little Rachel." He paused, and the look on Tom's face must have told him he found the right person, continuing, he said, "Maude, she wanted me to find you but you found me." He laughed softly. "How convenient."

"I don't understand. Maude?"

"We don't have time, we must go; she doesn't have much time."

"Who, who doesn't have much time?" Tom was more confused now than he had been.

"Maude. You drive. Come on."

The brawny man strode to the Camaro in lengths that took two of Tom's steps to catch up. The man was in the car before Tom could even complain – but something inside him said he must trust the man and take him wherever they must go.

The ride was primarily made in silence except for the periodic "turn right here" or "turn left here". Tom had not known what to say to the man and the questions that shot through his mind never escaped his lips, for he was afraid of the answers.

He suspected that Maude – he assumed would be the old woman who had been beaten by his brother – had informed this brute of a man of what he had looked like and that by coincidence, the brute had been standing in front of the restaurant at the same exact time as Tom had arrived. That simply had to be all it was – coincidence – for any other explanation would make him seem crazed and superstitious, of which he was neither.

They arrived at a hospital – St. Mary's. Once parked, the man, without a word, got out of the car and headed towards the front doors of the hospital, only glancing back once to confirm that Tom had indeed followed him. Tom had quickly followed. As the man guided Tom through the cold hallways and up the elevator to a room, Tom began to feel uneasy for the smell of hospitals had always disturbed him – the smell of sanitized cleanliness that Tom knew was used to only cover the stench of the dying.

The man stopped in front of a closed door and then, in a manner not unlike that of a guard, the man stood towards the right of the door, back straight, eyes forward.

Tom assumed he was supposed to go in alone. He glanced at the face of the man again but the man was focused on the wall across from him, not on the actions of Tom.

The room was dark when he went through the door, the irradiated light from the heart monitor glowing an eerie green as it lit his way towards the bed where the old woman lay.

A man sat next to the bed, hidden in darkness. Tom could only see that he held Maude's hand as lovingly as that of a son – perhaps Rachel's father – but as the man stood, he knew that this tall, gangly and unattractive man was not Rachel's father. The man flipped on the light above Maude's head with one stealth-like movement and the three winced in the sudden brightness, although the one light made little improvement on the darkness of the room. Tom could see the man now, probably late-30s, balding with a beak nose and unusually orange skin as if he used tanning lotion over his face and entire body. Dressed in a well-polished suit, the man looked at Tom once, shook Maude's hand, and walked out without a word. A briefcase, leather and expensive-looking, was in his hand.

Tom had surmised that the man was Maude's attorney, although he had assumed that it was in order to prosecute Junior for the harm he caused her. Maude had informed him otherwise.

She had waved at him very meekly when the man had left and then pointed to the seat where the well-dressed man had previously sat. Tom had noticed that Maude had casts on both legs that were lifted with a pulley system, but when he arrived by her side, he saw the real damage. Missing teeth and bruised, she was broken – but it was in her eyes that he saw she had given up hope, that she had discovered that this was her time to die.

"I'm glad you came." She said it so softly and meekly that

Tom had to lean forward to hear her better.

He smiled softly, hoping not to let his face reveal the guilt that he now felt.

"That man who left was my attorney."

"I thought so." Tom said, unsure as to what to say to the woman, unsure as to why he was brought here.

"The doctors don't seem to think so, but I'm dying. I had to get my final affairs in order. That is why you are here."

"I don't understand, ma'am."

She chuckled softly and he was reminded of his own grandmother who had died a few years past. So soft and caring and loving, he saw that in Maude and was happy that Rachel could have a grandmother just like his.

"You are a good kid." She reached for his hand and he offered it to her.

Her hands were cold and icy and he felt nothing more than sorrow that he had allowed her to be in this state. His inability to confront his brother had caused both this woman and his beloved Rachel harm.

As if she knew what he was thinking, she said softly, "It's not your fault. This was how it had to be, but…" She coughed, covering her mouth with her other hand. "…you need to take care of our little Rachel. She's in danger and you must protect her at all costs."

"But, how, I don't know anything about her – I don't even know where she lives."

She smiled softly, her hand losing its grip on his, and as her eyes drifted close, she mumbled, "Soon, my dear."

"I don't understand."

"Don't become like your brother and father."

Her eyes closed and her head tilted sideways as she drifted off into unconsciousness. Her heart monitor still beat a healthy tone, but Tom was unable to wake her – unable to get any kind of clarification about how and where to find his Rachel, and what she meant by her final statement. He was not his father or brother -- how did this total stranger know anything about his life?

Kimberly Thomas

Nineteen

She was able to sleep in because graduation practice did not begin until noon and would end at two so they could go home and get ready for the procession that would be later that night. Rachel had awakened, depressed and melancholy and thought to herself that it wouldn't be such a bad thing to just skip graduation. Yet, she knew she was obligated to be there – if not for herself, then at least for Maude who would no longer be able to attend. A tear escaped her eye.

She had stared at the ceiling most of the night, fighting sleep for with sleep were dreams of death and destruction. The sounds of death and destruction outside were enough for her on this warm May night – the shootings and sirens and screams, the constant reminder that life was not a fairy tale and her story was not becoming better with time but worse. Her happy ending surely would end badly.

At eleven on Friday morning, she put on a pair of sweat pants and a baggy t-shirt and walked to the football stadium where they would be holding their graduation ceremony.

The entire class was there, minus the two who had just died – and the twins would be given their graduation certificates posthumously, in respect for their untimely deaths. Rachel did not feel too out of place dressed in her outfit that truly indicated her living conditions because most of the students had not dressed up for this occasion and a large percentage of girls and guys alike were donned in shorts and t-shirts, as disheveled as if they were working in their yards or doing housework.

The practice ceremony was mundane and two hours later, the students, tired and restless, were sent home with a strict reminder to be back at five pm. With that statement, the students rushed towards their cars or homes like it was the running of the bulls – without care of whom or what they trampled in their wake.

Rachel slowly walked home, for there was no reason for her to rush; there was never a reason to rush. The warm May air was sticky and she regretted her choice of sweats on such a warm day, but as always her selection of clothing was minimal at best.

Rachel walked around the neighborhood that surrounded the school, avoiding Maude's diner – for fear that she'd cry – and avoiding her own home, for she did not want to be there right now. For an hour she passed by houses, beautiful with perfectly landscaped lawns and little happy children playing naively in their front yards, unaware of the anger and hatred in the world. At one home, an elderly couple sat in a swinging chair on their porch, his arm placed around hers and her hand on his thigh. They smiled as she passed and the old man said, "Nice day, isn't it?"

They too were oblivious to the anger and the hatred in the world -- they in their picturesque perfect world. Was she the only one who felt like this? Was she only one who seemed to leave death and destruction at every step? She wanted to yell at the old man and say, "Don't speak to me; don't look at me – for you will surely die." Yet, instead, she forced a smile and said softly, "Yes it is."

She sighed and glanced at her watch. It was 3:30 already and she had to go home and prepare for the ceremony.

She took the same long route back to the school and then back to her apartment. By 4:00 she had reached the outskirts of the apartment. As if her world had not grown strange enough, the vision of what lay before her as she reached the apartment complex left a sinking feeling in her stomach so great that she wanted to either pass out or vomit – neither of which was an option she had time to entertain.

Each of the hundred or so apartment doors had a single piece of red paper attached to the doors. She could only assume what was on them, and walked, with dread to her own apartment and slowly ripped the stapled paper off the door.

"*Occupant,*

This is a notice that you are hereby required to vacate the premises. You have thirty days to remove your belongings. We will begin demolition of these premises in forty days.

Sincerely,

Management"

It was not an official court order as she had expected, but she suspected that the management would go the low-dollar route first and then involve the sheriff's department later if necessary. It had been inevitable, but the timing of this was inopportune, for now this would cause Rachel to have to postpone college as she tried to find housing that was equally inexpensive and she would most likely have to find two or three jobs just to be able to support her and her mother. Of all the times to receive this news, this was not it – this was like a nail in the coffin of a week that would surely go down in her history as the worst week of all time.

She opened the door to the apartment and walked in. She wouldn't miss this apartment, that was for sure, but there were no apartments nearby that she would be able to afford on her minimal salary, and with Maude gone the possibility of her keeping her current job was very slim. She sighed and throwing the paper on the couch, she went to the bathroom and took a shower. She only had about 45 minutes to get ready for graduation and all her problems would have to wait until afterwards.

When she was done showering, she put on her black dress and walked around barefoot in the house, munching from the Fruity-O's bag as she had no time to eat and no food in the house besides the one bag of cereal.

Kimberly Thomas

The red eviction notice still lay on the couch seeming to stare at her with such scorn that she wanted to pick it up it and rip it into a thousand pieces. Instead, she glanced at her watch, and made an impromptu decision.

She sealed the bag of cereal and left it on the little card table and, grabbing the paper off the couch, went to her mother's bedroom door and knocked on it.

No one answered and she wasn't surprised.

She knocked again.

No one answered.

"Mom?"

No one answered.

She opened the door just slightly, enough only to see the corner of the dusty old bed. No one said anything – on any normal occasion if she had opened the door even slightly her mother would have gone on a tirade, but not today.

She opened the door fully in order to see the entire room – a twinge of panic passing through her with every push as she half-expected to see her mother fulfilling her promise and "lying dead in her bed". She was relieved when she saw that the bed was empty. She glanced at her watch, 4:30.

She entered the room – she had never been allowed in the room and entering it now was like crossing into enemy territory during a war; she could be taken down for this criminal trespass.

In the small, dark room, and lying on the simple blanket that covered the small twin-sized bed was a note and a black velvet box. The note was folded in two and on it, written in beautiful penmanship, was her name, Rachel.

She opened the letter and read it.

"Rachel,

I don't have much to say. The box on the bed is yours – your father would have wanted you to have it for your graduation. It is time for me to go.

Lisa"

Lisa – even in this short and to-the-point letter she had not even acknowledged that she was her mother. Her heart sunk in her chest

– she was truly alone on this momentous day in her existence.

Rachel looked quickly under the bed and noticed the suitcase was gone. She sighed – she didn't need this now, her mother was too sick – at least in the head – to be travelling around alone.

4:35 – she had to be going. She opened the black velvet box and inside was a beautiful diamond necklace; it glistened even in the dullness of the dimly lit room. She placed it on her neck, the little strings of diamonds hanging down in glittering beauty. She knew it had to be cosmetic jewelry for a necklace with real diamonds like this would have surely cost thousands of dollars and would have easily paid for food for months had her mother sold it. There was no way it was real but it was beautiful nonetheless.

Leaving the necklace on, hoping upon hope that it had indeed been a gift from her father, she left her mother's room. She went to the freezer and pulled the box of peas out of it to gather up the money. After graduation, she was going to have to find her mother and she had a pretty good idea where she had gone.

Vertueux.

Rachel sighed in disgust and threw the box across the room when she opened it. The box was empty – the money that had been in it was now gone. She wanted to cry, but couldn't – she was too angry now. Her mother had never been a mother to her, and now had stolen her money. What more could go wrong? How was she to find her mother when she had no money left?

Rachel grabbed her shoes from the box and put them on her feet, and then angrily walked towards the school.

When she reached the school, with five minutes to spare, there were flustered students everywhere. The practice earlier that day had not been enough – or perhaps the students had not paid attention as they were supposed to, and the students went around asking everyone where they thought they should be at, and no one seemed to know. Rachel knew where she was supposed to go of course, and headed towards the place where kids with the last name staring with O should be standing.

She passed by Randy in the hallway and he grabbed her arm as he passed.

Kimberly Thomas

"Can I help you?" She said it with disgust because he had not grabbed her arm softly but in a manner that portrayed a sense that he believed he was superior to her. She was in no mood for his callousness.

He looked her up and down as if he was looking to purchase a prized cow.

"I don't know, can you?" He winked.

"What are you talking about Randy? I don't have time for this."

He leaned up and whispered in her ear, his hand flirting dangerously with her butt. "I hear you're a good lay."

"WHAT?" She screamed it louder than she meant to and people around the two of them turned and looked as an odd hush fell over the once-noisy crowd.

"Well, that's what Danny said." He did not bother to whisper that response.

"Well, Danny's dead," and then she whispered, "and he lied."

She ripped her arm from his hand and continued walking, disgusted. Perhaps Danny was just like his sister after all.

The night drug on forever, and the Os, so far in the alphabet, took an hour and a half to get to and by that time Rachel was disgusted with the ceremony and just wanted to get up and leave.

Sitting in fold up chairs lined up in rows across the football field, with crowds and crowds of people gathered in the stands, she slunk under her graduation gown, trying to hide herself from the world – trying to withdraw. Her butt hurt from sitting there so long and she just wanted this all to be over, and regretted the decision to not skip the ceremony.

Finally, her row was able to go to the front, and they walked in single file to the stage where teachers sat in plush chairs and the principal stood at a dark tan podium. Name after name he called until finally, "Rachel Odium".

There was an odd feeling that overwhelmed her and she felt a presence next to her and turned, but saw nothing. Her hand felt warm as if someone held it but no one was there – then a whisper so soft and vibrant in her ear with the words, "I said I would be here", and she realized that Maude was with her after all.

Perhaps her over-stressed mind had imagined it all, after all, she did not believe in ghosts but she felt it as if it really happened – a beautiful and powerful emotional experience that erased the previous hopelessness that had overwhelmed her before. She smiled softly as she accepted the certificate from the principal and then proceeded back to her seat.

The warmness in her palm dissipated as she reached her seat and the presence she once felt near her now seemed to float away. She whispered softly, "Take care of her for me Dennis."

A cool gust of wind blew and she shuddered but she knew that Dennis had answered the only way he could, by providing a cool breeze on this hot and humid day. She smiled again and sat down. Perhaps death was not all that bad after all – Dennis and Maude had each other from the time they fell in love until after death and that, to her, seemed like perfection. Perhaps that ideology was more fantastical than she dared imagine herself ever to find – for that kind of love did not look foreseeable for her – but it still gave her hope.

The rest of the graduation ceremony ended an hour later and the students stood in the football field and waited as parents and family members came to gather them and take them home or just to congratulate them. Inundated with the massive crowd of people, Rachel simply tried her best to slip out of the arena unnoticed. She knew what she needed to do. She needed to find someone.

She needed to find Tom.

Twenty

*T*om had spent the remainder of the day driving around the town mindlessly, the words of Maude -- grandmother of his beloved Rachel and woman who's life he chose to not save – on his mind. He wished that he was strong enough to stand up to his brother but for the past eighteen years he had never once stood up to his father, so why now would he choose to stand up to his brother who was stronger and possibly more demented than his father had ever been.

Tom had never been a pacifist and even had a reputation in Vertueux for being the guy who would stand up for anyone. Too many times he had ended up with black eyes and bruised body for placing himself between the bullies at school who terrorized the younger and less-fortunate kids. He had never had to fight the bullies, the one blow inadvertently given to Tom was enough to stop the bullies from their barrage and send them on to other deviant acts.

It was not his fear of fighting or being hit that stopped him from protecting others from his brother – for in his life he had received so many blows from his father that he was pretty much used to the pain. He felt it had to be the brotherly connection, for Junior – as brutish as he was now – had at one point been the perfect big brother, always protecting his baby brother from harm, even taking the blows from his father just to spare his baby brother from the torture. That had been many years ago, and Junior had definitely changed.

Tom regretted now that he had not stepped in to help Maude – he knew she was dying, it was in her eyes. His brother, the murderer, was cavorting around town with mistresses while a woman lay dying because of him, his wife lay in ashes, and a man floated underneath the murky lairs of the lake, food for the carnivorous beasts that occupied its malodorous waters. Junior had definitely changed.

He did not understand the complexity of it all – how could he, his brother had left Vertueux at eighteen and eight years later was a man that Tom didn't understand. He knew it had something to do with Rachel – for those who had died were somehow connected to her – her grandmother Maude, her boyfriend, and the teacher who Junior had been upset with for saying something about her - but why her, why Rachel?

He had to admit that he had been enamored by her presence, in fact, from the moment he had seen her in his dreams he felt as if his world existed solely to be by her side. Meeting her had changed his world, for she was more beautiful than he imagined – but his brother, his brother had always chased the easy prey – too lazy to chase the big game – and Rachel was big game, he knew that. He hated referring to her as if she was a piece of meat, but in Junior's mind, that's what all women were – meat. To Tom, however, Rachel was the epitome of everything he had ever wanted in a woman – the woman he had saved himself to be with, the woman he could not live without.

A grumbling in his stomach reminded him it was now nearing 5 pm and he had not eaten all day. He pulled into a fast food restaurant, parked his car, and walked in. The young woman at the counter smiled at him, and leaning over the counter, asked softly, "What can I get you?"

"Number two with a Coke, please." He smiled softly.

The girl was pleasant to look at, but by no means as stunning as his beloved Rachel. With soft blonde curls, pulled back neatly with a bow, and big brown eyes, she was no doubt popular with the boys. Her smile was soft and pleasant and a single tiny dimple shown when she smiled. She looked maybe seventeen years old with an aura of naivety that would surely make her a wonderful lover.

The girl told him the total and as he fished out money from his wallet, he asked, "Do you go to the high school?"

She sighed, "No. I'm home-schooled." She was obviously not too happy about that idea.

"You don't happen to know Rachel Odium, do you?" He handed her the money.

"Nope, doesn't sound familiar." She placed the money in the drawer and handed him change. "Hold on, I'll ask Tony, he used to go to school there."

She bounced off, her curls moving in motion with her body. She'd make some guy proud some day, he thought.

He waited patiently at the counter while the girl talked to a guy in the back. He couldn't see the guy too well, but from what he could see, it was probably a good idea he was in the back because his hair was disheveled and all-in-all, he didn't look too terribly clean. He watched as the two looked back towards him and then talked again, and then the girl, still bouncing, came back towards Tom.

"He says he knows her---called her Wretched Rachel."

Tom looked puzzled.

"Oh, that was her nickname, something to do with her being poor or something, I don't know. Tony is kinda weird…"

"Does he know how to find her?"

"He said she works at a diner and lives at some---" She leaned closer to him and whispered, "-crappy--apartments near the diner."

"Anything else?"

She giggled, "He says she got hot."

He smiled; yes she had indeed "got hot."

"Thanks, you're a doll."

The food arrived and he grabbed the tray off the counter.

She leaned over the counter before he could leave.

"So is she your girlfriend or something?"

"No, no, just someone…" He wasn't sure how to explain what she was – he did wish that he could say she was his girlfriend, but that would be a lie and after all his other discretions this week, lying shouldn't be on his list.

She smiled a big grin obviously happy for the news of his singlehood. "I'm not supposed to do this, but you're too cute… do you think you'd like to go out sometime?"

He smiled softly, flattered.

"I'm actually only in town for a few days. I don't live here."

She still smiled, "Well you can have some fun while you're in town, I'll show you around." She winked at him.

"I'm flattered, really I am, but I just won't have time."

She fed some paper out of the printer next to the cash register and wrote something on it. Handing the paper to him, she smiled and said, "Just in case."

He smiled and put the paper in his wallet. "Just in case," he repeated.

He went to the table and ate his food in silence. The girl went back to her work, skittering about in the back like a moth around a flame. When he was done eating, and he placed his garbage in the trash and his tray on top of the trash can, the girl was nowhere to be seen. He slid out of the restaurant as quiet as a mouse, hoping that she would not see him. She did not or at least did not come after him.

His Camaro's engine roaring, he backed out and drove back to his brother's apartment.

When he arrived at the fourteenth floor apartment, his brother was home alone, sitting on the couch, drinking a beer, and watching television – wrestling. Junior had always been into more violent television shows while Tom had chose to not watch television except on rare occasions. Tom had preferred to stay out of the house, and watching television would require being home.

Junior nodded at Tom when he walked through the door.

"Want a beer?" Junior said it through slurred speech; apparently he had been drinking most of the day.

"No, that's OK."

"You're a pussy, Tom."

"Well thanks, Junior."

"Hey, I got something for you to read." He chuckled through the garbled dialogue and then reached over to the coffee table to grab some papers.

Tom took the papers from Junior's hands and read them. The papers were printed out from the local newspapers website; the headline read "Five dead in fatal traffic accident."

Tom scanned the article that pretty much said that two teenagers ran a traffic light, causing a major pileup and that the two teenagers died and that a mother, father, and their child died. Seven people were injured, one critical. Tom put the paper back on the coffee table, his stomach in knots.

"Pretty cool, huh? I did that." He smiled cockily. "I killed her." He motioned his head towards a picture of his late wife. "Then I killed that teacher. Then I killed that boy. That'll teach em to mess wit my Rach..." His voice trailed off and his head lulled downwards, the affects of alcohol taking too much toll on his body.

Tom shook his brother lightly. "Junior get up and go to bed." It was only 7pm but Tom really just wanted to lie down on the couch that his brother now slouched upon..

"What? What?" His voice slurred and tired.

"Go to bed." He helped his brother up off the couch and into the bedroom.

His brother now out of the room, Tom went back to the couch and lay down. Staring at the ceiling, he wondered if his brother felt any guilt for the body count that constantly seemed to grow – now at eight, how many more people had to die to satisfy his brother's thirst. Bewildered, he drifted off to sleep. He did not dream – he did not dare dream.

He awoke in the morning with the sun shining brightly through the patio window. Junior was up and about making too much noise when Tom just wanted to sleep.

Kimberly Thomas

"My head hurts." Junior cursed and swore as he opened up cabinet after cabinet.

Tom sat up on the couch. "What are you looking for?" He said it gruffly, upset that he was awakened.

"Something to make this hangover go away."

Tom muttered softly, "Try not drinking."

His brother thankfully did not hear him.

Tom walked to the bathroom, opened the cabinet, grabbed several types of pills, poured a few of each in his hand, and walked back to his brother.

"Take these, that's what dad always did."

Junior patted Tom so hard on the back, he almost fell down.

"That's my bro. You rock." He smiled widely.

"What time is it anyway?"

Junior turned around and looked at the microwave. "11:13."

Tom said nothing, amazed that it was so late and that he was still so tired. He really needed to get back to Vertueux so he could get back to school next week – it was already Friday, after all.

Junior interrupted his thoughts, "How long does it take for these pills to work?"

"A few hours – at least for dad that's how it worked. Why?"

"Graduation tonight – I have to go show my support, ya know?" He winked at Tom, as if Tom should get the joke.

He did not get it and he did not know why Junior would want to show support, because in a drunken stupor his brother must have forgotten that he admitted to killing his own wife. If he killed his wife, why would he show up to support her – unless – unless it was to get at Rachel?

Aware that Junior must want to go for Rachel, Tom asked, "What time is the ceremony?"

"Starts at 6 – you think this stuff will work before then?"

"Yeh, dude, you'll be your normal self by then."

Normal – there was no part of his brother that was normal. He would have to show up at the ceremony also, for if it was Rachel that his brother wanted, then Tom would surely have to step-in and protect her.

Twenty-One

*T*he excited atmosphere of the crowd grew as parents and extended family searched through the sea of blue graduation gowns to find their children, or friends, or relatives - and Rachel was alone, the castaway on a deserted isle. She had not searched for Mr. Crabtree or his brother Tom when she had sat sullen and depressed waiting for her turn to walk the stage; she had not searched for them when her spirits had been uplifted by the apparent visit of Maude. She did not expect them to be at the graduation anyway.

    She trudged through the crowd, avoiding eye contact, ignoring the sounds – everything was silent to her, as if she had been struck deaf. She did not know where she was going – the exit was the other way, and the exit would be the most logical place for her to go, but she continued inwards into the depths of the crowd of exuberant families as if following a homing beacon that would send her to her destination.

    She let her mind lead her towards Tom since she had no clue where he was; she let herself mindlessly walk through the crowd of people, staring intently at the ground below her avoiding the emotions that would surely overwhelm her if she were made aware that she was alone in this most exciting of times.

She mumbled "thanks" when people she passed said "Congratulations" – people she did not know who were only aware of her status as a graduate simply by her outfit – the blue cap and gown.

She was invisible here, more so than ever, because the sea of faces and the crowded stadium floor would surely lead a claustrophobic to a panic attack. She appreciated that she was able to blend in because she did not want to be noticed – she wanted to be the invisible Wretched Rachel once again.

After around ten minutes of searching, head down, only using her heart to search for him, she stopped and looking up, looked up straight into the face of Tom, his eyes glinting with a beautiful glow that spoke more words than could ever come from his mouth. Without a word, he grabbed her hand gently in his, and pulled her through the crowd of people towards the exit.

Muttering "Excuse me" as she pushed through throngs of people, she let him pull her towards the exit – her eyes focused, embarrassingly, on his butt that looked much too amazing in his blue jeans. She blushed when she thought about it.

When they reached the exit doors, Tom pushed them gently and waited as she passed through, and then with a glance backwards across the sea of people, he took her hand again and led her, without a word, to a white Camaro that sat close by in the parking lot. He unlocked the passenger door with his key and then opened the door and proceeded to his side. They closed the doors simultaneously and he backed up the car quickly and, tires squealing, pulled out of the parking lot.

He did not speak a word, only stared straight ahead with an intensity that was strangely comforting, although on any other person might seem frightening. She wasn't sure why she didn't feel uncomfortable with him; after all, his brother was someone that she knew was to be avoided.

At speeds that would surely attract police officers he headed away from the school, only slowing when at least ten blocks separated the two. He pulled silently into a gas station and parked at a tank, the bright glow of the lights overhead shining an eerie glow into the once dark car.

"Can you take me to Vertueux?" Her voice was meek like a mouse trying to portray his thoughts in a voice too soft to understand.

He said nothing, his hands firmly placed on the steering wheel in a grip that looked painful.

Fearing he hadn't heard her, she said louder,

"Can you take me to Vertueux?"

He loosened his grip on the steering wheel and turned his head towards her slowly.

His voice was soft and calm, unlike his demeanor which seemed stressed and perhaps even frightened.

"Why?"

"My mother – I believe she may have gone there."

"Let me pump some gas and then we'll talk about it, okay?"

She nodded her approval and he took the keys from the ignition and stepped out into the bright lights of the gas station without a word. Suddenly aware, now that things had slowed down, that she was still in her cap and gown, she slipped out of the passenger door and stood up – the bright lights of the gas station making her squint.

Tom turned towards her and smiled softly and as she smiled back, she unzipped the gown and then pulled it off and, folding it neatly, she placed it on the floor of the Camaro. After taking the cap off and running her hands through her hair to straighten it, she put the cap on the floor of the Camaro with the gown, closed the door and walked over to Tom who sat leaning against the car watching the numbers as they spiraled upwards.

He looked at her as she walked up, smiled, and then softly said, "You look beautiful tonight."

She smiled but the warmness in her face made her morbidly aware that she was blushing. "Thank you." Her voice was meek.

The pump clicked off, breaking the awkward silence and he squeezed off a few more cents to round off the dollar amount and then put the pump back on the tank.

"You want something to drink?"

"Sure."

He grabbed her hand gently, and wrapping his fingers within hers, he walked beside her proudly. The door jingled as they walked through it, and the gas station attendant, busy reading a magazine at the counter, looked towards them and then quickly put his head back into the magazine. Hand-in-hand, she and Tom walked through the cluttered isles. Tom grabbed a few things – bags of chips and pretzels and then opened up a cooler to grab a couple of waters.

"You want me to hold something?" She said it softly as she looked up into those beautiful gold-specked green eyes.

He smiled down at her and then kissed her gently on the forehead and then handed her, without a word, the bags of chips and pretzels he had picked up earlier.

They walked up to the counter, hand-in-hand, the other hands full of food and drinks. The gas station attendant placed his magazine down with a grunt, and without a word scanned their items and took their money. The two walked slowly to the car – she didn't want to let go of the magical feeling of having her hand intertwined with his.

It was odd – this feeling of passion that she felt now, after all, she was not one to fall in love or feel ardor for anything romantic. Yet, here with him, time seemed to stand still. The moments that they had spent walking hand-in-hand in the gas station had seemed like hours when, in fact, it had only been minutes. And now, as he walked towards the car with her and opened the door for her, she could only wish that moment would never end.

As he held the door, he turned her towards him and looked at her. He put his hand on her face and caressed it gently but there was a troubled look in his eye that betrayed the gentle, soft and caring, caress of her face.

She smiled softly at him and whispered, "Are you okay?"

He smiled, "No, no I'm not okay."

Rachel immediately became concerned and became unsettled. "What's wrong?"

She glanced nervously around her as if something lurked in the shadows around the gas station – something sinister and something surely named Junior.

His hand still held her cheek gently. "I want to kiss you."

She chuckled, suddenly amused that she had mistook his concern for something more evil. Smiling, she balanced herself on the balls of her feet so she could reach his face, and leaned in and kissed him gently on the lips – an ever so chaste kiss.

He returned the kiss with such passion that her body transformed into something warm and fiery, and she had a sudden urge to slough off her morality. He pushed her up against the side of the Camaro, avoiding the opened doorway, and explored her mouth. She wanted him to stop – and she didn't want him to stop. Her body screamed for him and her mind, her mind lost out. It was not like her to give herself to him so freely as she had only known him briefly but she could not stop, for it felt as if this moment, this very moment in time, was the culmination of years and years of history. As he pulled away, his eyes remained closed, his fingers still wrapped gently in her long black hair, he whispered softly, "I have waited my entire life for you."

She smiled softly as he opened his eyes and released her from his grasp. Her knees were weak, and feeling like she had just finished running a marathon, she still had enough energy to smile and say, "Are you okay now?"

He chuckled softly and smiled back and with a simple kiss to her forehead he said so softly, "I'll always be okay as long as you are with me."

Her heart beat loudly in her chest. She was not a romantic by any means but his words were what she felt in her heart also.

Kimberly Thomas

Twenty-Two

❦ ❦ ❦

*T*he silence in the car as they drove away from the gas station was not awkward. They both felt at ease and no words were necessary to disturb the ambiance of romance, desire, and lust that exuded from them.

Rachel sat looking out the passenger side window, watching as the world around her passed by in a blur, the lights of the city magnificent and beautiful. Tom drove, head forward, thoughts racing, but he dared not look at her for he would want to touch her, to taste her, to be forever part of her. He knew he should not rush this – this was something worth waiting for, something of which he had dreamed forever-perfection.

He broke the silence after a few blocks, the silence becoming awkward as his thoughts raced as fast as he did from this god-forsaken city and his brother.

"So your mother…"

She turned to him and giggled, "I had almost forgotten."

"Why would she be in Vertueux?" He looked at her briefly; her face was stunning in the dimly lit car and he wanted to kiss her full lips.

She paused, thinking, and then glancing out the window again, she said, "I'm not sure; it's just a gut feeling."

The light turned red and he stopped and watched her as she sat staring out the passenger window, her eyes shining in the reflection on the window. "I'm surprised you even know of Vertueux. Not very many people even know it exists."

She chuckled and glanced over at him. A horn honked behind him and he glanced up to notice the light had turned green.

She spoke, "Well, it's kind of a long and confusing story --- and really I'm just going on a hunch that she went there."

"Well we've got a long drive ahead of us, so you'll have a while to tell me that story." He smiled at her quickly.

"So, you'll take me?" She removed the top part of her seat belt and leaned over and kissed him on the cheek.

"Of course." Another red light and he slammed on his brakes to keep from running it, his mind and his eyes elsewhere.

"Are you hungry?"

"Sure, I guess I am."

She was used to being hungry.

He turned at the light instead of going straight and made a turn into a fast food restaurant and parked in the parking lot. She unbuckled her seat belt and sat waiting as he remained staring out the front window. It was the same fast food restaurant he had gone to just a few days before – he was not far enough away from his brother yet.

She reached over and softly turned his head towards her, her hand warm on his face. "Tom?"

He smiled at her, "We can't stay long; my brother…"

She smiled, "Yes, I know your brother is obsessed with me."

His eyes glazed over and he looked past her,

"It's more than that – it's much more than that."

He grabbed her face in his hands and pulled her close to him and kissed her fully on her lips.

Her eyes closed, imbibing in the aura of his presence and his kiss, she felt drunk on him as if she was intoxicated.

When he let her go, she still felt his lips on her.

"Do you feel it or is it just me?" He said it softly and his voice was so sad as if he was afraid the answer would be something he would not want to hear.

"Feel what?"

"Like we were meant to be together – like everything that has ever happened in our lives was meant just so we could be here now."

She smiled. She felt it but what if this was just hormones playing with them – making them think that this was meant to be, that their entire lives had been designed so they could be together. She couldn't live her life by what if's though…she knew that.

Without a word, knowing that words would be meaningless in this situation, she did what she had read in books – climbed out of her bucket seat and slipped onto his lap, kissing him so passionately that she felt that if they had not been bathed in the glow from the lights of the fast food restaurant that they would have surely gone farther than just less-than-innocent making out.

It was fortunate that a car pulling up interrupted them because she was not sure that she would be able to resist him. Still absorbed with him, she leaned backwards and said

"Yes, yes, I feel the same way."

She climbed off of him and crawled back to her seat. He smiled at her and leaned towards her and kissed her softly.

"I'm happy that you are mine."

He looked at the car that had parked next to them, the occupants which still sat in the car trying to nonchalantly watch them and then added, "I think we might want to go through the drive thru."

She laughed, "Yeh that might be a good idea."

He turned the car engine on and then backed out and pulled into the drive thru lane. A couple of burgers, fries, and drinks later they were back on the road, and getting onto the highway.

She held the food in her lap and stared at him as he drove. He yawned and she yawned in response. The food smelled delicious but she did not want to eat until he did – rudeness was something not in her vocabulary.

"You tired baby?"

He smiled at her softly.

"Just a little, I'll be okay."

"You want your fries or burger?"

He yawned again. "There's a rest stop in about 50 miles, I'll stop there and eat. It's hard to eat and drive in this car. You can go ahead and eat if you'd like." He yawned another time.

"Are you sure you're not tired? We can stop or I can drive if you'd like."

"Well I hope I don't sound like a chauvinist pig when I say this, but I really don't like other people driving my car."

She laughed. "No, no, it's okay…I understand. I wouldn't let me drive this car either."

He laughed. "You're too sweet."

"So stop and take a nap?"

He looked at the analog clock on his dash and then back at the rear view mirror – the city was growing smaller and smaller, a good sign that they were at least a decent distance from his brother. He yawned again. "A nap would be great; I haven't had a decent night's sleep since I came to visit my brother."

She smiled and then patted him gently on the knee. "So find us somewhere to nap."

She had assumed that he would pull into the rest stop and they would sleep in the car but instead he pulled into a motel and parked the car in front of the office door. Her heart fluttered in her chest with a loud thump that she knew he must have heard. As attracted as she was to him, and as apparent as it was that they both wanted each other, she was not ready to give herself to him and she hoped that he had not misinterpreted her desire for him as a willingness to sleep…well, have sex…with him. She wasn't sure she could trust herself with him.

He must have noticed her apprehension for he reached over to her and kissed her lightly on the cheek and said, "I don't want us to do anything more than sleep tonight, okay?"

She smiled.

"I'll be right back." He left the car running and went inside the office door.

In a few minutes he was back, key cards in hand. Putting the car in drive, he drove to the back of the hotel and parked.

"We're in room 253." He pointed to a room on the second floor.

The hotel was a small run-down place that looked like it catered to truck drivers who wanted a place to rest rather than vacationing families. It wasn't a horrible place, in fact, it looked cleaner and nicer than her own apartment complex but she was still apprehensive, not of the hotel itself but of the connotation of a hotel and what a man and woman would be doing at such a place – especially young teenagers.

She was silent as she opened the car door, carrying the food and drinks, and waited for Tom to gather a bag out of his trunk. She was breathless as they climbed the old iron stair cases that led to the second floor, each step creaking loudly under their weight. As Tom opened the door, she followed him into the dark room. Tom flipped a light switch on the wall and two wall lamps shone a dingy light on the sparsely decorated room.

There were two beds in the room covered in a blue paisley comforter that looked like it had survived years and years of abuse. The carpet, once probably a cream color was now shades of brown and tan, stained by liquids that no one would probably want to know. A small television set sat attached to a dresser and on the far end of the room was a double-sink that led to a room that contained a toilet and shower.

He watched her as she perused the room and then quietly said, "I'm sorry it's not the nicest room."

She laughed, "This is better than what I'm used to."

Sadly that statement was in all reality the truth.

She placed the food on the dresser while Tom sat his duffle bag on the bed closest to the door and opened it. Placing the two burgers and fries in neat stacks, she turned around and said, "Dinner's ready!"

He laughed and then walked up and grabbed a burger and started eating it. She grabbed the other burger and munched at it and then sat on the bed next to the duffle bag.

She ate a few bites and already full, she stood up and sat the burger back on the paper. Tom paced the floor eating his burger in small bites. She went back to the bed and laid down on it with her legs hanging off the end of the bed.

"What was your dad's name?" She asked unprovoked.

"Michael, why?"

"So your brother is Michael, Jr.?"

"Yeh." He turned to look at her, although her face was focused on the ceiling above.

"Apparently your father knew my mother a long time ago, like before I was born."

"How do you know that?"

"Well Mrs. Crabtree gave me some letters that she found in your father's belongings."

"And?"

"Well, they were love letters to my mom from your father."

"I don't get it, why would she give letters to you?"

Rachel laughed. "I don't know. But I think---I think your father might have had something to do with my mom moving to the city. I think he might have done something to my father."

Tom said nothing.

She rolled onto her side and looked at Tom as he stood staring at the curtained window of the hotel room. "I really don't know what to believe. My mom never told me anything about her past. I've never met my father and the letters said something about me and my mom and maybe my dad – but I don't know…I really don't know…"

Tom still said nothing.

She sat silently staring intently at Tom.

"I don't know anything about what my father did." His voice was gruff and angry.

She rolled back onto her back and stared at the ceiling, a tear escaping from her eye. "I'm sorry, I shouldn't have said anything."

He walked over to the bed and lay down next to her. She turned to him and he lay staring at the ceiling.

"I used to try to believe my father might have been a good man at some point but I think he may have always been a bad man. If he was anything like my brother is with you, then I can only imagine he did a lot of things that I don't know about." He sighed.

"You know, I get this vibe from your brother that freaks me out but in all reality he hasn't done anything that could be considered psychotic – I mean, honestly, all he did was give me money for clothes and some flowers. He's seemed a little like a stalker but it really wasn't much at all."

"I wish that was all he's done."

"What do you mean?"

"Well…" He paused and the pained look on his face said that he really didn't want to talk about it, but he continued anyway. "…he killed your substitute teacher – that one guy that was in the room when I met you. He killed your boyfriend. He killed your grandmother." His face still pointed towards the ceiling as if he was afraid of the response that Rachel would have to the news.

"Well I don't have a boyfriend or a grandmother."

"Maude wasn't your grandmother?"

"No." She leaned up and looked at him in the face. "Your brother did that to her?"

He looked away from her face. "Yes."

She was angry but she didn't want to show emotion. "Why?"

He shrugged. "I don't really know; all I know is that it seems to be anyone associated to you or that he finds as a threat to keep you from him will be targeted."

Her face contorted into a look of concern. "Who else? Who else did he kill?" She demanded.

"I don't know his name…he forced the kid and his twin sister into traffic and they died."

"Danny?"

"Yeh I guess. I assumed it was your boyfriend because I'd seen you with him one day."

She chuckled softly, although it didn't take away from the anger that welled up in her body. "No, Danny and I went out one time but apparently it was just so he could tell everyone that I was a 'good fuck'." She did her fingers in air quotes to emphasize that the "good fuck" was just a fabrication.

He laughed softly - obviously trying to change the conversation from something dire to something more jovial. "And are you?" He winked at her.

She laughed, "Well, I wouldn't know because I've actually never had a boyfriend." She leaned over him and smiled, her black hair falling around his face.

He smiled and said seductively, "You want one?"

"Only if you're volunteering for the job."

He chuckled, "I thought you'd never ask."

She was not prone to such flirtatious behavior – this was way out of character for her. In fact, she wasn't quite sure why she was being so abnormally forward with him. He was amazingly attractive and the feel of his firm body under hers was sending electrical jolts to her brain – tantalizing her imagination in ways she had never even imagined. A boyfriend – it wasn't the end of the world to have one, she thought.

Touching his face gently, she climbed off of him and walked slowly to the drink that now left a ring of condensation on the old furniture and took a sip from the watered down soda.

"Is it okay if I take a shower?" She said as she glanced at the bed where Tom still lay staring at the ceiling.

He laughed, "You don't need my permission."

"Okay then, I am going to take a shower. Do you think you can find something for me to sleep in?"

He looked at her longingly and with a twinkle in his eye that she knew betrayed his promise to keep this night's visit platonic. Perhaps she was indeed naive to ever think that the two could be in the same hotel room and remain innocent but she was adamant that no matter what strange emotions flooded through her, she would not give in to them – she would not sacrifice her virginity tonight.

The twinkle slipped into reality and he got up off the bed and walked over to the duffle bag, "I'll find something, go take your shower."

She slipped into the tiny bathroom which did not provide a

door for privacy. After struggling with the zipper on the dress and removing the rest of her clothes, she wrapped the dingy white towel provided above the toilet around her naked body. Grabbing her clothes from the floor, she held onto the garments and the towel and slipped back into the bedroom to neatly place the dress on the bed closest to the bathroom. It was important to keep the outfit clean since she had nothing else to wear. Knowing he would be watching her, she tried desperately not to make eye contact with Tom.

Tom watched her; watched as she moved and the towel opened and exposed a significant portion of her naturally tan thighs; watched as she clung to the towel so it wouldn't expose her nakedness to him. He wanted her – he wanted her to lose grip of the towel and have it fall to a pile at her feet or better yet, he wanted to rip the towel off her, throw her on the bed and have his way with her. He was ashamed at that thought – he was not his deranged brother and he was not his sexual deviant father. Yet he stared at her as she lovingly straightened her dress on the bed, holding onto the towel as if her life depended on it – and he knew it did, he would not be able to control himself if that towel fell.

He was glad when she returned to the shower and heard the water turn on because he knew that the moment would come when they could express their love in that most precious of ways, exploring each other's bodies with love and unfettered desire – that moment when they would know that they would spend the rest of their nights together in each other's arms. Tonight was not that night. He re-arranged himself in his pants, embarrassed that he had grown hard over the idea of taking her – his poor innocent sweet Rachel.

It seemed as if an eternity had passed when he heard the shower turn off and Rachel, body moist from the shower, hair wet and beautiful, wrapped only in a towel walked out of the bathroom.

When she approached him, he handed her a t-shirt and boxers, the best he could do on short notice. She smiled and thanked him and then walked to be the bathroom where she stood in front of the double-sinks and stared at the huge vanity mirror that was overly lit with multiple bulbs.

He watched as she held the towel with one hand and then attempted to pull the shorts on underneath the towel. She managed to get the shorts mostly on when the towel fell to the ground. He tried to look away and she tried to catch the towel in time but he saw her naked breasts in the reflection in the mirror for only a few seconds before she slipped the white t-shirt over her head and over her breasts. The shirt was a small, which was the perfect size for him, but for her, it clung to her still damp breasts tightly, leaving nothing for his imagination.

He tried to look like he had not seen the towel drop when she walked to the bed closest to the bathroom. She smiled at him softly, mouthed "good night" and then lay down over the covers and stared at the ceiling. He watched her for a moment, her chest moving up and down with every breath, her legs, long and slender, and her wet hair strewn across the pillow. He wanted to go to her, hold her, but he knew he would not be able to contain himself. So, instead, he flipped the light switch off near the door and with a soft "good night", he lay down on the other bed and stared at the ceiling, unable to sleep.

Twenty-Three

🦇 🦇 🦇

She awoke to the cacophony of birds outside and the sound of the shower nearby. She stretched and yawned and then glanced at the empty bed next to her. Sitting up in the bed, she rubbed her eyes and then ran her fingers through her hair to straighten it. The shower turned off and she listened as Tom stepped out of the shower.

He had expected her to still be asleep since when he had decided to shower he had been unable to wake her. When he walked out, rubbing his hair with the towel, his naked body exposed, he had not expected to see her sitting there watching him.

When she saw him, she fell back on the bed and covered her eyes with the pillow and giggled. She wasn't giggling because she was laughing at him but giggling because she had never seen a naked man before and she kind of liked what she saw – muscles wet and rippling on his stomach and arms and well, she had tried to not look any further down than that.

The pillow was pulled from her face in one swift movement and she sat looking up into his face.

"It's safe now little lady." He said in a voice reminiscent of classic westerns, as if he had saved her from the evil banditos.

She smiled and sat back up on the bed. He had put on a pair of boxers and nothing more.

"Hope I didn't scare ya." He leaned over and kissed her forehead.

"Nope, you didn't. That's not a bad way to wake up in the morning." She winked at him and then leaned over and kissed him softly just above his belly button on his still damp stomach.

He groaned softly and she proceeded to kiss him softly upwards up towards his mouth.

"You're making this difficult," he said softly.

She could hear his heart beat in his chest. Smiling, she said, "What am I making difficult?"

He kissed her softly on the lips and then said,

"I want you…I want you real bad." He ran his fingers through her hair.

She smiled and kissed him softly, tugging his bottom lip with her mouth.

Kissing her softly, he whispered, "We should probably go before we end up doing something we shouldn't…" Glancing at the dimly lit clock on the night stand, he added, "…checkout time is soon anyway."

He smiled at her longingly and then kissing her softly on the forehead, he walked away, adjusting himself in his boxers.

She stood up and faced the wall and then pulled the shirt off over her head, her naked back exposed to him. She slipped the dress over her head and then reached under and pulled off the boxers.

He stood watching her and as she turned towards him, holding the dress up to her chest, he started to dig through the duffle bag for clothes trying to look innocent.

"Can you zip me up?" She smiled at him softly as she walked towards him.

When she reached him, she turned her back towards him so he could access the zipper. He felt the urge to touch her back, pull the dress off of her, but he grabbed the zipper and after some effort, pulled it up to the top. When he was done, he grabbed her around the waist and pulled her back towards him; she turned her head backwards towards him and kissed him passionately.

She turned her body towards him as they kissed. His hands

gently grabbing her hair and then sliding down her back towards the zipper as their mouths explored each other. Her heart was beating as loud as his in her chest when he started tugging on the zipper. The zipper was down in a few seconds and the dress was on the floor in less time than that and he pulled away from her kiss to look at her longingly.

The knock on the door stopped them from going further. The maid, an elderly Hispanic woman knocked once and then slid open the door and when seeing Rachel reach in a quick swoop to grab her dress to cover her nakedness, she said in broken English, "So sorry. Checkout time eez eleven."

The woman did not leave but instead started cleaning the room while Rachel and Tom quickly dressed and left the room embarrassed.

When they were out of the room, Rachel said softly, "What time is it anyway?"

Tom glanced at his watch, "1:00"

She laughed and they got in the car and drove to the front of the hotel to turn in the keys and get on the highway.

The highway was virtually empty other than the plethora of big trucks which insisted on driving in the left lane and slowing down traffic. They passed a few families in mini-vans, off to some vacation, the kids in the back waving as they passed. Rachel would smile and wave back, which would immediately send the kids ducking out of view.

She watched as fields of corn and wheat and other crops she didn't know passed by, the lines dizzying if she watched them too closely. Tom was silent and she did not speak for fear that they would end up talking about what almost happened back at the hotel room. She knew too well that it should have never gone that far – she was here with Tom to find her mother, not to find love, if that was what was transpiring between them.

She glanced at him lovingly – she did believe she could love him but she didn't want to rush anything, after all, love was really not in her vocabulary.

He glanced over at her and said, softly, "What are you

thinking about?"

"Oh, nothing. I'm pretty much just looking around – I've never been out of the city before."

He smiled. "It's beautiful out here – the air is clean, the people are nicer. But – what were you thinking about when you were looking at me?" He winked at her.

She blushed. "I was thinking that I may have fallen for you."

"Really?"

"Yes."

"You're not just saying that?"

"No, why?"

"Well, I was thinking about that last night. I mean, I want your body and all, but I don't think that after all this is over that I could ever live without you. I think I may be in love with you too."

She smiled, unsure of how to respond. She knew too well that once this was all over she and her mom would go back to the city and she'd have to find somewhere else to live. Tom would be ancient history. There was no way she could afford to keep up a long distance relationship, and she only imagined that now that Maude was gone the diner would surely be closed so she'd be homeless and jobless.

She avoided the comment with a question, "How long till we get to Vertueux?"

"A few hours, three or four tops."

She nodded and then rested her head on the window and drifted off into sleep.

Twenty-Four

The sound of the phone ringing awoke her, although she did not stir. The phone rang once, then twice, and after the third, Tom answered.

"Hello?"

--- "I'm driving home."

--- "Because I have school on Monday."

--- "Why would I know where she is?"

--- "You're being paranoid."

--- "Are you driving?"

--- "Where to?"

--- "I'm almost home. Where are you going?"

With a muttered curse that Rachel could barely hear, Tom flipped the cell phone shut.

She turned towards him and rubbed her eyes with her hands. "Who was that?"

"My brother."

She rolled her eyes and looked out the window. They were in a small town now, no longer on the highway. The street they drove down was lined on both sides with store-fronts reminiscent of the 1950s, two story stores that looked like they could double as houses, blood red bricks accented with awnings that overhung the sidewalk in front advertising the name of the business. From thrift shops to a historical society, the little street stretched on for a few blocks and then ended abruptly as it fed its way into houses.

"I don't think it's a good idea to go to my house. I'm not positive he isn't already here."

"Who?" Rachel said in a voice so innocent it made his heart want her more.

"My brother – he's driving; he thinks I have you."

She giggled. "But you do."

"Yes, but he doesn't need to know that."

It was nearing five pm and they hadn't eaten all day and he was starving.

He continued, "I'm going to call my friend and see if we can drop by his house for some food."

He flipped his cell phone back open and dialed a number and waited on the line.

"Dude."

--- "Yeh, yeh, I haven't been at home."

--- "Can I drop by?"

--- "Sure we can go there."

--- "A friend."

--- "Yes, a girl." He laughed.

--- "I'll see you in a few."

Tom flipped the cell phone closed and laughed.

"That was my friend Alex. He's at his girlfriend's house right now."

Tom turned the car off the stretch of road and passed through housing developments where houses grew smaller and smaller and landscaping turned to lighter shades of green and then brown before they stopped in front of a small house where two small boys played basketball in the driveway.

"This is Andrea's house." Tom said as he quickly jumped out of the car.

He walked over to Rachel's door and opened it and she slipped out of the car, straightening her skirt and then her hair with her hands.

Alex, dressed only in a pair of basketball trunks, came bounding out of the house taking two steps at a time off the porch that was hid in shadows.

He patted Tom on the back, and then outstretched his hand towards Rachel.

"I'm Alex."

Rachel looked up into his green eyes and shaking his hand said, "I'm Rachel."

Tom, anxiously looking around, said in a hurried voice, "We need to go inside."

"Whatever you want bro, you disappear on me for a week and then bring a girl with you…you've got some explaining to do." Alex winked at Rachel as they walked inside.

Andrea, dressed in a white tank top and hot pink shorts, sat laying on the couch watching a show on television. When she saw Tom walk in first she waved at him and then got up when she saw Rachel.

She walked over to where they were and outstretched her hand towards Rachel, "I'm Andrea."

"Rachel."

"That is a beautiful dress."

"Thanks."

Andrea ran her fingers on the necklace that her mother had left for her. "Beautiful necklace – bet that thing cost your parents a fortune."

Rachel shrugged and the two girls smiled at each other awkwardly.

Alex interrupted the uncomfortable silence. "So there's some lunch meat in the fridge if you guys want sandwiches."

Tom replied, "Man that'd be great, I'm famished."

"Who says famished anymore, dude. You are such a nerd."

Tom laughed and the four walked single file through the narrow hall to the tiny kitchen.

When sandwiches were made, the four sat down at the little wooden kitchen table.

Alex began, "So explain."

"Well, my brother called me last Saturday to tell me my

sister-in-law had died."

"Damn. How'd that happen?"

"Written off as a suicide."

Alex scratched his head.

Tom continued, "Well, apparently my brother has gone crazy and is trying to find Rachel here."

Rachel piped into the conversation, "And I'm here looking for my mother who disappeared."

Andrea injected herself into the conversation, "Wow, you guys must have left out some serious portions of the story because you two are making no sense."

Rachel and Tom laughed and the look that they gave each other made Alex laugh and say, "Praise the Lord, Tommy boy has fallen in love."

Alex lifted his hands in mock praise and then patted Tom on the back. Tom and Rachel looking embarrassed lowered their eyes towards the table and the half-eaten sandwiches they had left there.

Andrea, always the talker, spoke to Rachel, "So, Rachel, why are you looking for your mom, here of all places?"

"Well, I think she came here."

"Why?"

"To look for my dad."

"Who is your dad?"

"I'm not sure."

"Then how do you know she's here?"

Tom interrupted. "Rachel's last name is Odium."

Alex pushed his chair back from the table and stood up. "Do you know what this means?"

Rachel replied, "No, I don't." Tom piped in, "Dude, don't" Alex, ignoring the plea continued speaking, "This means that all those rumors were true." "What rumors?" Rachel asked.

Rolling his eyes, Tom replied for Alex, "There were a lot of rumors about Jeremiah Odium." Looking towards Alex, he replied, "This only means one of them might be true and there's nothing saying that Rachel is his kid – it could just be coincidence."

Andrea leaned over closer to Rachel and said softly, "What they mean is that if you really are Jeremiah's kid, you are one helluva rich bitch." She laughed softly.

Tom looked towards Andrea and asked, "Can I ask you a huge favor, Andrea?"

"Sure thing."

"Can Rach stay here tonight? I need to make sure my brother doesn't think she's here. I need to go home alone."

"Sure." She looked towards Rachel. "You have a change of clothes?"

She chuckled, "No, it was kind of a rush decision to come here."

"Well, you're a skinny little white girl but I think you can probably fit in some of my clothes."

Alex, who had been pacing the floor, looked over and directed his question to Tom, "Do you need me to come with you?"

"No, no, I'll be fine. I gotta get going. I think my brother might be here already."

The four walked towards the door and when they reached the door, Tom grabbed Rachel around the waist and pulled him towards her and kissed her lightly on the lips. She wanted to hold him to keep him with her because she feared that if his brother was truly in the area that she may never see Tom again, losing him like she lost Maude and Danny and Mrs. Crabtree. She could not be in the shadow of death much more – she had been overshadowed by it since birth and in Tom's arms she felt as if life was rejuvenated, as if with him all the bad things would stop happening.

He let her go forlornly and walked through the open doorway, glancing back on numerous occasions at her face as she stood inside the door sadly watching him leave. Her eyes held that look of fear, the same fear that gripped at his chest – fear that this would be their final good bye.

Twenty-Five

His house was empty when he arrived. Although the sense of apprehension he had felt earlier was eased by the realization that his brother was not currently at their home in Vertueux, he was not entirely convinced that his brother was completely out of the picture. It was only inevitable for Junior to come for Rachel and it would be impossible to not face confrontation. He was already dreading the confrontation that would surmount between them, a knot grew in his stomach and made him tense and on edge.

He regretted leaving Rachel behind, for, with her, he had felt comfortable and peaceful – without her it seemed as though his life was in a constant state of turmoil. She was the ying to his yang.

His cell phone rang and he jumped, startled at the disruption in the morbidly quiet house. He pulled the phone out of his pocket and glanced at the caller ID. Work.

"Hello?"

--- "Yeh, I just got back in town."

--- "Sure, I'll come into work."

He sighed and hung up the phone. Again, wishing he had the ability to say 'no'.

He flipped the screen open and text messaged Alex. *"No one is at the house. I have to go to work."*

He went to the bathroom, showered, changed and then headed off to work.

There wasn't much of a crowd at the pizzeria and delivery orders were minimal when he arrived – unlike most times when Nancy would frantically tell him all the things he had to do when he arrived. Today was abnormally slow for a Saturday night as if everyone in the small town was overshadowed by the oppressive heat and humidity that had slipped in during the day.

It was nearing 10pm when Tom happened to glance out the window of the pizzeria while he was cleaning the tables. Alex's car was entering the parking lot. He watched as the car slid into a spot and then three doors opened on the vehicle and Alex, Andrea, and Rachel got out and walked towards the front door.

When Rachel saw Tom she ran to him and kissed him on the cheek.

Afraid that something had happened, he said, "Is everything okay? Did something happen?"

Alex slipped up to Tom and said, "No dude, we just got bored sitting around so we figured we'd come say 'hello'."

"It's not safe."

"You said your brother wasn't here."

"I said he wasn't at the house."

The clatter of a falling dish distracted them and they turned towards the source of the clatter. Nancy stood staring with jaw dropped at Rachel, shards of broken glass at her feet.

She spoke after a few seconds, "It was true all along."

Tom glanced towards Alex and whispered angrily, "This is why she needed to stay home. The more people who know she's here, the more likely my brother will find her."

Nancy stepped gingerly over the broken glass, as gingerly as a woman her size could muster, and walked towards Rachel hurriedly. Grasping Rachel's face in her bulbous hands, she cried, "You have his face and her eyes and her body – there is no doubt who you are."

Rachel perplexed, smiled at her.

Nancy continued, "How is your mother doing these days?"

Rachel, still baffled, said quietly, "She is okay; I came here to find her."

"She's here?" Nancy glanced around the restaurant excitedly.

Rachel shrugged and with disinterest said, "Somewhere."

Nancy shook her head sadly, "She probably went up to your daddy's place."

Tom muttered something under his breath and grabbed Rachel's arm. "You need to go back with Andrea."

Rachel pulled away from him. "Where is my father's home?"

Tom pulled her arm harder and she winced, "You need to go now."

Rachel struggled but Tom managed to pull her closer to the door.

They exited the door in a panicked rush although Rachel was oblivious to the urgency.

"What is your problem?" Rachel demanded.

"My brother just text me."

He flipped the phone open and shown it Rachel. The words on the screen were reason enough to explain Tom's urgency, although it seemed quite convenient that the text message appeared at that moment. *"Come out, come out, wherever you are."*

The three – Alex, Andrea, and Rachel – jumped back into Alex's car and Alex drove off at a hurried speed towards Andrea's house. Tom watched the car leave tread marks as Alex drove hurriedly away, a smile gracing his face.

When they were out of sight, he walked back inside the pizzeria which was soon to close, only to be rushed by Nancy.

"Things are going to change Tom."

Tom sighed, in no mood for her overly eager behavior. "What do you mean Nancy?"

"His wife *and* daughter came back – something either really bad or really good is going to happen."

A loud clap of thunder shook the restaurant as if God was sending an eerie warning that something bad was going to happen.

Nancy made the sign of the cross – always the devout Catholic – and then whispered, "Go home, Tom."

The first drops of rain started falling as he walked out of the restaurant and headed home.

Kimberly Thomas

Twenty-Six

The clap of thunder had shook the car in a violent motion and Alex sped up to get to Andrea's house before the rain fell from the sky. Rachel sat silently in the back of the car, her mind racing.

When they arrived at Andrea's house they slipped inside just as the drops of rain started falling from the sky. It was a beautiful sound, Rachel thought – the sound of drops of rain falling on the roof above.

They sat on the couch in silence – no television, just a dim light in another room that shone only faintly into the dungy living room.

Rachel spoke in a voice so hushed for fear that the ghosts and goblins in the room might hear her – although she knew that such things did not exist. "Do you know where my father lived?"

Alex sat staring at the ceiling, head leaned back on the couch and hand placed gently on Andrea's leg that was draped across his. He did not speak.

Andrea responded, "Everyone knows about the old Odium place."

"Except me." Rachel said, even though it should be obvious that she knew nothing about it.

Andrea laughed softly. "The house is supposedly haunted; people only go there on a dare."

"Haunted?"

"Yeh, haunted by your dead daddy." Alex said with such disgust that she wondered if he despised her.

Rachel said nothing in response to Alex, but prompted her question to Andrea. "So where is the house at?"

Andrea pointed to her left and said, "Like a mile that way on a little dirt road. The house is kind of creepy looking – only an idiot would actually go in there."

Alex glared at her, and Andrea covered her mouth and whispered, "Sorry", when realizing that Rachel's mother had probably gone to the house.

Rachel, ignoring the comment, said softly, "Oh ,OK."

Alex leaned over and whispered something in Andrea's ear that instigated a soft seductive giggle from her.

Andrea turned to Rachel and said, "I'll get you something to sleep in and a blanket, and you can crash on the couch, okay? We're going to go to bed."

She winked at Rachel and then stood up, followed by Alex, and then returned shortly with some shorts and a tank top.

Rachel mouthed "Thank you," and then went to the bathroom in the hall.

She heard them giggling and talking and then more sounds that she had never heard before and would not dare to guess the motivator of those sounds, and leaving the clothes in the bathroom sink, she opened the bathroom door quietly and tiptoed through the hallway to the front door, gathering up her shoes on the way.

She opened the front door softly as to not divulge her intentions and slipped outside and stood on the dark front porch. The rain still fell in a light drizzle and it glistened in the street lights as it fell, beautiful and serene.

"Left to the dirt road." She said softly to no one in particular as she proceeded from the house and onto the street to find her mother.

It was no time at all before her hair was dripping water and her clothes were soaked but she kept going – intently walking along the dimly lit street towards the direction of her father's home.

She was used to walking – that was what she had to do in the city – rain or no, it was a necessity. Here it was more than necessity, it was urgency. She could not wait for Tom to take her or anyone else for that matter, she felt she had to go to her mother and that time was of the essence. Perhaps it was just paranoia that brought about the sudden urgency but something in her heart said she had to go.

She had walked so far that there were no houses lining the street anymore, only a road that led towards open fields and darkness – complete and utter darkness. She kept walking – positive that she was going in the right direction. Noises exuded from the tall grasses – the sound of cicadas and crickets and more deviant animals that lurked for prey in the dark night. She was not afraid.

After what seemed like a hundred miles, but probably only had been one or two, she saw a dirt road with a mailbox to the right of it that read "Odium".

She was here. She traced her last name on the mailbox – this was where she had always been meant to be, this place, this home. She glanced down the small dirt road and noticed no house, just miles and miles of darkness. The moon, now hidden by dark rain clouds did not reveal the presence of any life in this dark foreboding land. She shuddered, the rain and cool air leaving her tired and cold.

A streak of lightening lit up the sky, revealing the large rain drops that glistened in its glow. In the glow of the brief lightening, she saw the road ahead that stretched for miles, dark red mud that shone and beckoned her to embark upon it.

The rain beat heavier, falling in torrents upon her and she hastened her step onto the side of the road to avoid the sinking and slippery mud of the old dirt road. She trudged on – her mind reeling, her heart racing. Each step brought her closer to the home of her father and hopefully closer to her mother; each step she felt brought her closer to her destiny.

Lightening illuminated the night sky on numerous occasions, each time revealing that she had not made it close enough to the house to see it. She was accustomed to the rain now, no longer shuddering from its harsh blows and cold touch. When the night was lit up by the magnificent show in the sky, she would envision movement in the tall grass around her and she'd quicken her pace for fear that this ground which felt unearthly would swallow her whole.

The ground squished beneath her feet, too much rain pouring down from the sky for it to soak it up quick enough. She paused and stood in the muddied grass and stared at her feet – desperate to rest even in the downpour. Even in the darkness she could tell her shoes were ruined; it was unfortunate for these had been gifts from Maude and she had vowed to herself to keep them forever – that was a vow she knew she had broken.

A flash of lightening lit up the entire night sky and she looked up and saw a man pointing across a field. She rubbed her eyes, for surely she had been mistaken. The man was dressed in a dark blue suit but was not drenched as she was – in the brief moment of light she could see no other discerning features about him.

Her heart beating loudly in her chest, confused but still not afraid, she looked towards where he pointed – a house, tall and magnificent, stood along the way -- the house from the pictures.

When she turned towards the man to thank him, he was gone.

She walked towards the house and stopped at a gated entrance that emptied into a graveled walkway, overgrown with weeds that led towards the entrance of the home. In the poorly lit night, she stood where the photographer had taken those pictures she had received and, glancing at that fateful window where the photograph had revealed an ethereal presence, she sighed in relief when she saw nothing there.

Music drifted from the house, the sound of a beautiful symphony engrossed in the eras of long ago by doing their homage to the classics. The sound was faint over the sound of the pitter patter of the rain, and as she walked along the graveled walkway the music grew louder and clearer. Her mind was absorbed with the music as if it put her into a trance and made her at ease in this place where ease did not come lightly.

Kimberly Thomas

When she reached the patio steps, she looked up towards the heavens, the rain falling on her face in large drops and then rolling off her face and to the ground. The house was magnificent and beautiful even in its state of disarray. The music pulsing from the home gave it an ambiance of old wealth where men wore powdered wigs and women wore dresses that cut off their breathing but made them look aristocratic and beautiful.

She stepped on the first step of the porch and the squeak of the wood underneath her weight sounded like it reverberated through the emptiness like a car engine. With that thought, the porch was lit up unnaturally, and she heard the car slam to a stop, sliding dangerously on the mud below.

"Rachel!" Tom's voice penetrated the darkness.

Twenty-Seven

"What are you doing here?" Tom looked nervously at the front door as if any moment the door would explode off its hinges and all the demons of hell would walk from its opening singing and dancing at the arrival of its new prey.

"My mother." She replied softly without looking at him, her eyes intent on the door and her ears still entranced by the symphony within.

"I was going to take you to find her tomorrow," he lied, knowing full well that he had no intention of taking her to this home where he had been forbidden for so many years to go. He continued, "You're soaking wet."

Rachel did not reply.

"Let's get you to Andrea's house to get you dried up – we'll come back tomorrow."

She shook her head in protest and walked towards the large wooden door, now peeling faded paint, the years having taken its toll. She placed her hand on the door handle – an abnormal coldness encompassed the handle and it felt charged with electricity.

Tom placed his hand on hers and in a whispered cry said, "Please…don't."

Not heeding his warning, she turned the knob as if she had not heard him and the door whisked open too quickly and too easily for a door that was as old and as large as this one. The music still softly played inside and Rachel crossed the threshold.

Tom wanted to grab her and throw her over his shoulder and run away. Too many horror stories had been told about this house; sad little urban legends that people had gone into this house and never returned. He had been told to never come here and he knew his dad's warning was not to be taken lightly. He felt something awkward here, perhaps not life threatening, but definitely not normal.

He watched her as she walked into the house without fear, looking around as if she was in a museum, her dark hair aflame in the abnormal light of the house – the house that should not have electricity running to it after so many years of vacancy.

She paused in the entrance way and stared at something on the wall to her left, something he could not see, and he knew that he must overcome his unexplained fear and enter the home with her. He could not lose her; he could not lose her to this house.

When he crossed the threshold, the door slammed shut and he jumped; Rachel still stood unmoved and entranced by the object on the wall. He looked at the object of her fascination – a painting so large that it was almost life-size of what he assumed was her mother and her father – for the woman in the picture was almost an exact duplicate of the girl he had fallen in love with and Rachel did favor the man in the photo, just like Nancy had said.

Rachel placed her hand gently on the painting and looked forlornly at it. Wiping a tear, or perhaps a trickle of rain, from her eye, she turned away and pushed herself into Tom's arms where she stood, not crying just simply being held – her wet hair and clothes soaking through Tom's clothes, but he did not care. He knew he could hold her for the rest of eternity and never tire of her. He kissed her gently on the top of her head.

The music in the house stopped as the song ended and then moved into a more solemn tempo as another classical piece reverberated through the large foyer. She glanced behind Tom into the dining room she had seen in her dreams – a table meant for royalty with at least twenty chairs around it. Her mother was not in the room as she had been in her dreams.

She looked up into Tom's eyes and whispered, "She's here; I know she is."

He kissed her on the forehead and said, "We'll find her." He had no faith they would find her, for the atmosphere in this home was characteristic of death and sadness, and he feared that her mother might have already become one of the urban legend's rumored fatalities.

She smiled at him softly and then grabbed his hand as she led him into the dining room.

Tom was frightened; there was no doubt in his mind that he was frightened. He was not a superstitious person and it perturbed him that this home flared fear in him. He walked staring around the room expecting something to come out of the walls and attack them. A crash of thunder outside followed by a flash of lightening that lit the room caused him to grab Rachel's hand tightly.

She chuckled softly, unafraid. He was embarrassed – had she known the stories told of this house perhaps she'd be afraid herself, he thought.

The foyer which had been unnaturally aglow with light was not the case for other rooms they entered. The dining room was darkened except for the glow from outside, which did little but cast foreboding shadows on the wall. The great room that followed was as dark as night and they stood there for a few moments as they adjusted to the darkness.

"Do you love her?"

He heard the soft voice whisper as a chill passed over him.

He pulled Rachel closer to him.

"Did you say something?"

She chuckled softly in that soft rhythmic laugh that he had grown to adore in these few scant hours together. "No, silly."

The voice so soft spoke again, "Do you love her?"

Rachel spoke, "It's cold in here."

He could see the glimmer of her arms as she rubbed them

with her hands.

"Yes, I love her." The question was so simple and so easy for him to answer. Yes, yes, he did love her – then and forever.

He thought the words but did not speak them and he grabbed her in his arms and wrapped his arms around her. Warmth flowed throughout the room in a rush and a single candle flickered on in the center of the room atop a grand piano that glistened in the movement of the flame.

He held her tight in his arms and she looked towards the flame and then into his face. With a huge smile, she said softly, "We did that."

Then she winked and pulled herself away from him and skipped haphazardly towards the flame and the piano. She looked like a little girl as her wet hair flopped from side to side. He smiled softly and then walked towards her saying softly, "Yes, we did do that."

The room was still dark except for the glow from the candle that did nothing but highlight the piano in the center of the room and Tom gingerly walked towards Rachel who had proceeded to sit on the bench in front of the grand piano and run her hands lightly over the keys. The light focused on her face, the rest of her hidden in darkness. Her hair fell into her face and as she pushed her hair behind her ears she glanced at him and opened her mouth to speak.

He had not heard the movement behind him and the pain in his head was the only indication that he had been struck. He fell to the ground in an instant and in blurred vision saw his brother and then darkness.

Twenty-Eight
🍂 🍂 🍂

She had seen him behind Tom but before she could speak she had seen the butt end of the pistol rise and then fall on Tom's head. Tom quickly fell to the ground in a heap – the blow having done its intended damage.

In an instant, she had pushed herself up from the piano bench and rushed towards the doorway that led away from the room and further into the house. In her movement, the candle blew out in a cold gust and the room was once again in complete and utter darkness. She had removed her shoes at the piano and now ran barefoot and silent across the hardwood floors of the old house, praying to herself that the floors would not squeak under her weight and praying that Tom was not hurt too badly. She knew she could not return to help him – not now at least.

She felt that Junior was behind her, his bulking weight running at speeds far greater than hers – but the darkness disguised him and she saw nothing but shadows of furniture in the pitch black house.

She ran until she ended at the foot of a staircase and knowing full well that upstairs did not lead to an escape, she passed it quickly and silently until all at once she was engulfed in light as she walked back into the foyer. The darkness had hid her movement from Junior but also disoriented her into making a full circle – something that was clearly a good move since here before her was the entrance to the home -- her only means to escape.

She heard a noise – a pained groan – reverberate throughout the house. She stopped. In her mad rush she had not noticed that the music had stopped and now in the utter silence she had heard Tom groan and she knew she must go to him. Without thinking, she rushed through the dining room and into the great room where she saw Tom struggling to get up.

She was at his side in a few bounds and grabbing his arm she helped him up to his feet. He smiled at her weakly. In a voice that was crackly and dry, he mumbled, "What happened?"

She glanced around the room nervously. "Your brother."

His eyes immediately grew wide with terror and looking around in the darkness, he put his arm over her shoulder and attempted to walk with her quickly towards the dining room. Still disoriented, he stumbled and nearly took her down with him in his attempt to rush the process of flight from this house.

Slowly they made it through the great room and back to the dining room. There was a red glow in the darkness and a face disguised by the darkened room. When they entered the room they saw her sitting at the table, talking to someone who sat with their back towards them. Dressed in red and grayish-black hair that fell to her waist, she was a stunning older woman who, after a moment, Rachel realized was indeed her mother. Not the mother who she had lived with her entire life, but a different woman who just happened to inhabit her mother's body. This woman was smiling – something that her mother never had done – and there was a light in her eyes that signified sanity – and her mother had never been sane.

Her mother turned towards her and with a smile, held her hand out towards Rachel. Rachel helped Tom struggle towards the table and then she reached out and grabbed her mother's hand and whispered, "We need to go, it's not safe here."

Ignoring Rachel's plea and in that soft and sultry voice that had never seemed at place before – but seemed apropos here, she said, "I have someone I want you to meet."

Her mother turned towards the chair that she had faced before Rachel and Tom had entered the room. Rachel and Tom both turned in unison to look into the ethereal face of Jeremiah Odium.

Rachel was not aware if ghosts could speak or not but Jeremiah Odium said nothing, a smile large and bright in his unearthly face as he extended his hand in a formal introduction so Rachel could shake his otherworldly hand. She grabbed it, although there was nothing there but cold air and her hand immediately closed upon itself.

Tom whispered in his broken voice,

"We need to go."

Rachel grabbed her mother's hand again and said with desperation, "We need to go Mom."

"But your father…" Her mother reached towards the ghostly figure and rubbed her hand on his face.

Rachel turned towards the forlorn figure and smiled softly,

"We'll come back, I promise."

Tom pulled away from her and leaned against the table with one hand, rubbing the back of his head with his other hand. Rachel bent on her knees in front of her mom and stared at her directly in the eyes, "Mom, for once, can you do something for me, please – I can't lose you too." She felt a tear fall from her eye, but her mom turned her head and looked towards Jeremiah, ignoring the pleas of her only child.

Tom leaned down and with a sigh said, "I love you Rachel."

In the darkness and in a burst of adrenaline Tom headed towards the foyer in a rush even before Rachel could say a word. When she glanced towards the door she saw Junior's bulking frame outlined against the brightness of the open foyer doorway.

The sound of the gun firing indicated where Tom had been headed. Rachel yelped and then watched as Tom fell into the open foyer, his tortured face aglow in the abnormal light.

Stunned by the loud explosion and suddenly aware that there might actually be danger, her mother stood up next to Rachel. The chair that once held her father was flung across to the back of the room violently, exploding in a thousand pieces against the wall behind it.

Junior had slipped further into the darkened room and was unaffected by the sudden movement of the chair. His gruff voice echoed throughout the darkened room,

"Come here Rachel."

Rachel muttered, "No!"

"Now you wouldn't want anyone else to get hurt would you?"

She whimpered, "No."

Her mother in a loud voice unlike her screamed, "Leave her alone, Mike!"

He chuckled, "Oooh…so you know, do you?"

Her mother grabbed Rachel's hand softly and squeezed it and then again in a voice filled with anger replied, "You took my husband; you are not taking my child."

This undeniably unusual behavior for her mother left Rachel stunned and she felt herself back further into the darkness as her mother's hand slipped from hers. Her mother walked up towards where the voice exuded from the darkness, confident and full of anger. Rachel stood there as if she was made of stone – incapable of speech or movement. She could simply watch as her mother, for once, stood up for her.

Another loud explosion and a flash of light and Rachel heard her mother tumble to the floor.

Now oblivious to the danger, she ran towards where her mother had been and in the darkness, sought for the damage to her, trying desperately to adjust her eyes to the darkness.

When she realized that her mother's breathing was now gurgled, she grabbed her mother's head in her hands. It was then that she felt the sticky hair as her fingers grew wet and warm. She was glad that the room was dark and she couldn't see for it was undeniable that her mother had taken a shot to the head. She was grateful she was unable to look into her mother's pained eyes – she had failed, failed to protect her mother from harm.

She lay her mother's head on her lap, uncaring that the dress Maude had given her would now be trashed. She reached for her mother's hand and held it – cold and clammy, it was obvious that her mother had very little time left. Tears fell from Rachel's eyes and her mother in a whispered gurgled voice said, "I'm sorry I wasn't there for you…I love you Rach."

"I love you too, Mom." She leaned her head onto her mother's chest and cried. Her mother gasped for air and then there was silence. The coldness that surrounded her mother in that brief moment signified that her mother had only suffered a short painful death and she was gone.

A waiflike figure escaped through the body and floated towards the back of the room – its red dress and dark black hair flowing beautifully around her. Her mother was dead and her spirit now existed with her father.

Rachel sat up and saw her father and mother floating above the table at the back of the room – holding each other's ghostly hands as they smiled lovingly at each other. As instant as that loving moment has occurred it was gone and the two ghostly figures' faces were contorted as they looked towards where Rachel sat holding her dead mother's hand and head.

The pain at the back of her head brought her back to reality and she remembered that Junior had not left, but simply taken a reprieve as she had sat mourning her mother. Junior had grabbed a fistful of hair at the back of the head and dragged her towards the exit, her mother's head and hand dropping noisily to the floor as she was pulled away.

With every step Junior took, Rachel screaming and clawing at Junior's arm, chairs began to float around the room dangerously, whishing by with noises that were too unearthly to have come from the simple movement of the chair. Each chair was sent flying towards Junior's head, but he successfully outmaneuvered each one as they passed and the chairs were sent splintering against the wall.

As Junior pulled Rachel into the foyer, the splintered chairs still followed crashing on the floor around her. Rachel saw Tom lying on the foyer floor, blood canvassing the tile entrance way. Pale and sprawled out in a position that looked surreal, Rachel could not tell if he was alive or dead. In hopes that he might still be holding onto life, she said loudly, "I love you Tom."

These were not the words Junior wanted to hear and Rachel knew she should have been smarter than that but she had to – for the sake of her love and for the sake of Tom. Whatever she had to endure for those words was well worth the pain.

In a fit of rage, Junior let go of her hair and grabbed her instead by the neck and lifting her two feet off the floor he held her up against the wall. She kicked her feet wildly and scratched at his arms with her fingers but his hand grew tighter upon her throat, like a python tightening its grip upon its kill. Weak, and gasping for air, she eventually slipped into darkness, her body limp and useless as he threw her over his shoulder, and opening the door of the house proceeded to his car.

Twenty-Nine

His eyes stuck together as he tried to lift his abnormally heavy lids. When finally breaking them free, his vision was blurry. He saw a shape lurking over him, dark hair flowing unnaturally in the air as if the woman floated under the ocean and her hair was caught in the current, beautiful and transfixed.

In a murmured voice, he whispered, "Rachel?"

The woman said nothing. He blinked his eyes a few times trying to focus on her, a warm liquid flowed on the side of his face and he felt faint.

He whispered again, "Am I dead?"

The woman again said nothing. A few more blinks and he was able to see her more clearly – Rachel's mother. She was different however and he couldn't quite place what was wrong.

Muttering as he reached his hand towards his head – a movement that sent pain reeling through his body, he said, "Where's Rachel?"

She pointed towards the open door to the house.

His hand rested on his head as he felt the sticky, warm substance that oozed from his head. He recalled the gun going off but not being hit; apparently his brother had just grazed him. Tom put his hands underneath his body and attempted to lift himself off the cold tile floor. A pain shot through his head that nearly made him double over but it was imperative that he go after Rachel.

Rachel's mother stood against the wall and watched him as he struggled to get up. When he finally was on his feet, his knees felt like jelly and he was on the verge of falling over but he grabbed the wall just in time to prevent him falling back towards the ground.

He felt his head begin to bleed again, incapable of handling the sudden rush of movement – although it had seemed to take years to get from the floor to a standing position. Rachel's mother, without a word, pointed to the shirt and then to his head and then made a wrapping motion with her hands around her own head. He knew what she meant; he needed to wrap his head so it would stop bleeding.

He pulled his t-shirt off over his head and then wrapped it around his bleeding head. The pressure to the open wound helped alleviate some of the pain, although his vision was still remarkably blurry. He glanced towards the dining room, expecting to see the ghost of Jeremiah Odium lurking around as he had been before, but instead saw the red dress of Rachel's mother – a lump that was obvious was a person lying on the floor. He turned towards her mother in the foyer and she was gone.

He stumbled towards the door – any person who had not witnessed the events prior would probably assume he was drunk. With pain shooting through his body with every movement, he staggered towards his car that was parked in front of the house and then fell into the driver's seat with relief as he started the car and drove down the dirt road towards his home.

He had to squint to be able to see where he was going – each sign that he passed was blurs of green and white and lights were huge and distorted as if he was on a bad acid trip and was existing in some alternate universe. He half expected to see some cartoon character sitting next to him who with a big gloved hand would wave at him and say, "Hey, hey, hey Tom, where you going?"

His mind reeled and raced as he headed towards his home –

aware that the roads were still dangerously wet even though the rain had stopped.

"I love you, Tom." Had he really heard her say those words? He was unaware how long he had been unconscious or how long ago Junior had taken her but he knew that time was of the essence.

There was no car parked in the driveway as he turned onto their road. He expected that his brother would take Rachel to their house because there was nowhere else in this town to go. Tom parked his car a few houses down as a precaution and wobbled towards the backyard of his house, crossing through other people's yards uncaring as to how they reacted. It was late now, probably past midnight – but Tom did not dare look at his watch for fear that the time would reveal that Junior had been with Rachel too long to not have already hurt her. He could not fathom arriving too late – he wasn't sure what he would do if his brother had taken his Rachel's innocence but, at that moment, he believed he would be capable of murder.

The alarm was enabled when he arrived at the house and he slipped into the house through the back door and entered the key code to not set off the alarm. The buttons beeped abnormally loud and Tom was afraid his brother would hear him. He heard no commotion inside the house.

He fumbled around the dark kitchen and reached up to one of the cabinets and grabbed in his hand a medicine bottle. Taking four pills out if it, as quietly as possible, he placed them in his mouth and swallowed. He listened intently, for any kind of noise, but there was nothing.

With every step the pain grew as he used every muscle in his body to walk as quietly as possible. His bedroom door was closed but his brother's bedroom door was open so he crept slowly across the room towards the open door and then peaked in. The room was dark with just a faint glow that lit the room just lightly from the street light that hung outside his bedroom window. No one was in the room.

He sidled over to his room and opened the door quietly. No one was there – the room had been left untouched since he slept in there last, which seemed like ages ago.

He crossed the house to the other side – towards his father's bedroom. The door was open and the light was on; Tom, stomach reeling, stumbled towards the open door.

His father had been a disgusting man – doing things to women that Tom could not imagine they actually enjoyed. He fancied himself the master of women and expected them to demoralize themselves for him – most of which were more than willing to do so. Because of this, his father had an eclectic collection of S&M supplies. Tom had intended on throwing them all out – perhaps burning them - but had yet to do so.

When he entered the room, he wished he had not procrastinated in throwing the articles away. Junior, surprisingly, was not in the room. Rachel, still dressed in her dress from graduation, lay curled up on the cold steel plate of a dog cage. When he approached her, he saw that his brother had put a large chain around her neck and wrapped it tightly around the foot of his father's large king-size bed. A piece of silver tape covered her mouth.

"Rachel?" He whispered it softly, for it was inevitable that his brother was somewhere around.

She did not respond. He went to the door of the cage and opened it, trying his best to not have it squeak and give away his location. When the door was opened, he reached his hand inside and pushed her leg gently.

"Rachel?" He whispered again.

She kicked and thrashed in the cage, making a racket that would wake the dead. He moved quickly to where she would see him and then put his finger over his lips to shush her. She quieted and calmed down.

"I'm going to try to get the chain loose, okay?"

She nodded, and the chain pulled against her neck and she winced.

Before he could move, she lifted her hands that he had not noticed were bound together as if she was forced to always pray and she held up nine fingers, her thumb on her right hand down against her palm. And then she held up her right index finger and then made fists and then held up her right index finger again.

9-1-1 - she wanted him to call for help. He fished in his pocket for his phone but it was not there – either in his car or lost in the scuffles back at the Odium place. His father had a phone near the bed. He picked up the phone and dialed the numbers.

"9-1-1 operator. What is your emergency?" The voice of the woman on the line was sweet and gentle.

"We need an ambulance and the police at 1420 Lakewood Drive."

"Is there an emergency, sir?"

"I don't know if he's still in the house, I can't stay on the line. Send help."

"Who is in the house, sir?"

He hung up without answering.

He ambled over to the bed and with astonishing strength – which he was quickly running out of – he lifted the heavy wood bed leg just enough to get the chain out from under it. Rachel moved forward in the cage and then carefully pulled the dog choke chain over her head so she could get out of the door.

She crawled out of the cage and lay on the carpet and Tom crawled towards her. He slowly peeled the tape off her mouth and then whispered, "Did he hurt you?"

She opened her mouth to speak but a broken crackle came out instead of words and she turned her head away from him. Her neck was shades of blue and black. He removed the ties from her wrists and ankles and then lay on his back next to her – too weak to move.

She leaned over and touched the t-shirt on his head and with concerned eyes that said "Are you okay?" She kissed his mouth softly.

In a remarkable reaction time, they heard the sounds of sirens approaching and then shortly heard the frantic knock of police at the door. He closed his eyes and drifted into the darkness - the feel of Rachel's hair on his face comforting him.

Kimberly Thomas

Thirty

She crawled towards the door as police banged on it – it was painfully slow and they seemed to bang on the door for hours when the window to the right of the door shattered into a thousand little pieces.

She fell into a lump on the living room floor and watched as a hand reached into the door and unlocked it and then as the door opened and two police officers, guns pointing, entered into the house.

They flipped on the light switch in the doorway and the lights blared on in the living room. She groaned as the bright light shined directly into her eyes and one of the two officers – the younger one – pointed with his gun towards her.

The older officer muttered, "Don't point that thing at people you dumbass."

The younger one looked at his gun and then at Rachel and then quickly put his pistol back into its holster.

"I'm going to go check the rest of the house. Go check on her." The older officer pointed to Rachel as he said it.

The young officer walked towards Rachel and then bent down on one knee. He looked her over and winced. "Are you okay?" He said softly.

She opened her mouth to speak and only the annoying squeak came out again.

"Don't try to talk. An ambulance will be here soon."

Rachel pointed towards the bedroom where Tom had passed out.

The officer, in a voice that sounded reminiscent of an adult speaking to a toddler, said, "Is there someone in there?"

She nodded.

"A bad guy?"

She shook her head to indicate that Tom was not the bad guy.

The officer still extracted his gun from the holster and crept slowly towards the hallway and towards the bedroom where Tom lay unconscious on the carpet. Rachel crawled after him, in too much pain to walk.

Rachel sat in the hallway, unable to go any further since the young officer now stood in the hallway staring blankly at Tom who lay in a growing pool of blood on the carpet – the t-shirt around his head having soaked up too much blood to hold any more. Shirtless and pale, Tom was either dead or dying and the young officer had never been exposed to anything more than typical domestic disputes, never death and definitely nothing as violent as this scene before him.

Three men and a young woman came into the house with two stretchers and the young woman rushed towards Rachel and leaned down on a knee to look at her. The young woman was pretty – green eyes with blonde hair that was tucked into a ponytail – but her eyes expressed concern when she saw Rachel and that concern flashed into anger when she explored the depth of the bruising around Rachel's neck and face.

The young officer turned towards the group of men. "I think this one might need you first."

The young officer, now pale, passed through into the living room and sat down on one of the couches and placed his head in his hand.

The young woman stayed by Rachel's side as two of the three men rushed into the bedroom and hovered over Tom and then slowly put him onto the stretcher.

When the stretcher rolled past her, she lifted her hand towards it. The young woman looked at her and then at the stretcher.

Rachel opened her mouth to speak and in a breathy whisper said, "Is" She gasped for air and then continued, "he" Again gasping for air she continued breathing out the syllables without using her voice, "O" The last syllable was a hard sound and came out more as "hey" than "K", but the young medic understood and whispered, "I'll go find out."

The woman stood up and the other medic brought another stretcher and laid it down next to her. He was a weathered man although he couldn't have been more than 30 – perhaps too much tanning or too much smoking or too much of both, but he had aged badly. When he smiled at Rachel, his teeth were yellow and his breath smelled rotten. She wished the woman would hurry back.

The man leaned next to her too closely for what seemed like an eternity and then the young woman finally returned.

"Let's get you on that stretcher, ok?"

She winced as the woman grabbed her ankles and the man grabbed her shoulders and lifted her onto the stretcher. Fortunately it was only inches away from the floor, otherwise she might have been in worse pain.

The woman pushed at the head of the stretcher and Rachel grabbed the woman's wrist. She looked up at the woman. It was obvious the woman was avoiding the news which only made Rachel fear that Tom was dead, but the woman finally spoke.

"They were gone when I got out there. The policeman outside said he's hurt pretty bad but that he'll be okay."

The young woman smiled at Rachel and then looked at her partner forlornly – Rachel knew what that meant – Tom wasn't okay.

The stretcher bumped along the house and then out the door and towards the opened back door of the ambulance. The two lifted the stretcher into the ambulance and then climbed in the back with her. Rachel stared silently at the ceiling, thoughts racing as the ambulance pulled away and headed towards she assumed a hospital.

Kimberly Thomas

She drifted off into sleep, weary and in pain from this entire ordeal. When she awoke she was lying in a bed, covered in a white blanket and her arm was attached to a machine that dripped fluids into her hand.

Her vision was blurry and she felt heavy as if someone lay on her chest. She squinted when she saw a figure at the end of the bed.

A rhythmic laugh, soft and beautiful, broke the air,

"Don't worry dear, that's just the medicine wearing off – you've been sleeping for a while now."

The woman went to the side of the bed and Rachel could see her clearer. She was dressed in blue scrubs, her hair blonde with streaks of grey but she was stunning nonetheless. "So how you feeling today?"

Rachel couldn't feel much of anything, so she said nothing.

The nurse smiled, "I'm Cheryl and it's an honor to be looking after you Miss Odium."

Rachel smiled but said nothing.

The nurse continued, "The doctor says you need to be eating some ice, it'll take some time for your throat to heal up but the ice will help you talk some, okay?"

Rachel nodded, afraid to speak – afraid that her voice might be forever gone from her.

"I gotta go look after other patients but I'll be back to check on you later." The woman faded into a blur and then nothingness as the door opened to a bright light and then closed again into darkness.

A few moments later another blurred figure came into the room. The blur walked towards the side of her bed and, once in a view, turned out to be a doctor, stethoscope hanging around his neck and white lab coat opened revealing a red and blue plaid shirt and a bulging belly that pushed threateningly at the buttons in front of it. He was an older man, balding and pudgy and he smelled vaguely of onions and Rachel didn't feel comfortable with him.

In a voice daunting, nasal and superficial, the doctor said, "So, how are you feeling today?"

Again, she felt nothing – and said nothing.

"Ah, the medicine makes you feel no pain – beautiful isn't it?" He beamed a smile across his pudgy face.

She smiled uncaringly.

"Other than the bruising around your windpipe and the cuts, you're going to be perfectly fine my dear. You're just going to need a few days of rest."

She opened her mouth and muttered, "Tom?" Her voice was so weak that she barely heard herself speak.

"Ah, yes, Mr. Crabtree." His voice was so snide that Rachel wanted to slap him aside the face. "He's doing remarkably well. He's still in ICU but he should recover."

She smiled.

"After all, he's got you waiting for him once he's all healed up." He laughed a haughty laugh that perturbed Rachel. "Now sleep child, tomorrow you have to deal with more important matters – like the police, etc etc." He waved his hand around in the air.

The doctor slipped away from the room and into the blurry expanse of the hospital and Rachel, as requested, drifted off into sleep.

She was vaguely aware that people came in and out of the room but she was in a dream-like state induced by medicine that made her feel no pain. She was appreciative of that – for if she had been lucid she would surely be thinking too much, and thinking was something that she did not need to do right now.

When the morning came and the medicine began to wear off she was more achy than in pain. Cheryl awoke her with a smile and a cup of ice.

"Mornin' Miss Odium."

Rachel smiled at her, afraid to speak.

"Another day and then you get to go home." Cheryl smiled as she busied herself around the room, checking machines and logging things on a paper on her clipboard.

Home – where was home now?

Rachel attempted to speak again, whispered and throaty, she said, "Tom?"

Cheryl laughed and her voice was so smooth and comforting that Rachel wanted to laugh with her – but couldn't.

"Love is a many splendored thing, child." Cheryl looked up to the ceiling. "I cannot remember who said that…dang."

Rachel smiled softly.

"You've gotta meet with some people this morning but this afternoon we'll take you to go see him, okay?"

Cheryl patted Rachel on the leg and then walked out of the room without a further word.

A man in a grey suit walked into the room, the door startling him as it closed behind him. He was a pudgy man with a big bulbous nose that glowed red as if he was some distant relative of Rudolph. He was primarily bald, although he had a few strands of hair on the top of his head that seemed to have been in denial of its occupant's baldness and stayed attached.

He approached the bed and sat in the chair that rested next to the bedside. Rachel pushed the button on the side of the bed to lift herself up in a sitting position. She groaned as the movement caused her pain.

"Hello Ms. Odium."

She smiled at him as she turned her heads towards him.

He continued speaking, "I'm Detective Young."

She nodded at him.

"They told me you shouldn't speak much but we're trying to find out who did this. Do you know who did this to you?"

She nodded at him and then in a crackled voice she whispered "Junior" but the letter n was too hard and it didn't come out sounding as expected.

"Juror?"

She shook her head and then motioned with her hand that she could write it. He reached in his pocket and grabbed a pen and then into another pocket for a small notebook. He flipped through the notebook until he found a blank page and then handed both to Rachel.

She wrote, "Junior" and then shown him what she wrote.

"Junior?"

She wrote again, "Tom's brother".

"Are you sure?"

She nodded.

She flipped to another page and wrote, "My mother is at the Odium place. Jr shot her."

"Did you see him shoot her?"

She shook her head. Flipping the page, she wrote, "He was the only other person there."

"That you saw. Who else did you know was there?"

She wrote, "Tom, my mother and my father."

He chuckled. "Is it possible that someone else might have been there?"

She shrugged.

"Junior is the one who reported that something bad had happened to you guys. He's the reason we got to the house in time."

She looked at him with a blank look on her face.

"If it weren't for him, Tom would probably be dead."

She shrugged and looked across the room at the far side of the wall, focusing intently on the door, hoping that someone else would step in and take this cold, callous man from her presence.

After a moment of silence, she flipped to another page and wrote, "What about my mother?"

"We'll send a squad car out there and take a look but I can bet ya that they won't find anything."

He laughed a haughty laugh and Rachel wanted him to leave.

He continued speaking instead, "It'll be a good deal for you if we find her though, that's a lot of money you stand to inherit if she's dead."

How dare him…how dare he insinuate that she would be in this for the money. Money was inconsequential to the devotion she had to her mother, her mother who had never deserved the title. She did not need the money – she wanted her old life back, that life where she was poor and unnoticed, not this life where she had to fear for her own safety and the safety of everyone around her. How dare he accuse her of anything insincere?

Screaming as loud as she possibly could with no voice, a

squeaky muffled "Out!" came from her as she pointed towards the exit.

He chuckled, rolled his eyes, and grunted as he pushed himself out of the chair and shambled towards the door. Without a word, he exited the room.

A few moments later Cheryl came in through the door.

"You okay, hun?"

Rachel shrugged.

"Mitch is a jerk, whatever he says it's just because he's jealous." Cheryl winked softly.

Rachel smiled and whispered, "Thanks."

Cheryl tucked the blanket up around Rachel's legs and then said, "You have one more visitor and then we're going to kick them all out okay – you still need your rest."

Rachel nodded and then placed the detective's pen and pad of paper next to her. In the rush to get out, he had not picked them up from her.

When Cheryl had left, a man in his mid-forties, handsome and tall, walked into the room. The man wore an expensive looking blue suit, tailored to fit his tall, thin body. His dark hair and amber eyes were accented by an olive colored skin and had Rachel been many years older she would have found the man to be devastatingly handsome. Rachel smiled at him and then laughed softly, but painfully, when Cheryl peeked her head through the door and mouthed "Yummy".

The man turned around just in time to see the door closing. He was probably used to that kind of behavior.

He walked regally to the side of the bed and sat in the same chair that the wretched Detective Young had sat in. He smiled at Rachel softly and then reached into his briefcase that he had brought in with him.

He spoke in a voice so soft but masculine that it sent shivers down Rachel's spine.

"First, I want to tell you that you have nothing to worry about with that policeman. Whatever inane accusations he threw were unfounded and I will make sure I speak with him personally about harassing you."

Rachel smiled softly at him.

He continued, "Second, I am the attorney for your father's estate. My name is Anthony Gillespi."

She smiled and then picked up the pen and paper and wrote, "How do you know he is my father?"

He laughed. "Ah, yes, we'll have to run a DNA check but we're making the assumption that you are his child for now."

She smiled.

He spoke again, "I came here to confirm that you will give us the permission to conduct a DNA test."

She wrote, "I can't afford it."

He laughed again, soft and rhythmic. "Don't worry about it. Do you agree?"

She nodded.

"Ok, then, we'll get that started right up then. Next order of business, until such time that we have proof of your heritage… Maude Tabor, your former employer…"

She looked at him perplexed.

"Well, as you know, she recently passed on."

Rachel nodded.

"Before her death she modified her will."

Rachel wrote on the paper, "With you?"

He chuckled, "No, no, with another attorney. I was requested to find you and your mother in your father's interest and by coincidence we found the attorney who had been contracted by Mrs. Tabor."

She looked at him, more perplexed with that response than not.

He laughed, "Don't worry about the technicalities. What I'm trying to say is that Mrs. Tabor's attorney has requested that I inform you that her probate hearing is tomorrow. Since you will not be well enough to travel I am requesting to be present on your behalf."

She wrote, "What does that mean?"

"Well, apparently Mrs. Tabor has named you in her will. That's how we found her attorney."

Kimberly Thomas

She smiled and wrote, "I can't afford you either."

He laughed again and she felt comfortable and relaxed.

"Don't worry about it."

He patted her softly on the arm and then continued, "Would you like me to attend the probate hearing for you?"

She nodded.

"I hear they are releasing you tomorrow. Will you be staying local?"

She wrote, "I have no where to stay here."

He smiled at her softly, "I'll have the utilities turned back on at your father's property and I'll have a driver pick you up and drive you out there."

She wrote on the paper, "I'm not sure I want to stay there."

He chuckled, "Understood. I'll have my secretary find you a place to stay."

She nodded and mouthed, "Thank you."

He patted her softly on the arm again. "Now rest and I'll take care of everything for you. When I return, we'll sit down and discuss your future."

She smiled softly at him, appreciatively. He stood up gracefully from the chair and with a nod good-bye he walked from the room.

Thirty-One
🌿 🌿 🌿

The room fell silent after the handsome attorney left through the door. Rachel huddled in her blanket, cold and tired. She flipped through the detective's notebook, reading her own scribbling and scanning the non-descript handwriting of the detective, useless notes that meant nothing to her.

The door swung open and Cheryl walked into the room pushing a wheelchair. She said with a voice excited and sweet, "Road trip!"

Rachel smiled and swung her legs out onto the side of the bed. Cheryl brought the wheelchair over and helped Rachel off the bed and into the chair. They proceeded in silence down the hall.

The hall was lit by harsh fluorescent lighting and imbued with the smells that reminded her of the visit to Maude. There were very few people in the halls that they passed. They headed towards an elevator and Cheryl pushed the down button. They waited in silence for the elevator.

The ding of the elevator was followed by the gliding open of the elevator doors, and Cheryl pushed Rachel into the open elevator cart. She pushed the one button and the doors closed and the elevator proceeded downward. When the elevator doors opened, Cheryl pushed the wheelchair again down another the hallway towards a room.

The door to the room was closed and the sign on the outside of the door read 123. Cheryl walked to the front of the wheelchair and knelt on her knees in front of Rachel.

"You won't be able to stay too long."

Rachel nodded.

Cheryl grabbed the door handle and pushed open the door and then pushed Rachel into the room.

The room was dark and cold. A single bed sat in the center of the room with an eerie glow from the machines illuminating the bed. She could see a lump on the bed – undoubtedly Tom.

Cheryl pushed her towards the bed. Tom's rhythmic breathing indicated he was asleep.

Leaning over, Cheryl whispered, "I'm going to go now but I'll be back, okay?"

Rachel nodded, although in the darkness she wasn't sure that Cheryl could see her. Rachel listened as Cheryl's softly padded feet walked across the bare floor to the door. The door slid open silently, and lit up the room, highlighting Tom's soft, bruised face – wrapped in white bandages. Rachel groaned as she lifted herself out of the chair to lean over the bed. She reached over Tom and kissed him softly on the cheek.

He murmured softly, incoherently. She wanted to crawl on the bed and lay next to him but the machines connected to him would surely be disconnected if she did that along with the fact that the nurses and doctors would probably frown on such behavior, so she simply stood next to him.

She touched his face softly and his eyes flickered then opened. He stared into the darkness of the room, not at her but at something unseen, something on the other side of the room. She turned to look but saw nothing – only darkness - but as if his eyes could see something that she could not, she shuddered as an eerie foreboding feeling passed over her. She had seen enough in the past few days to know that nothing was impossible.

His eyes turned towards her. In a voice soft and raw he whispered, "Rachel."

It hadn't been a question, more a statement.

She touched his face softly and placed her lips near his face. A tear escaped her eye and dropped onto his chin. In the darkness she could not see the extent of his damage, as well as he could not see hers. She had not seen her reflection in a mirror or been told the extent of her damage but she feared that she might be hideous now and welcomed the darkness of the room. He would surely run if she had been disfigured by the jealous rage of Junior – there was no way he would still love her. Even if half his face had been blown off, she would remain by his side; even if he was crippled beyond repair, she would remain by his side – but she did not have faith that he would return that devotion.

He touched her chin softly and pulled her towards him. He kissed her softly on the lips.

"Together, forever." He said the words softly.

She smiled although in the darkness she was not sure if he could see, then she said in a raw rough voice,

" Forever.".

She heard a scuffling noise behind her like the sound of rats running through the innards of a house, and turning around too quickly, her head reeled and she fell to the floor. But in the darkness, she saw nothing. She wanted to run to the lights and turn them on and unmask the hidden villain in the darkness, but she could not – she would not let the fear get to her.

She pulled herself up again and stood next to Tom's bed. He had fallen asleep as suddenly as he had awakened so she sat back down in the wheelchair and waited, listening to the rhythmic sound of his breathing, longing to hear that sound forever.

The door opened just as Rachel began to drift off into sleep. Glancing first into the darkened corner of the room and then at Rachel, Cheryl walked behind the wheelchair and wheeled her out of the room.

When they arrived back at Rachel's room, Cheryl helped her into bed and then said softly, "I probably won't see you before you leave so I just wanted to say it was a pleasure meeting you."

Rachel nodded.

Kimberly Thomas

Cheryl smiled and then wheeled the empty wheelchair out of the room.

The room, again, was silent and Rachel drifted off to sleep.

When she awoke, a young man, probably mid-twenties, somewhat handsome with dark blue eyes and sandy brown hair and a five o'clock shadow that Rachel assumed made him think he looked more mature stood next to her bed. He was dressed in a white dress shirt and dark blue navy pants. Holding a red gym bag, the young man stood leaning on the wall as she awoke.

When realizing she was alert, he walked towards the bed with a smile.

"Ah, Miss Odium, I'm glad to see you are awake."

She smiled at him and the expression she gave him was a look of inquisitive questioning that she could not express with words. She reached for the notepad that was still beside her but he continued speaking.

"Mr. Gillespi sent me." The young man tossed the gym bag next to her. "I brought you a change of clothes. The paperwork is being filled out for your release and we'll be leaving in about a half hour."

Rachel reached for the clothes and pulled out a pair of jeans, tank top, and underwear. No shoes.

The young man turned around and started walking out the door, but when he reached the door, he turned around and said, "Oh yeh, my name is James."

Rachel put one finger up to tell him that she needed a minute, and then reached for the paper hurriedly and wrote "Shoes?" in big letters so he could see it from across the room.

James muttered softly, but not so softly that Rachel couldn't hear him, "Dammit." And then in a voice so she could hear him said, "I knew I forgot something."

She giggled softly, something that didn't hurt as bad today as it had the past day.

When he left the room, she slipped the clothes on. Other than the pants being too long and the shirt too tight, the outfit was acceptable for leaving the confines of the hospital. She was excited to leave, but remorseful that she had to leave Tom behind. The doctors had said he would have to remain there for at least a few more days and possibly up to two weeks depending on how everything went. They were being cautious they said – she saw that as a sign of incompetence, not caution.

Rachel sat on the bed and was doodling in the notebook when a knock was heard on the door, proceeded a moment later with a head popping through the door.

He smiled at her and said, "Whew, you're changed. My dad would have killed me if I forgot your shoes and caught you changing." He laughed softly and she giggled in return.

She wrote in the notebook, "Who's your dad?"

He laughed in a soft and soothing voice.

"Oh, I forgot that. Anthony Gillespi is my father."

She looked at him quizzically because he looked nothing like the tall dark handsome attorney.

He chuckled. "I'm adopted."

She smiled.

"They have everything ready to go. You ready to get out of here?" She nodded.

A nurse walked in with a wheelchair, she stood and walked to it. The nurse looked down at her bare feet and then at James.

James responded with a chuckle, "I forgot shoes."

The nurse said nothing and then when Rachel was seated in the wheelchair she pushed them towards the elevator without a word, James quickly following.

When they were down to the ground floor, James rushed out of the elevator mumbling something about going to pull up the car and the nurse said nothing but continued walking. When they reached the wide doors to the hospital, she was surprised with the view. Vans with satellite dishes and antennas attached, with letters of radio stations or TV stations written in bright colorful letters on the side of the vans sat haphazardly parked in odd angles around the entrance. Women with manicured hair and pressed business suits sat like lions waiting for their prey at the entrance, microphone in hand. A few men, also in business suits, stood around the entrance way holding their microphones and a plethora of men and women with video cameras stood blocking the sunlight from entering the building.

The nurse stopped and Rachel looked up at her to catch the woman straightening her hair and applying a last minute coat of lip gloss – vanity before duty. A black sedan pulled into the driveway in front of the building and flashes flickered and women and men screamed questions that Rachel could not understand.

James jumped out of the car and ran inside the hospital and said breathlessly, "We're going to have to make this quick, the hyenas want a glimpse of the heiress." He glanced at the nurse and then Rachel.

The nurse pushed her quickly towards the door as James ran to open it and then past the crowd to open the passenger side door of the car.

A man's voice screamed over the barrage of shouts,

"Miss Odium?"

Another voice called,

"Miss Odium, over here."

And yet another,

"Where have you been?"

And still another,

"What do you plan to do with the money?"

And then a voice too familiar that made her pause mid entry into the car and glance frighteningly over the crowd,

"You can't run."

Amidst the flashes and sea of people, she saw nothing and James in an attempt to escape the mayhem pushed her softly into the car. She sunk into the deep leather seat as James ran to the other side and getting in the car, drove away quickly.

Thirty-Two

They drove in silence for a while until the town of Vertueux began to become familiar to her – remembering only a few days prior when she had roamed these streets with Tom. James stopped in front of a shoe store and turned to her and smiled.

"Shoes, anyone?"

She looked at her feet and wriggled her toes.

The store had ladies shoes lined up in the window, beautiful sandals and dress shoes that looked much too pricy for her. The concrete underneath her bare feet was hot and she walked on tip toes towards the entrance until James came up behind her and picked her up and carried her to the store and over the threshold as if they were newlyweds. Uncomfortable with the display, but appreciative, she smiled softly at him as he looked down into her eyes.

He chuckled softly as he sat her down on the carpeted floor, "Don't tell my dad…" He paused, "…or Tom."

She nodded softly and watched him as he walked towards the counter and then she went to the wall to look at the shoes displayed.

The first pair of shoes she picked up read $150 on the price tag – as if the shoes were on fire, she quickly put the shoes down and sat on the bench to wait for James.

A woman's voice interrupted the silence of the store.

"James, my boy, how are you doing today?"

Rachel turned around and the woman stopped hugging James and turned to look at her. The woman was a small woman, built like a stick without hips or breasts to make her shapely. She was probably mid-40s to 50s with graying red hair and green eyes. The woman walked towards her quietly and with a groan got on her knees in front of Rachel.

She grabbed Rachel's hands in hers and with tears in her eyes said softly,

"It *is* you."

She looked at James and then back at Rachel.

The woman stood back up and then walked towards the back of the store. A few moments later the woman came back with a few boxes in her hands.

She sat on the floor in front of Rachel and said proudly, "Size 7?"

Rachel looked puzzled and nodded.

"I thought so, same size as your mother."

Rachel smiled softly and then mumbled in her squeaky voice, "You knew her?"

The woman patted Rachel firmly on the leg and Rachel winced.

"Ah yes my dear, we all knew her – I used to work with her before…well, before she met your father." She laughed and looked away as if she was remembering a past time. "You're mother was a good woman, beautiful and smart."

While she spoke, the woman had placed a pair of sandals on Rachel's feet. Rachel looked down at her feet and nodded approvingly.

James spoke up and said

"So how much are those going to set me back, Lily?"

The woman stood up and sauntered over to the counter and rang in the shoes for James.

"Don't tell my dad, OK? He'll kill me."

Lily laughed and said, "You're secret is safe with me."

James and Rachel started walking out of the door, but Lily

called out behind them, "Hey, I know it's none of my business, but who did that to you?"

She had directed the question to Rachel but James answered, "We're not discussing that matter right now, Lily."

Lily smiled and then added, "Okay okay fine James. You're just like your daddy sometimes." She laughed, and then continued, "You two would make a cute couple though." She winked.

James laughed, looked softly at Rachel, and then placing his arm around her shoulders, he said, "Yeh probably would but she's already got herself a boyfriend here in Vertueux, don't think she needs another one."

She looked at him quizzically and he removed his arm from her shoulder.

Lily, curious as she had always been, said, "Oh really now, and who would that be? Wouldn't be my little Alex would it?"

James laughed, "Alex? Don't you wish? No. No. You were close though, she nabbed his best friend Tom."

Lily's face turned pale and she said nothing, just simply turned around and walked back into the stockroom. James shrugged and the two walked towards the car.

The car was warm in the heat and James rolled down the windows. Rachel sat with her head leaning against the window sill as her hair fluttered loosely against the outside of the car. Tiring of the warm wind on her face she sat back into the car and James looked at her lovingly.

"Where are we going?" She muttered.

He chuckled. "Dad got you a hotel room to stay in for a few days."

She looked at him puzzled.

"He said no one would guard you if you stayed at your dad's place."

"Guard?" She said in her weak voice.

"Well besides the press, whoever did this to you is still out there." She nodded.

"Tom?"

"When he gets out we'll let you know, okay? We'll keep you posted." He patted Rachel on the knee softly; his hand remained there when he was done.

James pulled into a parking lot with a big sign that read "Sleep Inn" in red neon lights that were turned off. The hotel was small -- maybe a 100 rooms -- each door facing either the street or the alleyway behind it. Every door was a bright blue and labeled with the room number.

James pulled under the awning near the front door and put the car in park and ran inside. A few moments later he came out again, and without a word, got in the car and drove back into the parking lot and parked at the end of the building.

He handed her a white envelope with the number 155 written on it.

"Your key, my lady," he said in a fake British accent.

She smiled and opened the car door to get out. He got out on the other side and walked behind her.

When they reached the door and after she struggled to get the card key to read, the door was opened and the two walked into the room. James looked warily around the parking lot before closing the door.

The room was similar to the one that she and Tom had shared – two beds, a small TV, a dank, dusky and disgusting room that only was different due to the small table and two chairs that sat next to the window. She wished Tom were there now.

She sat on the edge of the bed. James walked up to her and, sitting on top of the dresser, spoke, "I've got the second key. I'll be staying with you until my dad comes and until the full-time bodyguard shows up."

She smiled softly at him and looked away.

"Are you hungry?"

She shook her head and then stood up and walked towards the bathroom and the well lit mirror. James quickly hopped up and stood in front of her and touching her face softly he said, "Before you go in there I just want to say that everything will heal, okay?"

She looked at him perplexed, intrigued now, and then pushing him out of the way walked towards the mirror. Half of her face was normal, soft white skin; the other was a maze of bruises.

She wasn't disgusted by the view but it wasn't the most pleasant site to look upon. Her neck was bruised also but not as bad as her face. There was one thing she had wanted to see, however. She had a bandage on her left butt cheek that the nurses wouldn't let her remove and would not tell her why it was there.

She twirled her finger to tell James to turn around and then she unbuttoned her pants and slipped them down to her knees. She gasped when she started pulling away the tape slowly – knowing full well that she should just tear it off in one quick swipe to not cause so much pain – but she did it slowly anyway. With the sound of the gasp, James turned around only to blush when he saw her standing there pants down to her knees and underwear exposed. He turned back around and stared intently on the door.

He felt her tap him softly on the shoulder and he turned to look at her. He looked softly into her eyes and then up and in the mirror he saw that she still had her pants down at her knees.

In her squeaky voice, and with tears in her eyes, she said, "What does it say?"

He helped her walk back into the light of the mirrors and then bent onto his knees to stare intently at her butt cheek. He tried desperately to think of this professionally but what teenage male could seriously not be aroused when a girl's butt is in their face. He placed his fingers lightly on her soft skin and traced the markings that had been carved into her.

With each letter he traced, he told her, "M I N E"

Whoever had done all this other stuff to her had branded her, saying "Your ass is mine" in a crude manner.

She pulled her pants up quickly and stood leaning against the sink, tears falling down her cheek. In a squeaky voice she said softly, "Why?"

She paused and breathed in deeply, then leaned up against his chest and cried. He placed his arms around her softly and kissed her gently on the top of her head. He couldn't help but think that Tom was a lucky man – any man would be lucky to have her.

Kimberly Thomas

Thirty-Three

A knock on the door was a welcomed interruption for James. He wanted to hold her, to comfort her, but she was not his and he couldn't fall for her. She reluctantly had let him go when he lightly pushed her away to go to the door.

He peeped through the peephole on the door and then opened the door. Tall and handsome, Anthony Gillespi stood blocking the sunlight outside. With a quick movement, he flicked the lights on in the room and then walked inside and closed the door and locked it.

Rachel walked meekly towards him, eyes still leaking tears. Mr. Gillespi moved towards her and touched her lightly on the cheek. "Are you okay, child?" She nodded.

He glanced towards James who walked up and said, "That bastard carved into her ass, dad."

Mr. Gillespi sighed and said, "Yes, I know. But---" he placed one of his long fingers under Rachel's chin and lifted it up to force her to look at him, "---but there were things he could have done that he didn't."

She smiled softly at him – she knew he had not raped her but that news did little to comfort her.

"Come over here and sit, I have news for you."

She sat on one of the two small chairs that sat near the small table. Mr. Gillespi sat in the other and James sat cross-legged on the bed closest to the table.

"Well, first, I'd like to welcome you to the Odium family." He reached his hand over to shake Rachel's hand; she meekly placed her hand in his. "You're DNA was a positive match."

She nodded, not sure how to respond.

"Of course, we already knew that was going to happen." He chuckled softly. "Secondly, you are now the owner of a diner."

She looked at him puzzled.

"Maude Tabor left you her diner in her will – left it to you exclusively."

She smiled softly and then stared at the table top, unsure of what to say. Maude knew that Rachel wouldn't sell the diner and that Rachel would maintain its authentic historical value – anyone else would have sold it for real estate value alone.

Mr. Gillespi kept speaking, "As far as your father's assets go, you will be able to live in his house but I cannot release his monies to you until your eighteenth birthday. Until then, you will receive a monthly allowance for living expenses."

She looked at him and whispered, "What if I choose to not live here?"

"It is expressly stated that he did not want the home sold, but that is truly your choice. The property has been in your family for generations – it would be a shame to destroy that."

She nodded.

"What about my mother?"

"Her body was recovered from the house and was buried next to your father's as he had desired."

She smiled and said softly, "When?"

He frowned. "They buried her yesterday. I had asked to wait until you were out of the hospital but…"

 He shook his head.

She shrugged and changed the subject.

"What kind of assets did he have?"

James leaned in closer to the table.

Mr. Gillespi pulled a sheet of paper out from his briefcase and began to read through the sheet, "Ten million cash, home property worth five million, department store worth two million, income from store five hundred thousand annual, business property worth twenty million, rental income from those properties is around a million a year."

He ran his finger down the list that was longer than what he had listed, and then continued, "The list goes on and on."

She whispered, her voice hurting from overuse, "Who manages it all now?"

"It depends – I oversee it all but once you turn eighteen it'll be all yours to manage. You can hire someone to do it for you or you can do it yourself."

She glanced at James who stared at the list and then at the half-beaten girl who just became a multi-millionaire. He smiled at her and she returned the smile. She was sexy even beaten up but as a multi-millionaire she was a true catch – no wonder Tom had snagged her, he thought.

She whispered softly, "When can I go back home? After all the diner is mine now, I should probably check on it."

A knock on the door interrupted them and James walked up to the door and after peering through the peephole opened the door.

Mr. Gillespi stood up from his chair and walked towards the stranger. The man was short with a shaved head and arms wide and strong that were covered in tattoos all the way to the wrist. He was a reasonably young man, probably mid-twenties and was handsome in a punk rocker kind of way.

The man nodded his head towards Rachel and then grabbed Mr. Gillespi's hand and shook it.

Mr. Gillespi spoke first, "Brian! How are you doing today?"

In a voice uncharacteristic of a man whose days looked as if they were spent in the gym, the man said in a soft voice, "Not too bad Anthony, not too bad."

James shut the door and locked it and then sat again on the edge of the bed. Brian leaned over to Rachel and outstretched his hand.

Kimberly Thomas

"The name's Brian."

Rachel placed her hand in his and he shook it lightly. "Rachel." She coughed after she said it.

James jumped off the bed and ran to the bathroom for water.

Brian nudged Anthony in the ribs and whispered, "Looks like your son has a crush. I've never seen him run that fast."

The two men laughed and Rachel would have laughed had her throat not been on fire. She smiled instead.

Brian spoke again, "Oh, I did as you asked, and assuming that nothing comes up this week, Tom will be released in time to go to his graduation on Friday."

Rachel's face beamed – Friday, that was only a few days away. Rachel gratefully accepted the water from James and guzzled it in a few swigs, and then said softly, "What day is it today?"

Mr. Gillespi chuckled, "Monday."

She nodded and then stared blankly at the table.

Mr. Gillespi spoke again, softly, "So do you want to get out of town for a while, go check on the diner?" She nodded.

"We can get you back here for Friday morning if you'd like."

She nodded again and stared up into his face with a smile.

"Ok, well, I'm going to take Brian to go pick up one of your dad's cars. Do you have a preference?"

She shrugged; she didn't have a preference at all.

"Do you need a hotel to stay at there?"

She nodded.

"I'll have that taken care of for you. You and Brian will leave tonight. James will stay here with you for now."

James piped in, "Can I take her dad?"

Mr. Gillespi laughed a soft, caressing laugh, and said, "You have school, son."

James mumbled something under his breath and watched angrily as Brian and his father walked out of the hotel room.

Thirty-Four

Brian had selected a blue Aston Martin Virage. It was a sleek and beautiful car with its lustrous body and spoilers; it looked like something fit for the race track, not a road trip. The car looked barely used and when Rachel peeked her head in the door and glanced at the odometer, it had such few miles on it that surely an automobile collector would think it a travesty that they were going to drive the car the six hours to the city. Mr. Gillespi mentioned that Jeremiah Odium was one of the first in America to pick up the car and had it only a few months before his untimely demise.

Brian had yawned when he arrived back at the hotel with the car. Mr. Gillespi had followed with his black Lexus sedan and the black Lincoln Town Car still sat in the parking lot.

Rachel, having been watching out the window, asked Brian if he was tired when he entered the room.

He nodded and yawned again.

She cleared her voice, and then said softly,

"Should we stay here tonight? So you can sleep?"

He shrugged.

Mr. Gillespi spoke for him, "You're the boss - you tell us."

She stood up from the chair and looked out the window at

the three shiny cars that glistened in the setting sun. Yawning, she walked over to the bed and sat near James.

"Let's stay the night. We'll sleep and then get up early and leave."

A phone rang – a song from the 1980s blared loudly. Brian blushed and then grabbed the phone from his pocket. He glanced at the number and then excused himself to go outside and talk.

Rachel stood up and looked out the window. Brian walked rapidly away from the hotel room, ear plugged with one finger, the other ear with the phone placed up securely next to it. Brian glanced back at the hotel room and walked further away. Rachel was immediately uncomfortable.

She spoke softly again, "So, how about James stays here to guard me tonight and then Brian can come back tomorrow morning after he sleeps to take me home?"

Mr. Gillespi looked at her and then at his son. "Are you sure?"

She nodded.

"Is that okay with you?" He spoke to his son.

He smiled goofily and nodded.

"You'll be okay for school tomorrow?"

"Last week of school, dad, there's nothing going on this week."

Mr. Gillespi laughed.

"Ok, then it's a deal."

She whispered, "Leave the Aston Martin."

He looked at her perplexed but she had redirected her gaze back out to the man pacing the parking lot. She didn't trust him; he saw it in her face.

Mr. Gillespi walked up to her and placed his arm around her shoulder, "I've known him for years, you can trust him."

She stared outside the window, without a word.

Brian flipped the phone closed and walked back towards the hotel room. Mr. Gillespi met him at the door. "We're going."

Brian looked perplexed.

Mr. Gillespi spoke again, "Go home and sleep, come back tomorrow at---." He glanced at Rachel. "---7am?"

Rachel nodded.

Brian looked at her and then at James and then back at Mr.

Gillespi. "You're the boss. So, 7am, I'll be here."

Brian walked back out the door and back towards the Aston Martin. Mr. Gillespi called out to him, "Keys. You can take the Lincoln."

James, without prompting, tossed him the keys to the Lincoln. Brian reluctantly handed the keys over to Mr. Gillespi.

Without a word, Brian got in the Lincoln, backed up and drove off. Mr. Gillespi turned towards the door and said softly, "See you tomorrow."

The door closed behind him and Rachel watched as he drove off. She turned towards James and walked towards him.

"Take me home."

He looked at her perplexed.

She got on her knees in front of him and rested her head on his knees and stared up into his eyes. "Take me home."

He said nothing and she stood up and walked towards the bathroom. She looked at her broken and bruised face and neck and then saw James walking up behind her.

"Brian can take you tomorrow."

"He can't be trusted."

She grabbed a plastic cup from near the sink and filled it with water and then drank it.

"My dad said I couldn't take you."

She turned around and faced him; he was dangerously close to her.

"I don't trust Brian."

He placed his hand softly on her bruised face, "And I can't trust myself with you."

She smiled softly and he leaned in and kissed her softly on the lips. She pushed him away.

"I'm sorry." He mumbled and he walked away from her and sat on the bed.

She walked to him and sat next to him on the bed.

"No, I'm sorry."

"Want to go get something to eat?"

She nodded.

Kimberly Thomas

"Any preference?"

She shrugged, and then said, "Pizza?"

He smiled a smile that did not represent happiness, this smile was sad – he knew where she wanted to go, she wanted to go where Tom worked; he had no chance with her.

He grabbed the keys off the dresser and they walked out of the hotel room.

"You want to drive?" He said softly as they approached the car.

She shook her head.

He laughed, "Good, because I do. This is a kickass car."

He ran his hand softly over the hood of it and then proceeded to unlock the doors and climb into the car.

Rachel climbed in and buckled her seat and imbibed in the smell of newness in the car – its rich interior and perfection.

James threw the car into reverse, backed out and then sped out of the parking lot, yelling like a crazed banshee as the car responded remarkably quickly. Rachel laughed softly.

He pulled up to a stop light and a shiny red Miata convertible pulled up next to them with a stunning brunette in the driver seat. The girl honked her horn and James looked over. He waved but did not linger his gaze at her and immediately shot from the light as soon as it turned green. The red car grew smaller quickly as they pulled away at speeds most likely well above the speed limit.

When they reached the small pizzeria James pulled directly in front of the building. It was a Monday night and the place was virtually empty except for the woman she had met a few days prior and one customer who sat behind a newspaper reading.

Rachel fumbled with the seat belt as James rushed to her side of the car and opened the door. "Pizza, my lady?" His fake British accent nowhere near authentic – not that she knew what authentic British dialect would sound like.

She smiled and exited the car and followed him into the pizzeria.

The large plump woman waddled towards them and grabbed Rachel's hands in her face softly. "My poor, poor child, who could have done this to you?"

Of all the things Rachel couldn't stand, sympathy was one

of them. She backed quickly away from the woman and James placed himself between them.

"Now, now, Nancy, leave the girl alone."

Nancy backed away and walked towards the counter. A large man worked behind the counter and looked at them from across the room.

Nancy sauntered back towards them and handed them some menus. "Just pick a seat; I'll be with you in a second."

They picked a seat near the window and Rachel leaned her head against the window and stared up at the ceiling and placed her feet up in the booth. James sat and stared at the menu.

"You just want a couple of slabs of cheese pizza?"

She whispered, "Just one for me. And some water."

The light from a car outside shone into the building and she heard the car doors slam. She did not turn around to look. Nancy ambled her way over to the booth and James told her to bring out three slices of cheese pizza and a couple of waters. With a jot down on a piece of paper she returned to the kitchen.

The jingle of the door opening caused James to turn around – Rachel still studied the ceiling tiles which were worn in spots and had brown spots in places where something had leaked on them. Maude's diner never had such unappealing ceiling tiles – well, it was her diner now and she thought to herself, her diner would never have ceiling tiles so disgusting.

She turned when she heard a woman's voice say,

"Hey, Rachel."

Andrea, dressed in a short black skirt and tight red top that revealed a lot of cleavage, clung to Alex's arm. Alex nodded at her and from the looks on their faces were disgusted by her face.

Rachel moved her legs off of the bench and Andrea sat down next to her. Alex remained standing and said, "Is that your car out there?" He directed the question to James.

James shook his head.

"Nope, it's Rachel's now."

He looked at Rachel and then through the window at the car.

"That is one kickass ride."

She chuckled. Nancy moseyed her large body through the restaurant with a couple of waters and sat them on the table.

"Hey kids, you want something to eat?"

Both Alex and Andrea shook their head. Alex said softly, "We just dropped by."

Nancy directed her question to Alex, which Rachel thought strange, "So how's Tom? I didn't want to bother him by visiting."

Alex chuckled, "He'll survive. They are releasing him just in time to suffer through the graduation ceremony Friday."

Rachel drank some water and then crackled, "I saw him while I was there and he looked good for what he went through."

Nancy turned to her and looked at her sadly. Alex spoke, however, "I don't mean to sound mean but he looks like a beauty compared to what happened to you."

She laughed and then started coughing harshly, grabbing quickly for the water to drink.

Alex spoke again, "Well, we've got to get going. We have a movie to catch."

Rachel whispered through coughs, "Can you tell Tom I'll be back Friday?"

"You leaving town?" Alex asked.

She nodded and James answered for her. "Yeh we're having her driven back home. Her former employer deceased and willed her property – she needs to go take care of business. We promise we'll bring her back in time for graduation."

Nancy with a maternal look as if she was protecting Tom said, "Are *you* taking her?"

He laughed. "No. Dad says I have to go to school. He's hired a security guy to take her and protect her while she's there."

Andrea had stood up and was standing up near Alex, he put his arm around her and pulled her close to him.

Nancy spoke what they all were thinking, "Are you still in danger?"

Rachel shrugged.

James looked at her softly and then at the other three who stared at him with disdain. He spoke in a whisper, "We think so."

Thirty-Five

There wasn't much to say about the night. James had driven her home and they had slept on opposite beds and did not speak a word. It was remarkably ordinary – and she appreciated that.

In the morning the knock on the door woke them both up from deep sleep. Without thinking Rachel yawned, walked to the door and opened it. Fortunately it was Brian because in her trance-like state she had failed to confirm that it was someone not out to kill her.

She opened the door to him and went back to the bed and laid down, closing her eyes to the light that excruciatingly shot through the open door.

"Wake up sleepy head." Brian pushed her softly on the arm.

She yawned and turned over on her side.

She heard James sit up on the other bed and ask softly, "What time is it?"

"7:45."

"Oh, no! I'm going to be late."

The news of the time woke him up suddenly and he jumped out of bed, grabbed the keys from Brian and headed out the door without even a good-bye.

Rachel rolled on her back, stretched and then sat up in the bed.

"You ready?"

She shrugged.

He chuckled and then busied himself around the room picking up pieces of paper off the counter and tossing them in the trash.

The door was still open and the cool air smelled clean and fresh and she didn't really want to go back to the city where the air smelled of trash and excrement. She stood up and walked to the bathroom and threw water in her face, inspecting the bruises on her face. They'd heal, she knew that, but for now she was a horrid sight to see – someone with two heads would look better than she.

She slipped into the bathroom to use the toilet and closed the door behind her and then came back out – Brian was not in the hotel room. She walked through the hotel room and out the front door and saw him. He was leaning against the wall, his short stocky body propped up against the wall with his foot. He was smoking a cigarette and staring at nothing in the distance. She walked up next to him and leaned against the wall and looked at his tattoos on his arms.

"You want one?" He offered the cigarette package over to Rachel.

She shook her head. It was a filthy habit, she thought.

The tattoos intrigued her – from a distance they looked like a blob of color but up close they told stories – a girl dressed in a school girl skirt and button up shirt rolled up and unbuttoned to show a perfectly flawless stomach and amble breasts; a heart with a knife that protruded from it; and the weirdest one of all – a black hand and a white hand tugging at a flag. Forgetting that she did not fully trust the man, she placed her finger on it and traced it.

His breath came out in a sigh and she looked up at him but he had his eyes closed and his head tilted to the sky.

"What does it mean?" She said it softly, although her voice was not as fragile as it had been the days before.

"I was into some bad stuff when I was younger – skinhead stuff I'd rather not talk about."

She nodded and removed her hand from his arm.

"You ready?"

She nodded and he tossed his cigarette onto the ground and stomped on it with his foot. He glanced in the room, and then closed the door and they both walked to the car – he got in on the driver's side and she walked to the passenger side.

Buckled in, car engine roaring, he backed the car up and drove away. She rested her head on the window and drifted off into sleep.

A few hours later she woke when they arrived at a gas station. Brian chuckled as he got out of the car, "This car sure likes to guzzle gas. Thank God I'm not paying for it."

She smiled softly at him and exited out of the passenger side of the car to stand and stretch. "Where are we?"

"We've got about an hour or two left. Couldn't tell you exactly where we are, though.

He stared at the pump as the numbers grew higher and higher.

"I'm going to go use the bathroom."

He looked at her, and then glanced around the empty station parking lot, and then nodded at her.

The gas station was small and dirty, and the attendant at the counter was an elderly woman who looked near a hundred years old, although Rachel doubted she actually was that old. The old woman smiled a toothless grin when she walked in and then pointed to the bathroom as if she knew what Rachel was needing.

Rachel nodded and walked towards the bathroom, did her business as she held her nose to keep the stench from wafting in, and then after washing her hands thoroughly, she walked back to the car.

An attractive blonde woman – mid-thirties probably – with shorts that left little to the imagination and a shirt that covered less than the shorts, leaned on the Aston Martin and talked with Brian. Gas pumped, Brian, with his back towards Rachel, leaned against the car talking to the woman.

Rachel said nothing, just simply went to the passenger side of the car and got in and buckled in. She heard the woman laugh – a sound that did nothing for her since it sounded like a dentists drill – and then she handed something to Brian and he got into the car.

Rachel chuckled when he sat down, "She liked the car, didn't she?"

He laughed. "Who'd have thought?"

She laughed. "Who did you tell her I was?"

"Oh, you know, my kid sister."

She laughed.

She patted him on the shoulder. "Well, bro, thank you for taking care of me in my time of need."

He chuckled and turned the car engine on and then drove away, back onto the highway.

"So you gonna call her?" She asked the question at least a half hour after that incident at the gas station.

"Who, blondie?"

"Yes her."

"Nah. She was only interested in me for my body."

Rachel laughed. "I thought it was for the car."

"Yeh, that too." He stuck her tongue out at her.

No longer afraid to trust him, for after all, his exterior seemed to portray a man he was not, she laughed again. "You'd make a good big brother, Brian."

He fell silent, and unsure as to what to say, she rested her head on the window again and fell asleep.

He shook her and she woke up. They were in the city – home, again.

"Do you need to go your house to get any clothes?"

She nodded.

"Tell me how to get there."

She wasn't really sure where she was but after a half hour of driving around, she finally found a landmark that looked familiar – the city park where she had kissed Danny, where she had been betrayed. She guided Brian towards her apartment complex.

"This is where you lived?" The look on face was not disgust but surprise.

She shrugged her shoulders and said, "Yeh, why?"

He said nothing and he parked in a spot.

"Stay with the car, I'll go get my clothes."

He nodded and stayed in the driver's seat, car running. A few people's heads peeked out of windows and stared. Rachel ignored them.

There was a note on the door when she got there and she grabbed it and folded it up and put it in her pocket and then found the spare key in the hole that was next to the door awning and placed it in the keyhole to open it. The stench of poverty greeted her and she rushed inside and grabbed the box that held her few pieces of clothing. She did not bother locking the door behind her – there was nothing worth salvaging in that apartment anymore.

She would never return.

She rushed towards the Aston Martin and climbed into the passenger seat and threw her box onto the floorboard.

"Can we drop by the diner?"

He nodded and she guided him the few blocks to the diner. The diner was beautiful in the afternoon sun – shining magnificent like a silver can. The diner had few visitors on that Tuesday afternoon. Brian parked the Aston Martin and sat silently as she unbuckled and slowly exited the car.

"You hungry? We have a killer roast beef sandwich."

"I'm starving."

He exited the car in a quick motion and was at the front door of the diner before she even got close to it. He opened the door for her and then followed behind her. An older woman, mid-forties with graying hair, flirted about the diner with her pink poodle skirt and white top. Not turning around, and only responding to the sound of the chime that introduced another visitor to the diner, she yelled, "I'll be with you in a second."

Lou, short for Lula, was a single mother and only worked during the day while her kids attended school. Rachel had only worked with her on a few brief occasions. The double doors to the kitchen exploded open and Butch came running out to greet her.

He stopped when he saw her face. In a growl he said, "Who did this to you?"

She shrugged, assuming she was not supposed to discuss the events of that night.

Butch, just noticing the man standing next to Rachel, looked up at him with distrust. Rachel punched Butch softly in the shoulder.

"Butch, this is Brian."

Brian extended his hand and Butch reluctantly took it.

"Brian, this is my surrogate father."

Butch chuckled and then blushed.

Trying to avoid the topic, Butch said, "So, I hear you're my new boss."

Rachel laughed and then coughed, her throat dry from too much talking.

Lou came up to them and handed her a glass of water, "Here ya go boss."

Lou looked at Butch with a look that said "I'm not working for no kid," and then walked away.

"Who's working today in the kitchen?" Rachel directed her question to Butch.

"Nick's back there."

"You think you could get Nick to whip up a few roast beef sandwiches?"

He chuckled, "He'd be more than happy to do so."

Rachel took a swig of water and then looked at Brian, "Go have a seat and I'll meet up with you, okay? I need to talk to Butch."

They walked to the back and then stopped by the kitchen to tell Nick to make a few sandwiches and then proceeded to the office in the back.

When they reached the office, she closed the door behind them.

"Who did that to you, Rach?" Butch asked the question again.

"It's a long story, Butch, and really I just don't want to talk about it."

He nodded.

"So, I need to ask you a huge favor."

He nodded again.

"I need you to watch this place for a while until I can get back. I know Maude kept all her financial records in a book, so I'm going to find that and take a look at it. If you can manage the place till I'm gone, keep a mutiny from uprising, I'd appreciate it. Once I look at the numbers I can tell you what I can pay you for your time."

He smiled at her softly.

"It'd be my pleasure."

"Thank you."

She flipped through some papers on the desk and then a couple of books on the shelves until she found what she was looking for – Maude's financial records. She grabbed it and waited as Butch opened the door to the office. She walked towards the kitchen and grabbed the sandwiches that Nick had made and said softly, "Butch is in charge for a while until I get back."

Nick looked at her but said nothing. She threw some fries on the plate and walked out to the dining area. Brian sat at a booth typing on his phone. She walked towards the booth and placed the plates on the table. He immediately flipped the phone shut and reached below the table to put it in his pocket.

He smiled at her and said, "After this, you want to go get settled in?"

She laughed, "Sure, where are we staying?"

"An apartment – friend of mine found it."

"Is this something permanent or just for the week?"

"Just for the week. The person that was in the apartment is just letting us borrow it while they are out of town."

She nodded and then grabbed her sandwich. They ate in silence.

Butch walked out when they were done eating and grabbed the plates; Lou had disappeared. He looked at Brian and said, "So you gonna protect my little girl here?"

Rachel laughed and Brian said, "That's what they paid me for."

Butch smiled and then placed his big hand on Rachel's head and ruffled her hair.

The two got up from the booth and walked towards the exit. She smiled and waved at Butch as she left; Butch looked stoic, like a statue built of stone, but with a soft smile he waved back.

They got in the car and drove off silently to the apartment. Rachel had never been to the part of the city that Butch drove through. In fact, she doubted that she would have ever had a reason to go to this part of town because the stores were brands she knew she could have never afforded and the cars parked along the street were all expensive foreign imports. As if he was familiar to the area, Brian pulled into a parking garage and grabbed a ticket and then drove through the darkened driveways up and up and up until he found a spot nestled under a bright light.

She grabbed her box from the floor and followed him doggedly towards the staircase. The staircase led to a hallway that had two elevator doors; Brian pushed the button to go up and when the bell chimed that the elevator had arrived and the doors opened, he walked into the elevator silently. Rachel followed close behind.

A tall blonde woman was in the elevator and she smiled seductively at Brian when he walked in and then looked disgustingly at Rachel when she followed close behind. Rachel stood on the opposite side of the elevator while Brian stood in the center. The woman's hair fell softly into her face and onto the cream colored jacket that she wore. The jacket was long enough to cover down to her mid-thigh. Nothing showed underneath it and nothing showed at the small opening at the top. The woman held the neck line loosely.

She glanced at Rachel's face and then moved her hair out of her face exposing a black eye that was now fading into purples and yellows. Giggling she said, "Look, we're twinkies – although looks like you had more fun." She winked.

Rachel smiled but said nothing, disturbed by the woman's ignorance.

The woman giggled again, "You forgot to push what floor you're going to."

The elevator had already started going up.

Brian spoke, "We're going to fourteen." His voice was rough and calloused as if he didn't want to speak to the perky blonde who pushed herself up against him.

"I'm a going there too!"

Rachel rolled her eyes when Brian glanced over at her

and he chuckled.

The elevator dinged and the doors opened up to the fourteenth floor. The young woman let go of the neckline of her jacket and made an unfortunate, at least to Rachel, revelation that she was completely naked underneath the jacket. Rachel wasn't sure if Brian enjoyed the scenery, but she couldn't imagine what man wouldn't. The woman bounced out of the elevator and skipped down the hallway, her naked butt cheeks slipping out from underneath the jacket with every step.

Brian and Rachel walked out behind her and Rachel followed Brian as he walked down the hall. Brian stopped at a door and Rachel looked down the hall to see the young woman fiddling with the lock on the next door down the hall.

The door had unlocked finally for the blonde and she looked up the hall at Brian opening the door and she yelled out, "Oh my God, we're neighbors. That's great!!"

Rachel rolled her eyes, and Brian popped the door open and walked inside. Before Rachel could get in the door the woman yelled out, "Maybe you two can come hang out with me and my boyfriend sometime."

Rachel looked at her, and said, "Sure," although she didn't really mean it. Brian grabbed her arm and pulled her inside.

"She'll keep you out there all day talking if you let her."

She laughed and then closed the door behind her. He locked the door and placed the chain in place.

She glanced around the room. It was a beautiful apartment – the furniture was all black leather, there was a TV that was bigger than the couch in the living room, the kitchen that was just past the sunken living room was all stainless steel appliances and accented by a dining table that showed the person who lived here was cultured and had friends. She smiled and walked inside and sunk into the leather couch.

Brian grabbed a remote on the coffee table and walked to the couch and flopped himself on the other end and turned on the big television. He flipped it to some movie and she rested her head on the side of the couch and fell asleep.

Kimberly Thomas

Thirty-Six
🍂 🍂 🍂

She woke up to the sound of explosions on the television and excused herself to go take a shower. The only bedroom was off to the left of the living room and in it was the master bath which was bigger than her old apartment. It had a full size Jacuzzi tub and a shower and a phone next to the toilet. She felt out of place but sinking herself into the tub and turning on the jets, she didn't really care.

A knock on the bathroom door interrupted her peaceful bath and she called out, "Yes?"

"You got a phone call."

"Ok, one second."

She grabbed a towel off the rack next to her and quickly dried her body off and wrapped the towel around her. Opening the door, Brian looked her up and down and then handed her the cell phone. He walked away.

"Hello?" She said the words softly.

"Rachel?"

"Hey, it's Alex."

"Hey." She wasn't sure what to say to him.

"I got this number from James. I have someone that wants to talk to you."

She chuckled, "Okay?"

There was a pause and after a reasonable amount of time, she said "Hello?"

A muffled voice came on the line, "Rach?"

"Tom?"

The voice cleared up, "Hey baby, how are you doing?"

"I'm good. I'm back home but I'll be back for Friday, okay?"

"Yeh they told me about that. Where you at now?"

"At some apartment."

"In the city?"

"Yeh, Brian said his friend found it."

Tom said nothing.

"It's a nice place."

She could hear Tom breathing on the line but he still said nothing.

"There's this dumb blonde who was next door. She was wearing just a coat in the elevator. It was pretty funny."

Tom's voice was somber when he spoke again.

"Do you know the name of the building?"

She thought and then after a brief pause, "I don't remember seeing it."

"What floor are you on?"

"Fourteenth."

He didn't say it to her but she heard it anyway. He said the word, "Damn."

"Is everything okay, baby?"

After a brief pause, he said, "Yeh. Just be careful, okay?"

"I will."

He paused and then added, "I love you."

Her heart beat loudly in her chest and she said softly, "I love you too."

He hung up the phone and Rachel, grabbing tightly at the towel, walked into the living room and handed the phone back to Brian who glanced at her and then looked again at the television.

She grabbed her box of clothes off the living room floor and walked back into the bedroom to change. She did not go back into the living room after she put on a sundress but instead laid on the big king size bed in the bedroom and stared at the ceiling in the darkened room.

She heard the banging on the wall first, a soft thump-thump that sounded like someone knocking and then she heard the voice of the blonde woman not moaning but screaming and Rachel grabbed her pillow and threw it over her head to block out the sound.

When she braved taking the pillow off her head, the theatrics next door had stopped and she sighed in relief and looked towards the clock to see the time. It was nearing midnight and she had slept so much during the day that she couldn't sleep now.

She got up and walked into the living room. The television was on but Brian lay on the couch softly snoring. She went back to the bedroom, grabbed a blanket and wrapped it over him and then softly walked to the television and turned it off. Brian did not stir - his rhythmic breathing and soft snoring the only sound that interrupted the silent room.

She walked back into the bedroom and lay on the bed and eventually drifted off to sleep.

She awoke in the morning to the smell of bacon – a smell she was all too familiar with from weekend after weekend of cooking bacon at the diner. She slipped off of the bed and straightened her yellow sundress and walked into the kitchen where Brian stood over the oven.

"So, you cook?" She said it softly as she walked up behind him.

"Been single a long time." He chuckled.

He grabbed a couple of plates off of the counter and placed some bacon and eggs on the plate and handed it to Rachel.

She smiled at him softly and walked to the table to sit and eat.

He was done cooking in no time and brought a plate over to the table that was filled with at least three times the amount of food she had. They ate without speaking.

She pushed her plate away from her after eating about half the food. "So, are you going to go hang out with your friend while you're in town?"

He looked at her puzzled and said, "My friend?"

"You know silly, the one who got you this place."

He chuckled, "Oh, him."

She said nothing.

"Do you trust me?" he said softly.

She chuckled, "Well, to be totally honest, I didn't at first. But, you're an okay guy I guess; I think I can trust you."

He said nothing.

His silence disturbed her and she fiddled with her hair nervously.

"You sound better today." He said the comment out of context of the conversation.

She smiled.

"Your bruises are healing up nicely too."

In a voice that sounded much too wise for her, she said, "Some bruises never heal, Bri."

He smiled at her softly and then looked down at his food, the pile now significantly smaller than when he had brought it over. He looked up and in a voice almost like a whisper he said, "Who did that to you?"

"A guy."

He chuckled softly, "What guy?"

"I'm not sure I'm supposed to say."

"I will rip his throat out if I see him."

She smiled and then softly said, "He's a killer you shouldn't mess with."

A soft knock on the door interrupted their conversation but Brian ignored it and said, "Just tell me his name."

She stood up and silently walked to the front door. She heard him push his chair out and follow behind her. She glanced through the peephole and saw the blonde woman from the day before. She rolled her eyes and then grabbed the chain to open the door.

Brian quickly put his hand on hers to keep her from opening the door and glanced out the peephole. His response was the same to hers, a roll of the eyes. Without releasing her hand, his body pushed up against her back, he looked down at her and said softly, "A name."

He moved his hand from hers and as she turned around, and grabbed the door handle, she said in a whisper, "Junior."

Thirty-Seven

*W*ithout even an invitation to come in, the bubbly blonde walked into the apartment, pushing Rachel's arm out of the way. The blonde walked directly to Brian, who stood wide-eyed and terrified.

He grabbed her arm and aimed her towards the door. In a voice more harsh than his regular voice, he said, "You need to leave."

She stuck her bottom lip out in a pout and then looked at Rachel, "So, did you enjoy our performance last night?"

Rachel looked at her puzzled.

She pretended she was moaning and groaning, and then continued, "He said that was all for you." The blonde rolled her eyes in disgust.

Rachel said nothing.

Brian grabbed her by the arm and said forcefully, "Who said that?"

"My boyfriend."

"Who is your boyfriend?"

The blonde struggled as Brian's grip grew tighter on her arm.

Rachel, afraid that Brian might take it too far, said, "Bri, you need to let her go." She touched him softly on the small of his back.

He looked at her softly and the fire went out of his eyes and he let the blonde go so quickly that she nearly fell to the ground.

The blonde pushed herself up against Brian and whispered loud enough for Rachel to hear, "You know I like it like that." She giggled and then winked at Brian and then looking at Rachel she said softly and with a look of disgust on her face, "I was told to tell you that it's your turn next."

And as quick as she had come into the apartment, she was out the door and back into hers – disappearing without a trace.

Brian rushed to the apartment door and slammed it shut and locked it again. He leaned on the door and said softly, "Get your stuff, we have to go."

"Why?"

"We'll talk about it later. Hurry."

She ran to the bedroom and gathered up her few belongings and then walked back out into the living room where Brian stood nervously by the door, keys to the car in hand.

"We must leave quietly." He said in a whisper.

She nodded.

He looked through the peephole of the door and then opened the door locks trying his best to not have them click loudly. He swung the door open quickly and quietly. Brian stuck his head out in the hallway and looked down both sides and then motioned for her to come out. He closed the door softly behind them but did not bother locking the door.

They moved swiftly but silently down the hallway and then waited patiently at the elevator doors, both constantly gazing down the hallway for a sign of the blonde woman or her boyfriend -- neither of which appeared before the elevator announced its arrival with a ding.

They both sighed in relief when the doors opened and the elevator car was empty. She wasn't sure why they were in a rush to leave, why the name Junior had sparked a response from him, why the blonde woman appeared to be such a threat but something in her heart knew they should leave.

They walked into the elevator quickly and Brian pushed the "Door Close" button in order to expedite their departure and then pressed the button for the parking garage level. The door closed shut and the elevator proceeded down towards normalcy – towards freedom.

The door opened up to the hall that led towards the parking garage and as they exited the elevator car they both froze in their steps.

Rachel's heart seemed to stop in her chest.

Junior, dressed in jeans and a tight t-shirt, stood leaning against the wall. He looked relaxed like a cowboy who leaned against a fence post chewing on a piece of straw. He stared at the ground and for a second, Rachel thought they might just be able to pass him, thought maybe that they wouldn't be noticed. But that was a fleeting thought when Junior looked up and directed his gaze towards the two of them, his eyes cutting into her with more veracity than she had ever seen.

"Brian, Brian, Brian." Junior walked up towards her guardian and patted Brian on the shoulder. "You come in town and you don't even say 'hello'." Junior shook his head.

Brian said nothing and Rachel slid behind Brian.

"And who is this you brought with you?"

Brian still said nothing, his teeth clinched in his mouth.

Junior grabbed Rachel's arm and pulled her to the front of Brian.

"Did you bring me a present?" Junior smiled wickedly.

Rachel glared up at Junior as if the glare was enough to knock him down.

Junior ran his huge hands over Rachel's bruised face. "I missed you." He reached down and kissed her sloppily on the lips; his breath smelled of stale alcohol.

She pushed herself away from him, dropping her box of clothes, and he reached his hand up to slap her but Brian stepped in his way and he hit Brian's arm instead.

In a flash, Junior produced a knife from behind his back and he placed the cold steel point under Brian's chin. "Stay out of this," he slurred.

Rachel pushed between the two and touched Junior's chest soft and seductively. Junior removed the knife from Brian's chin and focused his attention on Rachel.

Kimberly Thomas

She cooed softly, "You don't want to hurt him."

He looked down at her and in a drunken smile, he spat, "You are so beautiful."

Her face bruised and beaten, she was not beautiful – not today at least. She could not argue with him, however. She ran her fingers down towards his belt and wrapped her fingers around a belt loop. "Give me the knife." She cooed the words softly and seductively.

He gave her the knife as requested. She took advantage of his moment of weakness and slammed the knife blade into his forearm. He screamed in pain and in that brief moment, she ran – Brian close behind her.

Breathless from running down the staircase, she said softly, "Call 911?"

It was more a question than a statement because she wasn't quite sure that 911 would be useful in this situation. He said nothing in response but instead responded by fishing for his phone in his pocket and pulling it up, flipping it open and muttering, "no signal."

When they reached the final set of stairs – three flights down – they were greeted by Junior, knife still protruding from his arm. She wasn't sure how he had arrived before them but the question was not much of a concern – for once again they were confronted by the madman.

They stopped in their tracks and then tried to run past him but their attempt was thwarted as Junior grabbed Rachel by the hair and pulled her to the ground. She hit the ground hard, her head hitting the concrete with a thump. She yelped and tried to focus on her surroundings as the blackness tried to overwhelm her vision.

Spitting and slurring, Junior pulled the knife from his arm and then pushed it up against her already bruised neck. "I told you that you couldn't run."

She could not see Brian – perhaps he ran off or perhaps he backed away because any movement he made would surely mean harm to Rachel. She lay there, panting – refusing to cry or scream. He sat on top of her, his heavy body on her legs.

Her head throbbed and in a whisper she said, "I will never be yours."

The knife pushed closer to her throat and she lay still, trying not to breathe because breathing would push the knife closer to her neck. His free hand slid up her thigh and towards her panties.

He leaned his face into her and kissed her again, sloppily licking her lips and biting her tongue. He pushed his body completely against hers and whispered in her ear, "I should have taken you when I had the chance."

The force of his heavy body against hers pushed the knife into her skin and she cried softly, "Don't hurt me."

It was a sign of weakness – she knew that and she also knew that he would find that weakness erotic and she would not be left unharmed this time. If only Brian would risk her safety to protect her, but the knife on her throat could kill her and he surely would not take that risk.

As Junior's fingers slipped into her panties and towards private places no one else had ever touched before, a tear escaped her eye. Junior moaned seductively and removing his fingers from her, released the pressure of the knife on her neck by moving it down farther. He sat up and cut the dress, opening it up so he could see her partially naked body. He ran the tip of the knife up her exposed upper body, she gritted her teeth as the knife nicked her body and little streams of blood pooled and then dripped down the side of her.

Brian seeing an opening for saving her walked closer and grabbed Junior by the hair. In a voice filled with anger and hate, he screamed, "Leave her alone."

The knife went from her body to Brian's arm and as the knife cut his skin, Brian released Junior's hair. The knife immediately went back up to Rachel's exposed throat and Brian grasping his arm backed away.

He kissed her again, shoddy and messy, and she wanted to puke, she wanted to cry, she wanted to scream, but she could do nothing with that knife against her throat. Her partially naked body was being explored by his free hand, his rough large fingers grasping at her body as if it were silly putty to be molded. She could feel his desire for her rubbing against her through his pants. Helpless, the knife pressing so sharply against her throat, she cried.

She heard him unzip his pants one-handed. She felt him against her, rubbing himself on her bare thigh like a dog humping its owner's leg. Her breaths came in fits now, like a small child who had cried for hours and now had no breath left to scream anymore. Grabbing her by the hair again, he pulled her off the ground and pushed her forcibly against the back of the car. He ripped the already cut dress off of her and then cut her panties off in a moment so quick she didn't have time to scream. The knife was away from her throat now and Brian, seeing the opportunity arise, ran towards him and tackled Junior like a football player.

The patter of footsteps on the staircase should have made evident that it was time for Junior to flee, but he did not – instead the two large men fought -- one avoiding the lunges of a knife and the other avoiding the throw of a fist. Rachel grabbed her shorn clothes from the floor and, grasping them to cover her nakedness, she hid in the darkness waiting for Brian to win this fight so they could leave.

The sound of footsteps grew louder and then her heroes were there – dressed in navy blue with holsters at their hips and guns pointed in the direction of the two men fighting. One man's voice firm and strong said, "Drop the knife, son."

Junior lunged the knife towards Brian in response but with the sound of the guns being cocked, he raised his arms in the air and the knife dropped with a cling to the floor. Brian had already raised his hands in the air.

Rachel watched him from the darkness, fully aware that even in the darkness he could probably see her. His hands now crossed behind his head, he looked bored as if the police had inconvenienced him rather than caught him in the act of a crime. He looked towards her in the darkness with a look that said more than words could ever say – it wasn't over. She grabbed the clothes closer to her body.

When they finally dragged Junior away, he had gone without a fight. There were four police officers remaining and Brian who sat on the staircase with his head in his hands. She did her best to cover up her nakedness but there was little she could do with her destroyed clothing.

She glanced over at the remaining officers and in a weak voice said, "I left a box of clothes three floors up near the elevator, can one of you go get them?"

One of the four ran up the stairs to get her clothing while the remaining officers watched her silently and did not say a word. She really expected that they should say something – at least to tell her an ambulance was coming or another officer or something.

She walked towards Brian, fully aware that her naked body was partially exposed – it did not matter now, what innocence she had left was minimal, at best. He looked at her softly and then at the three officers who did not hide their ogling of her. He remained seated on the staircase and grabbing her hand gently, he pulled her towards him and sat her in his lap, wrapping his arms firmly around her in order to cover up any exposed areas that might be left in the view of the officers.

She leaned her head back on his shoulder and smiled back at him. The officer returned with her box of clothing and handed it to her. Brian released her only enough to allow her to pull the new dress over her head. Once her naked body was no longer exposed, he released her from his grasp. Now, no longer the object of attention, she stood up and leaned down to help him up, softly she said, "Are you okay?"

He looked at her with eyes filled with tears, and said, "I'm sorry."

She smiled softly at him but said nothing. There had been little he could have done to protect her.

One of the four officers walked up and tapped her on the shoulder. He looked to be having a hard time making eye contact with her when he said, "We'll need you to make a statement if you are choosing to press charges."

Kimberly Thomas

She rolled her eyes, "Yeh, whatever you need."

Brian spoke up, and in a choppy voice said, "How'd you guys know to come?"

The man pointed to a camera on the wall.

"Expensive neighborhood – they are paranoid for a good reason." He chuckled.

Brian spoke again, "We'll follow you to the police station, if that's okay."

The police officer nodded and Rachel and Brian walked to the Aston Martin.

Thirty-Eight
🦇 🦇 🦇

*T*he pudgy little man sat across from the desk that was cluttered with too much paper, his hair as sloppy as his desk. His gums were black although his teeth were unnaturally white and his breath smelled like cigarettes. He was polite, however, which was better than the cop she had talked to back in Vertueux.

After the typical barrage of questions, "How did she know him, why did he attack her, who was that other fellow that was with her," the questioning finally ended. He stood up from his desk with a groan and said softly, "I'd suggest you get a restraining order against this creep. We can hold him for now because of the video surveillance, but I can't guarantee he won't post bail when it's set."

She nodded, shook his hand and he escorted her out of his office. One of the young men who had been at the scene was sitting on a desk talking to a few other guys – guys who had not been there. She smiled at him softly, and when the other guys turned towards her she knew they had been talking about her. She wanted to stick her middle finger up at him, but refrained – always the good girl.

Brian still sat in another office, door closed. She could not see the man who sat at the other side of the desk.

The pudgy officer that she had not caught the name of went and tapped on the window outside the guy's office. Apparently being told he could go inside, the pudgy man stuck his head in the door and said loudly, "We're done."

She saw Brian stand up and when he reached the door he turned around and said, "Do we need to stay local?"

She heard from the man she could not see,

"We'd prefer it."

Brian walked inside and handed the man a card and Rachel heard him say, "Miss Odium has business she needs to attend to in Vertueux. If you need her, you can contact her attorney."

There was no discussion between them and Brian turned around and walked towards Rachel, grabbing her arm softly and tugging her towards the door.

He released her arm when they started walking and they walked out of the police station and towards the parking lot where they had parked their car. Another one of the four officers stood near the Aston Martin. He was inspecting the car as if he was searching it for bombs.

When they got closer to the car Brian said,

"Can I help you?"

The officer turned around and looked at them. He was a middle-aged man with thinning brown hair, thin with eyes that were too close together, he squinted at Brian and then looked longingly at Rachel. He turned his gaze back towards Brian and in a nasally voice said, "Is this your car?"

"No."

"Then why you drivin' it?"

"It is Miss Odium's car and she has allowed me to drive it."

"Who?"

Brian pointed towards Rachel.

The officer walked up to Rachel threateningly and she backed up a step.

"How's a little lady like you own a car like that?"

She said it in a voice that was meant to be condescending and rude, "My parents died. I inherited it. Do you have a problem?"

He shook his head and backed up a few steps,
"No, no, that's a nice car 'tho'."

She smiled at him and then walked to the passenger side. Without a word, Brian passed the officer and unlocked the doors so they could get in. With a turn of the key, the car sprung to life and the roar of the engine made the officer jump.

Rachel laughed and Brian turned towards her and smiled.

She looked at him and said softly, "We going home?"

"You mean Vertueux?"

She chuckled, he was right; it wasn't really her home – not yet at least. "Yes, Vertueux."

He nodded and then backing the car up, he drove away from the police station. The sun had already begun to set, the buildings glowing in its fiery burial. The day had been wasted but Junior was behind bars and for now she was safe.

Kimberly Thomas

Thirty-Nine

Alex had calmed him down enough to convince him to not go to the city to find Rachel. It was, after all, probably only a coincidence that she was living in an apartment on the fourteenth floor – there were probably at least a dozen apartment complexes that had a fourteenth floor. It was probably also a coincidence that Rachel's bodyguard was named Brian who had been one of Junior's best friends back in the day – in fact, those two had always been in trouble. Alex was right though, it was all just coincidence. With that thought, he had done as requested, remained at the hospital until they would release him.

Alex dropped by Wednesday night as he had every night since he'd been admitted. Sometimes Andrea would come along but usually it was just Alex. Tonight it was just Alex and he brought a big bag of candy stuffed inside his pocket.

"I want to call her." Tom said softly with a mouth full of candy.

Alex laughed and then pulled his phone out of his pocket and dialed the number for Brian.

"Can I speak to Rachel?" Alex spoke the words before Brian could even say anything.

A moment later her voice came on the line, "Hello?"

"Hey, baby."

He imagined that she smiled longingly while on the phone, her beautiful face aglow with love, but instead of the typical return of the greeting, she greeted him with

"You're brother is in jail."

"What?"

"He attacked us."

"Are you okay?"

"We're coming back to Vertucux."

"Are you okay?" He repeated the question because he had to know, he had to know if his precious Rachel had been hurt – she was not dead but he could not bear the thought if she had been hurt in any way.

"Yes, we're okay."

A nurse walked into the room and told him he couldn't use the phone.

"I gotta go. I'll see you tomorrow?"

"Yes, tomorrow."

He hung up the phone and immediately regretted not telling her he loved her.

He handed Alex the phone and Alex said, "What happened?"

"My brother's in jail."

Alex laughed, "That's not a first."

His brother had been in jail on and off since the age of sixteen – drunk and disorderly, driving under the influence, domestic disputes -- the charges had always been dropped.

"She's coming back too." His face lit up and Alex chuckled.

Alex stood up and stretched.

"See if that nurse will let me walk around." They had removed the monitors a day or so before, he just had to have permission to move around.

Alex ducked his head out the door and called to the nurse, who responded that he could walk around. Tom was out of the bed before Alex could turn around.

In the light of the hallway instead of the dimly lit room, Tom looked worse. He was pale and thin and part of his hair had been shaved off where they had to stitch the gash in his head from the bullet that grazed him. Even in that state, however, he was still typical Tom – bright and energetic and overly friendly.

A nurse passed by him and said "Hey Tom."

He replied, "Guess what? My girlfriend's coming back tomorrow." The smile on his face more than told everyone around that he was truly in love.

The nurse stopped, chuckled, and in a sing song voice said, "my girlfriend's back and we're gonna get married…" She walked off still humming the tune.

Alex chuckled and said, "Isn't it 'my boyfriend's back'?"

Tom laughed. "Doesn't matter dude."

They kept walking until they reached the end of the corridor and then turned back around. His doctor was standing in the hall.

Tom made his voice all deep and masculine, "Doctor Reynolds, how are you feeling this fine day?"

Dr. Reynolds chuckled and said, "Not as well as you, I'm afraid."

Tom laughed. "Well my girlfriend is coming home tomorrow."

"I know, I know, I think the whole hospital already knows." The doctor laughed and patted Tom on the back.

Tom chuckled. "I only told one person – well two including you."

"Well, your girlfriend is a veritable celebrity now, you know. Anyway, how about I discharge you tomorrow morning? Looks like you're doing fine."

Tom's eyes lit up. "That'd be fantabulous!"

The doctor laughed. "Well then rest, otherwise I'll keep you here for another month."

Tom laughed and then walked along with Alex back into his room.

Tom climbed back into bed and stared at the ceiling, and Alex, still standing said, "So dude, I'm gonna get outta here."

"Tell Andrea I said 'hi'."

Alex chuckled, "Will do."

Alex walked out the door and Tom drifted off to sleep, wishing that he could dream of his beautiful Rachel.

Forty

The drive was unbearably boring and the cuts on Rachel's neck and chest and the dull ache at the back of her head where she had hit the concrete were annoying and painful. Tom had called but she had not been in the mood to talk – her head aching and her body cold and then hot. She did not want to bother him with the details; she just wanted to get home.

When they stopped for gas, she asked Brian to buy her aspirin – the pills helped some and she drifted off to sleep. Her dreams were filled with monsters and demons and prison breaks where Junior led an army of rapists and serial killers directly to her doorstep.

She awoke to the sound of the car stopping and the window rolling down. In a voice burdened by sleep, she said softly, "What happened?"

He grunted, "Got pulled over."

She chuckled, "How fast were you going?"

"Like 5 over."

She had always heard they never pulled over for anything under 10 over. The police officer leaned into the car and Rachel immediately recognized her – the blonde woman who had been flirting with Brian at the gas station on the trip down.

The woman looked at Rachel and then at Brian. "You never called."

He chuckled nervously. "Yeh we've kind of had a crappy couple of days."

Rachel leaned over and looked the woman in the face. "I don't believe you're allowed to flirt with people you pull over, Officer---" She leaned over and glanced at the name tag, "---Gutierrez."

The woman by no means was of Hispanic descent – Scandinavian most definitely, but not Hispanic – the woman was either married or divorced or perhaps adopted but Rachel figured it was one of the first two options.

The woman rolled her eyes at Rachel, "Well then, I'm going to give you a warning." She leaned closer to Brian's ear and whispered something that Rachel could not hear.

Brian chuckled and said, "Yes, officer. I'll be sure to do that."

The woman went back to the car and Brian rolled the window back up.

"You know you could have actually made me get a ticket by saying that?"

Rachel laughed, "It was a chance I was willing to take." She stuck her tongue out at him.

He chuckled. "You know if I were ten years younger…" He didn't finish his statement.

She laughed, "What would you do if you were ten years younger? Huh?" She smiled at him and then continued, "Wouldn't that make you like fifteen?"

He laughed heartily. "How old do you think I am?"

"Twenty-five-ish?"

"Twenty-eight baby girl. Twenty-eight." He flexed his arm showing off his huge muscles. "I look damn good, don't I?" He laughed.

She couldn't help but laugh with him.

He finally drove away from the side of the road and they drove in a silence for at least an hour. She sat busily watching the houses and fields whizz by and wondered if other people's lives were as strange as hers.

She finally broke the silence. "So you knew him, didn't you?"

He jumped, startled, the sudden break in the silence frightening. "Who?"

"Junior?"

"Yeh I went to high school with him. We were really good friends a long time ago before he moved away."

"Is he the one who got you that apartment?"

"Yeh." He paused, silent for a moment, and then continued, "I'm real sorry about that. I didn't know."

She said nothing, contemplating if she should be angry with him or just forgive him for his mistake. She chose the latter.

"He was an aggressive kid – always got in fights. We used to pick fights together, but he was never a total psycho."

"I'm not mad at you."

He chuckled, "Well you should be. His dad was a weirdo. Always drunk, always beating up women and his kids; I guess Junior just turned into his dad – it happens to the best of us. We always end up like our parents." His eyes glistened with sadness – or possibly tears.

She reached over and placed her hand on his knee. "Not all of us do."

He smiled at her softly and then reached over and ran his hand over her hair, pushing a stray strand out of her face.

She smiled softly at him and removed her hand from his knee. "Well at least it's over." She said the words confidently.

He looked at her quickly and then put his eyes back on the road. "Not exactly. He's got to have bail set, a hearing, and maybe he'll get some time for assault and battery but it'll not be long enough – he won't go away for life."

She reached over and patted his bulky arm, "Well then can I hire you as my body guard?"

He softly said, "I couldn't even protect you last time."

"But we survived, eh?"

"We just got lucky."

The conversation ended and they sat in silence. She wanted to reach over and hug him and tell him that there was nothing he could have done, that he did the best job he could, but it would have gone unheard – she knew he was beating himself up because he had placed her there. He had trusted someone he shouldn't have trusted.

He was right, they just got lucky.

The moon shone high above in a perfect sphere, beautiful and magnificent. There was not a cloud in the sky and the moonlight shone on the bare fields that lay below it. She drifted again into sleep.

The light of dawn awoke her along with the ring of the telephone that Brian promptly answered. She looked out the window to see the town of Vertueux appearing above the horizon.

Brian hung up the phone, she had not been listening.

He turned towards Rachel and spoke, "Anthony – Mr. Gillespi – said that Junior's bail was set pretty high so it's doubtful he'll make bail."

Rachel nodded and turned towards him.

He continued speaking, "Tom's being released at 9am, which is like two hours from now. We can go get some breakfast and then pick up a different car and go get him, if you'd like."

She nodded again. Her head ached and she wanted more aspirin.

Brian drove through the town and pulled into a restaurant. They got out of the car and walked into the restaurant; the few older couples who were eating turned to stare and then immediately turned to each other and started whispering.

Brian leaned over and whispered in her ear, "You're a celebrity here."

She chuckled, and her head felt like it was going to explode.

When they sat down she asked for a glass of water and took a couple more aspirin that she had brought in with her and laid her head down on the table.

Brian reached over and pushed her hair out of her face, "Are you okay?"

"Just a headache. I'll be fine."

He ordered for the two of them and when the food arrived she ate a few bites and then lay her head back onto the table.

"I think you should see a doctor when we're at the hospital."

She lifted her head up and shook it. She did not want to see another doctor. "I'll be fine, I promise."

He chuckled. Waving the waitress over, he got the check and paid it.

He grabbed her arm gently in his when they walked because she was swaying gently, as if she was about to pass out. She wrapped her arm around his waist and leaned against his big burly chest.

He helped her into the car and then got onto his side of the car and drove away. He drove the car to a warehouse and parked in front of a door. Typing a few numbers into a keypad, the door opened slowly and noisily. Once the door was opened enough, he drove the car inside and into the darkened warehouse. Lights went on automatically as he neared them.

There were at least a hundred cars in the warehouse – most were classic automobiles, some were everyday cars others were cars that weren't even legal on American streets. He parked the Aston Martin where he had picked it up and going to the passenger side of the car, helped Rachel from the seat as he let her lean on him as she walked.

They came to a black Taurus – which seemed out of place in such luxury – and Brian opened the door, keys of which were always inside the car, and then helped Rachel to the other side to get in.

She curled up in the front seat and fell asleep.

It was nearing 9am and he had to race towards the hospital to make it in time but they pulled up to the main entrance just as the clock struck 9. He put the car in park, grabbed the keys from the ignition and walked over to the passenger side and shook Rachel who grunted and moaned and then opened her eyes.

She squinted at him, her vision blurry. He grabbed her under the arms and lifted her up out of the car – she was remarkably light – and then he held her for a few seconds as he struggled to close the door, her body leaning up against his, her head resting softly on his chest, her arms wrapped around his thick waist.

He stood there for longer than he probably should have, her

warm body pressed up against his. He was so entranced by her arms around him that he had not seen Tom being pushed out by the nurse; he had not seen Tom rushing towards him either with his fist in the air. He by no means had known that Tom was flinging that fist towards his face until the fist hit him squarely in the eye.

The hit only stunned him, after all he was used to fights and Tom had the throw of a teenage boy not a full grown man. The hit stunned him enough however, that he lost his grip on Rachel and she slipped towards the ground, tumbled like a ragdoll onto the hot concrete.

Tom and Brian both reached for her but both missed and she hit the ground with a thump. The nurse came running also and Brian scooped her up in his arms and ran with her towards the entrance.

The nurse and Tom followed closely behind.

Forty-One
🌿 🌿 🌿

*H*e wasn't sure what possessed him when he hit Brian square in the jaw. He didn't even realize until later that it hurt his hand. It had been a split-second decision, after all that old man had his arms wrapped around his precious Rachel and Rachel's head was buried in his chest, her arms wrapped around his body. He loved her with all his heart; he couldn't bear to see her with another.

When she fell to the ground he realized that he had seen it all wrong. He had followed closely as Brian carried her into the hospital, stayed nearby in the waiting room with Brian when the doctor's examined her, and then sighed in relief when they told her she was suffering from orthostatic hypotension which was probably caused by dehydration.

They had put her on an IV drip and they allowed them to visit her periodically during the day as they monitored her.

He watched Brian as he looked at her; he watched silently as they spoke of things that happened on their trip. He couldn't tell what he saw between the two but he knew he didn't like it.

It was a few hours before she was able to be removed from the IV and the doctors agreed she could go home. When they did, she grabbed his hand in hers, fingers intertwined, and he walked by her as they wheeled her out of the hospital. Brian walked a few steps behind.

She sat in the back of the car this time and Tom sat next to her. She leaned over and rested her head in his lap and he brushed her hair gently with her fingers. Brian went to the front of the car and asked them where they wanted to go.

Rachel said softly, "Home."

But neither of the two men knew what home she meant and both remained silent.

Rachel turned on her back and looked up at Tom her eyes full of love. She did not know he had hit Brian and he wanted it to remain that way.

He saw the cut on her perfect chest, a single line that went from her neck and then down into her dress. He ran his finger down it softly and whispered, "What did he do to you?"

She had fought back the tears, he could see that. She looked at him with eyes that were full of caring and love and said,

"Those will heal."

He knew she meant something more by those words but he did not want to hear them.

He saw Brian watching in the rear view mirror and he had the sudden urge to kiss her, to make Brian feel like a voyeur, to make Brian jealous, but Brian spoke before he could say anything.

"So what 'home' do you want to go to Miss Odium?"

She chuckled, and then sitting up said softly,

"My father's house."

Brian said nothing, he did not smile or laugh, he remained professional and began to drive towards the house where no one in their right mind would ever enter.

Rachel sat up next to Tom and he reached over and kissed her softly on the lips and she kissed him back, her leg sliding in between his as she moved herself closer.

"I missed you." He moaned softly as his hand drifted dangerously up her skirt.

She pulled back a little from him and smiled softly, "I missed you too."

She looked up at his head and the shaved portion and then ran her fingers through the remaining part of his hair. She reached up and kissed the scar forming on his scalp and then leaned back against the seat and stared blankly out the front window.

He leaned over and whispered, "Can we ditch the bodyguard?"

She chuckled and then leaned forward, "Hey Brian. Why don't you drop us off at Tom's place and we'll get his car and you can go home, okay?"

He looked back at her in the rear view mirror.

"You sure that's okay?"

"The world's a safer place now because of you." She leaned up over the seat and kissed him softly on the cheek, a move that would have made Tom upset had he not been staring at the miraculous view of her butt as she leaned over.

"Well, you're the boss."

She laughed and Brian made a quick U-turn and headed towards the opposite part of town.

When they reached the Crabtree residence, the Camaro still sat in the place he had left it. The keys were fortunately in his pocket because neither of them wanted to go back into that house.

Without a word, Brian drove off quickly and Tom and Rachel climbed into the Camaro. School was letting out and young kids were walking in clusters and buses were driving around their red stop signs and flashing red lights on at the most inopportune time.

"I gotta go stop by and see Nancy. I promised her I would." Tom said the words as he drove away from the house.

She nodded. She did not mind because Nancy was apparently a mother to him like Maude had been her grandmother – no blood, just connection.

They pulled into the pizzeria that was packed with kids and adults and teenagers, two of whom were Andrea and Alex. Alex came walking up to them.

"Seems like we always see each other here." He chuckled softly as he gave Rachel a hug.

Tom spoke, "What are you two doing here?"

"Oh nothing, grabbing some pizza and then we're going to

the lake."

Rachel grabbed Tom's arm and pulled him closer.

Alex spoke again, "What are you two doing?"

"Came to see Nancy."

Tom glanced around the restaurant and noticed Nancy busy taking orders and dealing with the massive crowd of people. The noise in the pizzeria was deafening.

Tom continued, "Guess it's a bad time."

Alex chuckled, "Yeh I guess so. You two lovebirds want to go to the lake with us?"

Rachel looked up at Tom, who, in turn, looked down at her.

"You down for a trip to the lake?" He brushed her hair softly out of her face.

She nodded.

Alex headed back towards Andrea and yelled back, "Then a date is a date."

Forty-Two
🍂 🍂 🍂

*T*hey had gone to the lake following closely behind Andrea and Alex. The sun was still shining brightly and Andrea laid a blanket on the soft ground and her and Alex lay next to each other. Rachel stood and watched while Tom grabbed a blanket out of the back of his car and walked a ways away from the two who now lay kissing each other passionately. He placed a blanket on the ground and then sat down. Rachel came and sat down with him, her eyes inquisitively focused on Alex and Andrea who, with each passing moment, grew more passionate.

Tom leaned up near her and whispered, "Don't worry about them."

She looked towards him and he grabbed her face softly in his hands and kissed her lightly.

She smiled at him softly and he touched her bruised face gently. "I'm so sorry."

"For what?"

"That my brother could do that to you."

"It's not your fault."

He smiled at her and then reached over and kissed her again softly.

Her focus on Tom was distracted when she heard movement nearby. She jerked her head towards the sound and saw Andrea taking her pants and shirt off. Alex soon followed her and both stood there in their underwear for a moment and then in a flash they raced for the lake and with a whoop they jumped in, laughing and splashing.

She chuckled. She turned and watched the two and Tom pushed her hair away from her neck and kissed her softly.

"Would you like to go in?"

"The lake?"

He laughed, "Yes, the lake. Just go in your undies, they'll dry by the time we leave."

She laughed and then leaned into him, "I don't actually have a bra on. Your brother kind of destroyed the only one I had."

He chuckled, "Ah well then just go in topless."

She blushed.

"Okay, okay, fine, you can use my t-shirt."

He pulled the t-shirt over his head and held it. She turned her back towards the two in the lake and pulled her dress over her head. Exposed to him, she reached her hand towards him for the shirt but he wouldn't give it to her. He just smiled wickedly.

Alex yelled out, "Hey Rach!"

Without thinking she turned around and then realized that she had done exactly what he had wanted – exposed her nakedness to him.

Andrea smacked him across the head and the two laughed and disappeared under the water.

Tom reached up behind her and grabbed her stomach and pulled him into her. He pushed her body into his, his naked chest against her naked back. He kissed her neck softly. His hands reached up to cover her breasts. She melted in his arms.

"Do you love me?" He whispered the words softly in her ears and a shiver went down her spine.

She sighed, her heart beating loudly in her chest, his hands tantalizing as they cupped her breasts. She didn't want to answer.

He leaned back down on to the blanket taking her with him and then turned her towards him. They kissed softly at first and then more passionately, his hands sliding down towards his pants and then towards the front to unbutton and unzip them.

She wanted to stop him, wanted to just go back to the guise that they were going to go into the lake.

She heard Alex and Andrea get out of the lake and did not care that she was exposed to them. She heard Andrea say

"Well, looks like Tom's losing his virginity tonight."

She heard Tom chuckle as his kiss became more fervent and more impassioned and his hand wrapped in her hair to pull her closer to him. She tried to pull away, but her body – her body wanted this, wanted to give herself to him.

He grabbed the edge of the blanket and wrapped them up in it, their remaining clothes somehow now lost in the tangled mess. They kissed and groped each other's naked bodies for what seemed like forever and then he slipped himself inside her.

It wasn't how she expected – she wasn't sure how she expected it to happen. She enjoyed making love under the stars, the cool night air their fan and the grass their bed. It was painful and ugly and then it was comfortable and beautiful and then she wanted more, she wanted it to never end.

When it was over, they held each other, their bodies sticky and achy – neither of the two being fully healed. She did not mind.

She wanted to never leave his embrace for at that brief moment she felt safe.

He kissed her softly and his hand drifted to the letters carved on her butt. "Did he do that too?"

She nodded and turning her back towards him, curved herself up against his warm body and stared blankly into the night. They drifted to sleep together without a word, his arm wrapped around her waist and the sounds of the night were a soothing soundtrack.

Kimberly Thomas

Forty-Three

Alex and Andrea pushed at Tom and Rachel to wake up. The morning sun had arisen and today was graduation day. Andrea stared at the letters carved into Rachel's butt and whispered silently to Alex, who nodded. Andrea looked saddened.

Tom forgetting he was naked stood up and then quickly reached for his clothes and put them on. Rachel had slid her dress on as soon as she woke up.

Alex looked at his watch and said, "Tom, we have to get going, practice starts in an hour."

Rachel was busy picking up the blanket and folding it. Tom grabbed her by the waist and pulled him towards her and kissed her gently, "Did you want to go to your house or go to my practice?"

She smiled and kissed him softly,

"I will go wherever you go. There's nothing for me at my house anyway."

"Ok, well we're going to have to stop by my house for a change of clothes, at and at some point I'm going to have to shave my head." He chuckled and ran his finger through his hair.

They walked towards the car and he followed her to the passenger side of the car and opened the door for her. She smiled sweetly at him and he pushed her towards the car and kissed her.

In a whisper he said, "Thank you."

She chuckled, "For what?"

"For being here with me; for making my life complete."

She smiled softly at him and did not reply. She climbed into the seat and waited.

He drove slowly to the house, his hand resting on hers and he pulled up to his house and, opening the garage door, pulled his car into the empty garage. Her heart beat loudly in her chest.

When he opened the door and got out, she remained seated, seat-belt still buckled. He leaned his head in the door, "You gonna stay in the car, baby?"

She didn't want to go in the house but she didn't want to be alone either. Her fingers clutched tightly to the door handle and Tom closed his door and walked to hers. He opened the passenger side door and got on his knees near her. Kissing her softly on the forehead he said, "Are you okay?"

She looked at the closed door that led to the house and then at Tom, his face sweet and innocent. She unbuckled her seat belt and he took her hand to help her out of the car. Like a young child, she grabbed his arm and walked close to him, never letting go of him. They walked into the house through the door in the garage and she placed her head firmly in his back.

She did not open her eyes until they reached his room and he pulled away from her to look around the closet for clothes. She sat on his bed and then lay on it, staring silently at the ceiling - afraid to look around, afraid that Junior might have escaped jail or posted bail and was waiting in the house for her. The fears were unfounded.

He leaned over and kissed her softly and then removed his clothes. She tried not to watch but he was as beautiful as a museum sculpture - stoic and perfect. "Oh what we could do if we had more time." He threw his shirt at Rachel's head and blocked her view.

She chuckled and imbibed in the smell of him. When he was done changing and had grabbed his clothes for the graduation ceremony later, she slipped off the bed and they walked hand-in-hand through the house towards the garage. She dared not look around for fear that something would remind her of what had happened only a few days prior. Although Junior had branded her, she would not nor would she ever be his.

She smiled and pushed herself closer to Tom. When they were safely back in the Camaro, however, Rachel was finally relieved and in a sigh let her worries go.

He backed up and drove towards Vertueux High and managed to get to the building five minutes before the rehearsals started.

Rachel was a third wheel at the rehearsals and in an effort to stay out of the way; she went into the stands and dozed off in a chair. Her rehearsal only a week prior had been painfully boring, this one was even worse.

An hour had passed and then two and finally Tom walked up into the stands and with a gentle nudge told her it was over. "A couple of my friends are going to catch some lunch, wanna go?"

She nodded and rubbed her eyes gently.

They walked hand in hand towards a group of people and when they were nearby the group stopped talking. A beautiful dark-haired girl walked up to Rachel and stretched her hand out.

"Hey. I'm Mica."

"Rachel."

"Is it true?"

Rachel looked at her puzzled and then assuming she was referencing her relationship to the Odium household she said,

"Sure."

"So you two did do it." Mica chuckled and Rachel turned a bright shade of red.

Tom grabbed Rachel around the waist and pulled her close to him and kissed her softly on the lips. Turning to Mica he said,

"You jealous?"

Mica's face distorted into a face of anger and she flipped her hair over her shoulder and stomped away in a huff. Tom chuckled, amused.

They followed closely behind a group of teenagers. There

were six of them – three girls and three guys. She did not see Alex or Andrea in the group of kids. The eight of them walked out to the parking lot and got into their cars and drove away – Rachel drove with Tom in his Camaro.

The two drove in silence – each so enamored with the others presence that words would have sullied the moment, made it more real and less surreal as it felt right now. Tom's phone interrupted the silence.

"Hello?"

She could hear the loud voice on the other end all the way to her side of the car, but she could not recognize the voice.

"Hey. Can I talk to Rachel?"

"Who is this?"

"Brian."

"What do you want?" Tom's voice immediately became cold and calloused.

"I have to pass a message to her."

"From?"

"Her attorney."

Tom rolled his eyes and without a word handed the phone to Rachel.

She spoke softly, "Hello?"

"Rach?" His voice was softer now, and she doubted that Tom could hear him.

"Hey Bri."

Tom looked at her with a look that she felt was more with disdain than love.

Brian spoke again, "I dropped the Aston Martin off at your house."

"My house?"

Brian chuckled, "Your father's house."

She smiled although he could not see it. "Why?"

"Well I figured in case you wanted to get around town by yourself."

She chuckled. "I wouldn't even know where to go."

"Well it's there if you want it."

"Thanks."

"Oh, and I put a cell phone in the car too. Mr. Gillespi said it's important that he has a way of contacting you."

She laughed, "I'll see if there's a way I can get out there sometime today."

He said, almost in a whisper, "I put my number in the phone. Call me if you need anything, okay?"

She smiled and said, "Will do, Bri."

"Bye, Rach."

"Bye."

She flipped the phone closed and handed it back to Tom. She had not realized that he had parked in front of a sandwich shop. He looked at her sternly and said harshly,

"So it looks like you two got pretty close on your little road trip."

She chuckled nervously. "He's a good guy."

"I bet." Tom looked out the window, his fingers gripped tightly around the steering wheel.

"Are you mad at me or something?" She said it softly and then leaned over and placed her hand on his thigh.

"Why did he call?" He did not respond to her question, a sure sign that he was mad at her for some unknown reason.

"To tell me he left a car at my dad's house and that Mr. Gillespi left a phone for me."

Tom's breath was loud and ragged and he turned towards her, his eyes aflame,

"That was it?"

She rubbed his thigh softly, nervously. "Yes baby that was it." She leaned towards him and kissed him softly on his cheek. "What's wrong?"

"Nothing." He said the word sullenly and sorrowfully and then released the steering wheel, grabbed his keys, got out of the car and slammed the door and walked towards the sandwich shop.

"Like hell, nothing," she whispered and then got out of the car and walked away from the sandwich shop, towards her father's house.

She did not take a direct route, instead went left at the light and then right at the next one and straight for two more blocks and then left at the next light. She knew that once Tom figured out that she had not stayed in the car nor had she followed him into the sandwich shop that he would come find her. Right now, she needed the air – she needed time to think.

Her mind was filled with racing thoughts – she believed she might love Tom with all her heart, her mind, her body, her soul wanted to be with him but unfounded jealousy was a demon that overpowered even the strongest wills and she could not love Tom if he were to become like his brother, angry, violent and insane.

She was ten blocks away from the sandwich shop when the Camaro pulled up next to her. She ignored him and kept walking; his car edged inch by inch along with her stride.

Tom leaned over and rolled the passenger side window down and said softly, "Where you going, baby?"

She did not look at him, she simply said softly and sourly,

"Home."

"Why?"

"Why do you think?"

"Because I was being a jealous jackass?"

She couldn't help but smile. She was never an angry individual and she couldn't hold grudges if her life depended on it. "Yes, exactly…because you were being a jealous jackass."

She stopped and turned towards the car. He stopped the car next to the curb and smiled out at her.

"I'm sorry, baby."

She leaned over into the car and said, "Don't do it again." Opening the door, she slipped into the passenger seat.

He leaned over and kissed her passionately and all the anger, the jealousy, the regret slipped away in a moment.

"Do you love me?" He whispered it ever so softly as he held his face in her hands, his eyes closed, mouth centimeters from hers.

"Now and forever." She said it softly and then kissed him gently.

He smiled. "So home?"

She chuckled, "Yours or mine?"

"How about ours?" He winked at her.

She chuckled softly, "Well how about my father's for now."

He laughed and put the car in drive and drove towards the old Odium house. They talked about graduation and what they had planned to do after graduation before their lives had been turned upside down. He had planned on attending college at the state university; she had planned on going to community college. She wasn't sure what she planned to do now – probably college but she had businesses to run and a fortune to maintain now. He wasn't sure what he wanted to do either because he couldn't bear to be away from her for any length of time.

When they arrived at the turn-off for the old Odium place, the mailbox was full. Tom stopped and Rachel glided out of the car and grabbed the package of papers and placed them in the car. She flipped through them – most of the mail was junk mail, advertisements for businesses or coupons for junk she would never need. When they arrived at the house, she had not managed to make it through half of the papers.

The Aston Martin sat in front of the house, beautiful and glowing in the midday sun. Tom looked at it longingly and said softly, "That is one hell of a car."

She chuckled, "That's what all the guys have said."

He frowned disapprovingly and then trance-like walked towards the car and placed his hand on it. Rachel sat the pile of mail on Tom's seat and walked towards the car and opened the door. The keys had been placed in the front floorboard along with the cell phone that Brian had mentioned. She grabbed the phone and keys, tossing the keys to Tom and flipping open the phone to look at it.

She was flipping through the options on the phone and leaning on the car when she said suddenly,

"What time do you have to be back for graduation?"

"Six p.m."

"You want to go inside?"

He glanced up at the eerie foreboding house and then down at his watch. They still had around three hours before they had to go back.

"I guess so."

She laughed, "Scared?"

He chuckled, "Yeh, maybe a little."

She ran back to the Camaro and grabbed the pile of mail and then walked up the porch and to the front door.

Tom followed closely behind.

Forty-Four

There were no angry outbursts of malevolent spirits when they entered the house. The door pushed open and they pushed it shut – nothing abnormal about it. Tom sighed in relief.

The house was abnormally bright from the sun outside and the dusty gloom of the unused home was apparent in its brightness. Rachel did not look to her right into the dining room; she feared to see her dead mother still lying on the floor. Tom glanced in there, but saw nothing.

Rachel walked forward into an alcove that led to a staircase. She walked upstairs and he followed her closely, his hand touching hers as they both ran their hands against the dusty wall to steady themselves. Rachel's hands were full from the mail she held and he regretted that he had not offered to help.

When they reached the second floor, there were a selection of doors to choose from and Tom, in a frightened state, felt that he was on a game show where the wrong door would lead to certain death – perhaps all of them would. He had no time to choose, however. Rachel walked towards the end of the hall and entered a room. She had not said a word since she walked into the house – it was as if she was sleepwalking, her body taking her places without her knowing.

Tom followed her closely. The room that Rachel had entered was apparently the master bedroom – beautiful and magnificent; the furnishings were fit for a king, the bed plush with pillows that seemed to reach to the ceiling.

She glanced around the room and then turned around, seemingly disappointed.

She did not look at him when she passed him – she was in a spell. Tom followed her down the hall to the room opposite the master bedroom. Rachel opened the door slowly and walked in; Tom had to side step just to keep from being slammed into the door. Rachel walked towards a smaller bed and sat on it, a cloud of dust floated around her.

Tom walked towards her and sat next to her. He coughed.

She looked at him and smiled softly. Softly she spoke, almost in a whisper, "Do you think I should keep it?"

"Keep what?"

"The house."

He touched her face softly. "That's up to you."

She lay down on the bed, her feet dangling off the edge. Even after years of no use, the bed was still more comfortable than she was used to, for no expense had been too great to furnish this large house.

He lay down next to her and grabbing the mail off of her stomach tossed them on the floor. The dirt that had long since been dormant now flew about in a flurried frenzy.

She turned her head towards him, her eyes wide and beautiful, and said softly, "It's just so big."

He leaned over and kissed her full lips, longing to hold her and caress her but also vaguely aware that he had once thought he'd seen the ghost of her mother and father in that house – although looking back now it almost seemed less than feasible. He wasn't going to take the chance, however.

He said nothing in response and she continued to speak, "Mr. Gillespi said the house has been in the family for years."

He touched her face softly and said nothing in return.

"I wouldn't want to be the one who got rid of it just because it was so big."

He smiled softly at her. "There is a lot of history here – a lot of pain…"

"…and a lot of love," she added.

She leaned in and kissed him passionately, her hand slid up under his shirt and she ran her nails gently up and down his muscled abdomen.

He sighed.

Her eyes closed and with her hand still gently rubbing his abdomen, she whispered, "Are you okay?"

Before he could speak, she rolled over and straddled herself across his waist. He grabbed her waist and smiled up at her. He spoke softly, "I'll always be okay as long as you are here with me."

She leaned over and kissed him softly and then more passionately, instictively grinding herself down on him until he began to paw at her dress, lifting it up slowly, but never letting go of her kiss.

There was a knock on the door – not the door to the room they were in but a knock on the massive doors that led to the house.

She groaned and then sat back up.

He said in an annoyed voice, "Who the hell would be out here?"

She walked towards the windows that faced the front of the house and peering out the dirty windows said softly, "Delivery person it looks like."

An old white car sat in the driveway with a magnetic sign attached to the side – she couldn't read what it said. She straightened her hair and dress and walked with Tom to the front door. She swung the door open in one big swing and startled the boy who apparently assumed no one was home and was already walking rapidly to his car. He grasped his chest and said meekly, "Holy crap; you guys scared me."

Tom recognized the guy and said, "Hey, Zach."

Zach nodded his head towards Tom and then said, "Hold on a second, I got something for you two."

She looked at him oddly but he said nothing more, he simply turned around and scuttled off like a frightened mouse to his car.

He was an odd looking fellow, balding at the age of sixteen, eyes that were too big and too far apart and a nose that was wide and long. He was nice enough but was moody and rarely made eye contact, something that Tom felt made Zach not trustworthy.

Zach returned - his feet shuffling as he brought a bouquet of red roses and a bouquet of black roses. Zach stared at the ground as he handed the red roses to Rachel and the black roses to Tom.

In his shaky frightened voice, Zach said softly, "So have you seen him?"

Rachel laughed softly and Zach turned towards her, making eye contact. Rachel spoke in a voice that was like an aphrodisiac, "Who, my father?"

Zach stared at her – Tom did not like that. Zach nodded like a school child enamored by his kindergarten teacher.

She smiled at him. "Yes, yes we have."

In more words than Tom had ever heard from the meek teenager, Zach said, "You know, it's funny that you guys are out here. I told my boss that no one was going to be out here and he said that he had been given viable information that you would."

Rachel said softly, "It's my house now."

He nodded.

Tom, annoyed with the attention that the ugly boy was paying to his beloved Rachel, walked over to her and kissed her softly as he took the red roses from her.

Rachel looked at Zach and said, "Do you know who they are from?" She nodded back towards the roses that Tom held awkwardly.

Zach shrugged his shoulder and said, "I don't know. Should be on the card. I'm not on the 'need to know' list." He smirked as he made quotes in the air with his fingers.

Rachel laughed softly and Zach laughed with her. Tom had never heard Zach laugh before - he wanted to punch him but he refrained.

Zach glanced at Tom and then his watch and then back at Rachel. "Well, I really have to go."

Rachel smiled at him softly and said good-bye as Zach rushed towards his car and drove away.

Kimberly Thomas

Forty-Five

*R*achel turned towards Tom. "So, what does your card say?"

He sat the roses down on the porch and pulled the card out of the bouquet. He flipped open the seal of the envelope and then pulled the card out and read it. Without a word, he quickly grabbed the card off of her bouquet, flipped the seal, and read it.

His face was immediately distorted into concern and anger – a mix that frightened her.

"What do they say?" Rachel inquired.

He tucked the notes in his pocket. "It's not important."

She walked towards him and placed her hands seductively in his pockets but his hand grasped the notes tightly. Keeping her hands in his pockets she bent down on her knees and ran her nose along the pocket, her mouth nipping gently at his arm and hand.

He looked down at her, the concern and anger that once distorted his face was now replaced with lust and desire. She removed her hands from his pockets and looked longingly into his eyes. Before she could go any further, he took his hand from his pocket and grabbed her under the arms and pulled her up to him and he kissed her, pushing her against the door of the house until it fell open under their weight.

They toppled onto the tile floor of the atrium laughing.

The life size painting of her mother and father staring at them did little to enhance the mood, and they lay on the cool tile floor staring at the ceiling, saying nothing.

After a few moments, she turned on her side and looked at him, "Please tell me what the cards said."

He pulled the cards from his pocket and handed them to her and looked away.

She opened the envelope labeled 'Tom Crabtree' first.

In perfect block letters was written the words, "She's mine." She opened the envelope labeled 'Rachel Odium'.

In the same perfect block letters, the card read, "See you soon." She whispered the name, "Junior."

The house shook with a rumble as if affected by an earthquake; the windows rattled and the floorboards creaked and in a gust of cold wind the front door blew shut, the reverberation from the noise echoing noisily throughout the house.

Tom sat up quickly, frightened and suddenly aware that they had never been alone in the house. He stood, grabbing Rachel's hand to pull her up and out of the door. They raced to the Aston Martin and Tom climbed into the driver's seat and she climbed into the passenger's seat. He started the car and drove off quickly.

Tom did not look back but Rachel, turning around in her seat, looked towards the house that had been so disturbed by the name. She smiled when she saw them looking out the upstairs window – her mother and father – they had not left, they had stayed there for her.

From two of the windows on the upstairs floor, equally apart in distance, flowed a bright red substance and from the distance they were now from the home, it appeared to Rachel that the house was crying tears of blood.

She turned around and dared not tell Tom what she saw – her heart beat wildly in her chest and she wondered if that house would ever be normal enough to be occupied by the living instead of by the dead. Perhaps her parents would always be there but her need for normalcy would not be satisfied by occupying a house that was haunted by the ghosts of her deceased parents. This place might never be her home.

When they had reached the comforting housing developments of Vertueux, Rachel spoke softly, "It's not over, is it?"

Tom shook his head. It was inevitable that this would not be over until Junior or Rachel was dead and Tom could not bear the thought of losing either of them.

She leaned over and patted him softly on the knee. It was nearing time for graduation and without second thought Tom drove to Alex's house to borrow a set of clothes – having left his in the Camaro which still sat in front of the Odium house.

She knew the house was frightening and worrisome but it held her past, her heritage, and she knew that she could not part with it. Her mother and father would surely not hurt her – they would be more likely to protect her if she were to stay – or would they? Perhaps she would be better losing herself in the city, becoming one of the many unknown faces there rather than the celebrity she had become in this small town.

When they arrived at Alex's house, Alex led Rachel to his sister's room to pick out an outfit and he took Tom to his room to find some clothes. She borrowed a black V-neck dress. Alex's sister was fifteen, tiny in height and weight and lacked the curves of the normal teenager. Most of the clothes that she owned were not meant for someone with Rachel's body. The V-neck dress was made of stretchy material and even though skin tight managed to fit without making her look either like a skeleton or a fatty. In fact, checking herself out in the full length mirror, she looked pretty damn good. Alex and Tom's reaction confirmed that she looked amazing.

Alex waited at the house for his parents while Tom and Rachel left for the school. They were silent, unsure as to what they should say to each other. She knew that Tom was thinking about the times to come when Junior would be back and she was thinking the same thing, afraid but unafraid. She had survived these past few weeks; surely she could survive the rest of her life even if Junior prevailed.

Kimberly Thomas

Randomly, she reached over and kissed Tom gently on the cheek.

"Don't worry."

He chuckled. "About what? Graduation?"

She laughed, "No, about your brother."

His face was somber. "I can't help but worry."

"Today is a happy day – let's keep it that way." She leaned over and kissed him softly on the cheek and then his chin and then down his arm until she could bend over no further.

He chuckled and placed his hand on her head and ruffled her hair.

"Do you love me?" He said the words softly as she sat back up in her chair, her face aglow with a smile.

"Forever and always, baby."

He smiled at her and grabbing her hand in his, he placed it up to his mouth and kissed it softly.

"I love you my beautiful sweet Rachel. I will do whatever it takes to make you mine forever."

She laughed and said, "I love you too."

In the back of her mind she couldn't help but feel strangely reminiscent of his brother's emotions – controlling and destructive. But as they parked at the school parking lot and he reached over and kissed her, she melted in his arms. They were young, and time would tell if this was real or not – neither of them would rush their love.

She was sad when they had to part ways – him to the throng of students, her to the swarm of parents and friends and families. She found her way through the crowd to a seat secluded and away from the happy mothers and fathers and bored brothers and sisters. The crowd eventually found her, however, the seats in the stadium filling up at an exponential rate.

She felt someone sit by her but did not stray her eyes away from the empty stadium floor for fear that they would recognize her and want to speak and the ceremony was still fifteen minutes from beginning. There was plenty of time to have a conversation about her life.

She recognized the voice as soon as he spoke. "Hey there."

Without turning her head, she rested her head on Brian's shoulder.

"Hey, Bri."

He chuckled, "You know you're the only person I'd ever let give me a nickname."

She laughed and turning to look at him batted her eyes at him.

"Awww."

He laughed.

She placed her hand softly on his eye.

"What happened?"

"Got punched."

She looked at him incredulously and then rubbing her hand on his big muscles in his arms, said softly, "I just don't see someone catching you off guard."

He chuckled and then nervously said, "Well, yeah I was a little distracted at the time."

"Ah -a girl?" She punched him softly on the arm.

He laughed, "Yeh, actually, if I remember correctly, it was you."

She chuckled. "Really? When did this happen?"

The music started and the roar in the stadium became too loud for her to hear; Brian stopped talking.

She watched as the students passed slowly and sat in their seats and then as the principal and honor roll students were given special awards and as others spoke and she wondered if all graduation ceremonies were as dull as this one.

She glanced at Brian periodically – he always seemed to be watching her, rather than the proceedings.

There was a brief silence before the graduates were awarded their diplomas when Brian leaned over to her and whispered, "I need to tell you something."

The first group of kids walked to the front of the stage and the roar of the crowd amplified to a crescendo. Rachel leaned over to Brian's ear, her upper body flush up against his huge arms. "What is it?"

"Duane Abel."

The first name was called by the principal and a roar of friends and family screamed across the stadium.

Brian put his finger up, indicating that they should wait.

The first line of graduates passed across the stage and then the second and then a few more until they were nearing the Cs and Tom's approach to the stage.

The crowd hushed as another one of the principals approached the stage to hand some of the diplomas out to the graduates.

Brian leaned towards her ear again,

"I have two things to say."

She turned her head towards him, forgetting that he was so near to her, her face graced his, her mouth touching his softly but innocently. He backed away, not in disgust but out of respect.

She smiled softly at him and then he leaned again before the crowd started again. His breath was warm and ragged against her ear, and he spoke softly, "I think I might be in love with you."

She said nothing but did not back away, her ear remained flush against his lips, his breath warm and more labored.

The crowd roared again as another student was announced and she crossed the stage.

Over the roar he said softly, "The second thing is…" He paused before he spoke. "…Junior posted bail."

She did not look at him and she did not respond to either of these new discoveries. Brian sat sullenly staring at the proceedings.

She stood when they called "Thomas Crabtree", clapping her hands exuberantly.

When he reached the podium, Tom did something the other students had not – whispered to the principal who, muffled over the microphone, they heard say, "I shouldn't."

Tom whispered something else to the principal and the principal's muffled voice came over across the crowd, "Just this once," and then the principal handed Tom the microphone.

Tom stood there with the microphone for what seemed like an eternity, the roar from the crowd hushed so that every sneeze or cough was magnified a hundred fold.

Then Tom spoke.

Kimberly Thomas

"Rachel Odium, will you marry me?"

To her it seemed as if the entire stadium turned towards her and stared but in an instant, Tom had handed the microphone back to the principal and walked off the stage back to his seat to await the rest of the proceeding so he could find her and be told his answer. The crowd roared and every person in the stadium stood up it seemed – except for Brian.

Rachel said nothing to Brian when she stepped over him and walked quickly up the steps to freedom. Her head was ducked, fearing that eye contact with any of the attendees would cause her to be recognized and forced to make an answer. When she reached the hallway she kept going until she had pushed the glass doors open and was outside – the cool air blowing on her face.

She heard the door open and the steps behind her but she did not turn around. Brian walked up behind her and placed his hand softly on her waist.

"Do you love him?"

Without turning around, she walked towards the wall and leaned up against it and then slid down to the ground and sat on the concrete. Brian followed her and sat next to her. She leaned over him, her face inches away from his, her body pushed gently up against his muscled chest. She spoke softly as she placed her hand gently on his black eye. Brian winced in pain.

"Did he do that to you?"

"Who?"

In a move she meant to be purely maternal, she leaned over and kissed his eye softly. His breath became labored.

Without pulling away from his face, she whispered softly, "Tom?"

He nodded and then pulled her face to him and kissed her gently and softly on the lips – she did not pull away but instead returned the kiss with more passion than he had intended.

Eyes closed, he whispered, "I will walk away right now and never bother you again if you just say it. Just tell me, do you love him?"

"Now and forever."

Eyes closed and heart racing, she thought the words but could not say them out loud.

She wasn't really sure anymore.

To be continued…

Kimberly Thomas